A Royal Encounter

Natlie Bartholomew Pitt

Roaring Seas Press—Big Bear Lake, CA
ISBN: 978-1-7369938-8-0
Library of Congress Control Number: 2021908033
Title: *A Royal Encounter*
Author: Natlie Bartholomew Pitt
Digital distribution | 2021
Paperback | 2021

This is a work of fiction. The characters, names, incidents, places, and dialogue are products of the author's imagination, and are not to be construed as real.

Originally created on 5/14/2015
Reedited on 03/10/2021

Dedication

For Lily.

Chapter One

A soft wind graced the branches of the gorgeous cherry blossom trees at the Promenade Mall in Temecula. It was an especially beautiful day in April, the perfect day to become acquainted with an unfamiliar town. Her cousin Bella was out and about with her new date, and hasn't yet found the time to show Natalie around. Despite being the new girl in an upper division neighborhood in California, Natalie was curious and determined. Nothing would keep her indoors on this beautiful spring day. It was about a twenty minute walk to the Mall, a regular hot spot. Having been brought up mostly in England and having lived a sheltered life, she was always driven places, picked up or dropped off somewhere, by Maureen, the family Chauffeur. Natalie had to get to the Mall and this time she would walk. An idea that made her feel spontaneous and free.

The short time she's been in the States, the local shopping Mall was the only part of town she's visited with her cousin. On most days she was stuck at home, hoping that Bella would make more time for her. Being away from London made her feel a freedom she's never felt before and for the first time in forever she had privacy. Natalie was hardly tired when she arrived and could hardly wait to get to her favorite store. She jumped onto the fast moving escalator to the second floor of the Mall, a speedy ride to her favorite store Reference, to purchase a new scarf and gloves for the surprisingly cool weather outside. She strolled into Reference and was greeted warmly by the friendly staff as she searched through the becoming collection of women's clothing. Her experience was always quite lovely, with the help of a friendly staff who's always genuinely helpful, something she always looked forward to.

Having been raised in England, everything about this new environment wowed her. She came to America for change, to escape her reality, and to discover the unknown. There was no better time for adventure, young and beautiful, only twenty-one and ready to discover the secrets of life. Natalie is strong minded as she is beautiful, a trait that defines her perfectly. As Natalie continues to enjoy her shopping spree, she is constantly greeted with smiles or the occasionally pleasing stares. She noticed the difference and immediately agreed that Californians are a naturally warm friendly people: Despite this fact, one would be blind to not notice this striking beauty; her beautiful figure, tall petite body and angelic face was something impossible to ignore. Natalie's tall confident walk and fine choice of clothing separated her from the norm.

After shopping, she stepped gracefully onto the escalator to the first floor of the Mall and headed over to the Cafeteria to have lunch. Placing an order without her cousin's help took a little while, but she finally did and sat down to dine. As she sat dining, she notices an individual walking briskly toward the cafeteria. Why did it seem like he was headed in her direction? A handsome Caucasian male who appeared to be in his late twenties. His blue shirt looked rumpled, but that didn't take away from his charming appearance. *He's handsome*, she thought. She took her gaze away from him returning to her lunch.

As she sipped on her ice tea, she was interrupted by a soft…

"Hello, I'm Philip, my friends call me Phil. What's your name?" Surprised she looked up.

"I'm Natalie, is something the matter?"

"Oh, I'm sorry I didn't mean to startle you. Nothing's the matter. I've seen you here at the mall a few times before and I've always wanted to say hello." Noticing her accent…

"Are you from London?" he asked.

She responded...

"Umm?"

Noticing that she was shy he said…

"You're the most beautiful girl I've ever seen; any chance I can get your number? I tried approaching you before, but you walk very quickly and are always in a hurry."

She smiled in agreement.

"From the moment I saw you," his eyes drifted to the floor. Then he looked at her directly. "Are you seeing anyone at the moment, I would love to take you to dinner sometime," he said.

Natalie smiled, feeling a bit awkward.

"Sure that would be lovely. I'm Natalie, and I'm very new to the States. Would you like to show me around?"

Philip's eyes lit up as though it was the best news he's heard his entire life.

"Absolutely, I would love to!"

After exchanging numbers, he explained that he had to get back to work.

"I would give you a ring tomorrow," she promised.

"Not if I phone you first," he replied.

Natalie Stared after him as he hurried off. He looked over his shoulder at her one more time and smiled before slipping out the door. She returned to her lunch curious but pleased. What a nice chap, she thought, and so very bold to come up to her like that.

The six short weeks she had been in the States, many men had expressed interests in her, but she has only dated on a few occasions. She enjoys going out on dates, however, her stubborn personality never allows any of her previous dates a second chance. Having been brought up within a very strict British family, Natalie has set very unrealistic standards for herself. Her friends always doubted that she would ever find Mr. Right, being this picky. It's been a week since her last date, but somehow she had a great feeling that this would be different.

Her phone rang around 8:30 a.m. Saturday morning. She hesitated to answer, and on the fourth ring, she reached for the handset.

Still half asleep, she answered, "Hello." It was Philip. He was taking the day off today and offered to show her around Temecula. She responded with a yawn.

"Is it ok if I return your call around noon, I'm still in bed."

"Absolutely," he replied. At 12:00 noon on the dot, her phone rang again. There's no doubt that it was Philip, and of course it was. It wasn't difficult to tell that he was very much into her. She hasn't had anyone express such genuine interest toward her while in the U.S and she became nervous that it may not last. Natalie wanted a real date, someone who can handle her beauty, and yet behave as a gentleman.

"Hi Natalie, can I swing by in an hour?" he asked excitedly.

"Sure," she said excitedly, but there's one condition.

"And what's that?" he asked.

"Promise me it would be different," she warned.

"And I hope that you're ready for the time of your life," he replied. They both laughed before hanging up. Natalie knocked on her favorite cousin's door, to let her know her plans for the day. As stubborn as she is, she felt it was proper to inform her cousin about her whereabouts. After all they lived together and her cousin Belle is her only relative in California. As always, Natalie knocked twice and opened her cousin's door.

"Good morning cuz, are you up?" she called.

She responded with a half-awakened...

"What's up, I'm asleep, and I don't have any little babies to care for, please leave me alone."

"I'm headed out for the day; just thought I should check on you before I leave."

Her cousin sat up in bed, she appeared exhausted. Although her hair was a mess and her face was still covered in makeup, she looked beautiful.

"Why, you look fabulous, where are you headed?" she asked, appearing annoyed, yet happy to be awake from her sleep.

"I have a date. I met someone yesterday and he's going to show me around," Natalie said blushing.

"How exciting for you, does he have any friends?" she asks, with that knotty expression on her face.

"Not sure, but I'll ask. By the way aren't you seeing someone?"

"Whatever," she replied.

"Some Angel you are cuz." They laughed. A few moments later, the doorbell rang.

"I think my date's here, I love you. I'll be back before dark," she said. After giving her cuz a smooch on the cheek, she headed out in a hurry.

Chapter 2

Phillip greeted her with a comforting hug. "You look great," he said.

"Thank you, you look like a proper gentleman," she replied. He smiled at her British charm. Philip's brand new Land Rover was parked in the driveway. After helping her into the car, he put on a Dean Martin CD and began shaking his head rhythmically.

"Where to?" she asked.

"It's a surprise," he replied with a glimmer in his eyes. While they traveled, every now and then he would glance over at her. He could hardly process what a beautiful woman she was. He's had quite a few interests but had very few dates over the past few months. Since his arrival in California he's dug deep into his new company and has only dated on a few occasions. Overtime, he became much too busy to care. He was approaching his mid-thirties and his Uncle Ben and Aunt Becky, were beginning to wonder if he would ever find himself a nice girl to settle down with. His tight knitted family did not agree when he'd decide to move to California, but this didn't take away from his motivation. He always wanted to move to California and knew that he had to leave Michigan in order to achieve his dreams. Philip was very passionate about his pursuit as a gaming Artist and has ignored every possible distraction in order to accomplish his goals-up till now. As they drove Natalie broke the silence.

"So tell me a little about yourself."

"Absolutely, I grew up in a small town in Wayne Michigan. My mom's name was Elizabeth and my dad was Andrew Albert Lane. My mom was a registered nurse and my dad was a math teacher at a public school in Detroit."

He paused after this.

"I was about seven years old when a horrible accident took both my parents."

Natalie's face became as pale as though she'd seen a ghost.

"I'm so sorry, you don't have to talk about it if you don't want to," she said, touching his shoulders.

"Don't worry, it's much easier to talk about it now. I was very young when it happened, and besides my Aunt Becky and Uncle Ben are the best parents that anyone could ask for," he said with a smile. They drove for about ten minutes and suddenly; there were vineyards everywhere. They are the largest, most beautiful vineyards Natalie had ever seen.

"Whose are these?" she asks.

"These belong to the Rockwell's, they own a Winery across the way," he replied excitedly.

"I can tell that you love this place."

"Truly," he replied.

"We call this area, Temecula Wine Country; it's the heart of the Inland Empire. This is a very popular spot, lots of folks come here on the weekend, to dine and enjoy the fine wine."

"Sounds lovely," she said excitedly.

He winks at her as he parked his Land Rover in the parking lot in front of Rockwell Creek's Winery. It was a beautiful evening and the Winery was very busy, yet not overly crowded and everyone was having a lovely time. As they walked into the busy room, Philip held Natalie's hand. She can tell that he was already being very protective of her. They strolled into the tasting room and it was almost impossible to place an order. Despite the crowd, Philip was surprised to have found somewhere, where he and his beautiful date could sit to enjoy the wine tasting.

As they chatted, Natalie gazed at the beauty of the place; it was the perfect setting for a first date. There were couples everywhere; some sitting in beautiful flower gardens, while others took shade under the finest built gazebos she'd ever seen. There's a magic about this place; everyone's smiling, laughing or chatting and having a great time. Everything about this place is beautiful, which reminded her of her childhood garden. There are times when she misses her home in England and all the people that contributed to her upbringing, but she needed this and was happy to be away, for however long.

A short while later, her date strolled up holding two bottles of Rockwell Creek's finest commodities; their highly requested Almond

Champagne and their newest favorite Chocolate wine served in glasses made of pure milk chocolate.

"This can't be what I think it is," she said excitedly. "Chocolate glasses, how marvelous," she beamed.

"I'm surprised that they had these in their collection, these are very much in demand," Philip replied.

After pouring each a glass of Champagne, Philip tossed a few jokes here and there about his previous experiences visiting this Winery. He is well known by the owners, and is one of their favorite customers. Although approaching his mid-thirties, Philip had this very youthful almost boyish way about him. He could easily pass for someone in his mid-twenties, the fact that he's always asked to provide Identification when ordering alcoholic beverages.

Already so deeply in love and so distracted by her beauty, Philip must have forgotten to order lunch. Having had very little to eat, the couple started feeling light headed, but that didn't prevent them from drinking the entire bottle. Natalie felt terribly embarrassed as Philip while attempting to stand, tumbled out of his chair. Both laughed as bystanders look on. Some joined in the laughter, while others simply looked on curiously. One of the owners of the winery was made aware of the incident and he came hurrying toward the couple.

"Oh, it's just Philip," he giggled. "Nothing new folks," Benny said, joining in the fun. Attempting to help Philip up also landed Natalie on her biscuits, and the laughter continued.

"Isn't she beautiful?" Philip yelled.

At that, he reached over and gave her a smooch on the cheek.

"She's gorgeous," someone called.

The laughter was followed by supporting applauses, as the young couple finally got up and strolled out of the winery.

"Want to walk this off before grabbing lunch?" he asked.

"Sounds great," Natalie replied cheerfully.

The two stumbled upon a dirt trail leading toward an acreage of Orchard groves. The sound of birds and the smell of blossoms filled the air. Natalie playfully tossed an orange at Philip and took off running.

"That's what you get for getting a fine British girl drunk on her first date," she laughed.

"I'll get you for this" he joked and took off running toward her. But Natalie was fast and she soon disappeared among the groves.

7

"Where'd you disappeared too?" he called. He searched for a few minutes and couldn't find her. As he was about to give up the search... he heard a muffled sneeze, which gave him an idea. Philip began imitating the Wolf man, walking slightly hunched over with his shoulders and arms protruding in a comical way, searching the groves as an angry beast eager for its prey. This scare tactic he's created has managed to scare adults and children alike. Natalie peeked at him from behind a thick brush. She laughed uncontrollably, suffocating her laughter in the cleft of her arms, trying not to reveal her hiding place. How could such a handsome face transform into something this horrid? Yet no one has ever made her laugh this hard in forever. Suddenly, Philip remembered a rumor that British girls were terrified of Snakes. Slowly backing away in horror, with his eyes wide open, he yelled...

"OH MY GOSH, this place is crawling with snakes. Look at the size of them, it must be the oranges!" Then he heard a rustle and looked just in time to see his date fleeing the orange groves in utter horror. Philip called after her...

"Hey Nat, wait up!"

But she didn't stop until she reached the dirt trails.

"Phil, come away quickly, they might be poisonous!" She called. Philip walked briskly toward her, she looked petrified. He almost felt bad seeing her so terrified, yet it was difficult to ignore how innocent she appeared. He laughed uncontrollably.

"There you are I swear you'd disappeared in thin air. At least now I know one of your weaknesses."

Realizing that he was toying with her, she stared at him with narrowed eyes. She strolled toward him and playfully reached for his collar. Unable to resist her charming presence, he cupped her face and kissed her passionately. Taken off guard, she couldn't resist and sunk in his strong embrace.

They held hands as they enjoyed the stroll back to their car at the Winery.

"Hungry yet, I know the perfect place," he said.

"I'm starved," she replied jokingly.

They got into Philip's car and drove for a few minutes. It was almost difficult to keep his eyes on the road having such a beauty sitting next to him. He didn't want her to notice how often he stared at her.

They pulled up in front of what Philip said was the finest Italian restaurant in Temecula. Natalie was impressed and thought the place was quite exquisite. Although she would have eaten at a less expensive restaurant without penalty, she realized that he was trying to impress her and she blushed. They were greeted by a friendly waiter, who showed them a table in a less crowded area of the restaurant.

"That's perfect," she said.

After lunch the couple headed over to the movie theatre to watch the new release of "An Evening to Remember." Natalie loves the unplanned events surrounding the day. Everything about this date was surprising and unexpected. It was only her first day spent with Philip but it already felt like she had known him a lot longer. This has never happened to her before. She felt adventurous and excited and didn't want the day to end.

During the movie she noticed Philip glance at her on more than one occasion. She didn't want him to realize how attracted she was to him or the fact that it was their first date and how she already felt about him. It scared her. Being only twenty-one she wondered if he might later find her too young. She knew Philip was much older than she was and she wondered if he would be able to tolerate her youthful stubbornness, and if so for how long. Philip glanced at her again, this time he asked jokingly...

"What are you thinking about?"

He then leaned over and whispered into her ears... "You are so beautiful." And for the tenth time today, she blushed. When the movie ended it was already late. The two agreed that the day was well spent and they headed home. As they pulled into the driveway, Natalie thanked Philip for a fine evening. They stood out front and chatted for a while before he walks her to her door.

"I'm not leaving until you agree to a second date," he said, slightly sarcastic, yet his eyes suggested otherwise.

Natalie giggled.

"How does next weekend sound?"

"Sounds perfect," he replied.

He then kisses her one more time before forcing himself to leave. As Natalie slipped inside, Philip thanked her for a fine evening. It was the most fun he's had in a long time.

Natalie was exhausted and after checking in with her cousin who was having dinner with a friend. She went to bed and didn't awake until the following morning. She slipped on her robe and headed to the kitchen to start coffee and was surprised that her cousin was already up.

"Good morning sleepy head, up early?"

"I can say the same to you. What are you up too?"

"Oh nothing much, just thought I'd have tea with you, it's been a while since we had breakfast together," she replied.

"How very sweet of you, thank you, it smells delicious," Natalie said taking a seat at the table. During breakfast, Natalie couldn't help but notice something different about her cousin. There was a smile on her face as though she'd reach a place of acceptance in her life. The short time she's been in the States she's been wonderful to her. Although they'd never met before that, her father had mentioned her cousin Belle in California on a few occasions. She remembered how excited she became when Belle invited her to California. It was the perfect timing. Recently widowed, and having no children of her own, she was thrilled when Natalie agreed to come for a visit.

"So how was your date?" she asked.

Natalie smiled. "Oh it was fantastic. Philip seems great; I like him a lot."

"You blushed when you said that," she said smiling.

"So where did he take you?"

"Oh boy, somebody's being nosy," Natalie said touching her cousin's nose playfully. After filling her cousin in on the previous day's events, there was almost a glimmer of jealousy on her face.

"Let's see how long this one would last."

"You said that when I first moved in with you, and I'm still here, putting up with you, am I not?"

She laughed. "Am I really that bad?"

"Try asking me again in a month, I might have a different answer then," Natalie jokes.

"You're wild about me and you know it," she said, pouring Natalie some more tea. Just then her cell phone rang. Natalie stood up quickly...

"I'll be right back."

"That must be Philip," her cousin replied.

Natalie answered, sounding a little bit out of breath from running up the stairs.

"Hi, it's me Phil." Natalie melted at the sound of his voice.

"You were the first thing on my mind this morning," he admitted. He wanted to know if she would like to spend the weekend with him. Natalie became nervous and excited at the thought of it. Were they moving too quickly?

"Sure, why not? I'll be ready in an hour," she replied.

Philip was thrilled. She hurried down the stairs, smiling broadly.

"Yep, it was Philip alright," her cousin said smiling. "He misses you already. Sounds like you found yourself a real catch."

Natalie was beaming with excitement.

"I'm spending the weekend with him; sounds like you will be all by your lonesome," she teased, hurrying up the stairs to get ready.

Her cousin giggled.

"He's headed over; you'll get to meet him."

"Wait a minute, he's headed over now?" her cousin asked surprised. "But sweetheart, my hair is a mess. I'm not ready to meet anyone."

"Then I suggest you get ready darling."

"This does not give me much time," she called.

A short while later the doorbell rang.

"I got it," Belle called.

"Hi, you must be Philip, come on in."

"Thank you, you can call me Phil."

"Pleasure to meet you Philip, Natalie told me a little about you. Please, have a sit, she'll be down shortly."

Belle is a tall slim brunette with a few blond stripes in her hair which she wore up in a ponytail, defining her face perfectly. Philip thought she looks a bit like Natalie.

"Beautiful home," he said.

"Oh thank you. I've lived here over two decades. When my husband passed away two years ago, even with devoted friends, it got very quiet around here and it was so amazing that Natalie agreed to come for a visit. She's got more brains than most politicians I know." Philip giggled at her remark.

"Sorry to hear about your husband, I'm sure Natalie is great company."

"Oh she's been a wonderful blessing. But don't worry, you can have her for the weekend, I'll be having company soon," Belle replied. A short while later Natalie came down the stairs. She looked adorable in sunglasses with a full length pink spring dress. Her shoulder length, caramel blond hair was back in a ponytail and a white handbag slung over her shoulders.

"Hey cuz, I see you two have officially met."

"Yep," they replied simultaneously.

"Well, you two have fun, let's all get together sometime for a BBQ."

"How about next weekend?" Natalie replied, embracing her cousin Belle tightly kissing her near her lips. They all agreed.

"I'll call you later cuz, I love you."

Natalie blew her a kiss before getting into Phil's convertible.

"Nice ride," Natalie said, removing her ponytail.

Chapter 3

The couple headed over to Temecula where Philip has a Townhouse. Later, they drove over to a local store to purchase items for dinner. Natalie was fascinated.

"This place is amazing and there's so much stuff, wow."

"I love shopping here; it's a popular favorite for most families. You can find almost anything here," Phil said, placing more items in their shopping cart. After shopping, they headed over to the electronics department to pick up a couple of DVD's for later.

"Wow, I love this place!" Natalie shouted, catching the attention of other shoppers.

"I love her accent," one couple replied.

"Where are you from?"

"Grenada, but I grew up in England," Natalie replied.

"Very nice, we've been to Grenada. What a great coincidence."

"That's incredible," Philip replied.

"We loved it there; my husband and I spent three months in the northern parts of the island and we fell in love with it. We've been thinking of moving there and opening up a restaurant. We heard that it's is the perfect place to start one. We also heard that Grenada sees lots of visitors from all over the world, especially during the summer."

"You've done your research. By the way, I'm Natalie, and this is my friend Philip. I'm here visiting and he is kind enough to show me around."

"How nice, by the way I'm Symone and this is my husband Greg. We've been married almost twelve years now."

"Very impressive," Philip said.

"It was very nice meeting you. Here's our card, maybe we can all get together sometime and you can tell us more about Grenada."

"That would be great," Natalie said smiling.

"You two would make an adorable couple," Greg said.

Natalie and Philip looks at each other and smile.

After picking out a couple of movies, the two headed back to Philip's place.

"Let's show you around," he said politely. It was a comfortable place, very clean and everything in its rightful place. There were lots of Star Wars and Indiana Jones toys and posters lining the walls. Philip's bedroom was also perfectly kept, and his closet was nicely organized. It seems he has over fifty pairs of shoes and his Tuxedos are arranged so neatly that it reminded her of her father Richard's closet. Phil's Garage was almost filled with boxes, most of which had Star War images on them.

"What are all these?" Natalie asked.

"Oh, I'm a collector; I collect Star Wars magazines and toys. I've been collecting these since I was about ten years old. One day, they will be worth a lot of money," he replied confidently.

"Wow, have you tried evaluating some of these yet, there's quite a few. Pretty soon, you won't have any room for them," she teased.

"Someday soon," he replied. He was still attached to them and wasn't sure he would ever sell them.

After the tour, Philip went to the kitchen to get dinner started. Natalie sat on his comfortable black, leather recliner reading one of his Star War magazines. She noticed that Philip seemed quieter than usual. There was definitely something on his mind. Suddenly, he broke his silence. He was getting used to having her around and was wondering how long she was visiting for.

"How long are you visiting for?"

She looks up from her magazine.

"Umm, my visa is good for another four months."

"Do you plan on extending your stay, or will you be heading back to England?"

"I'm not quite sure yet, since I'm a first time visitor, I'm not sure that U.S immigration would approve an extension; but I can have my cousin look into it." She knew why he asked and was thrilled. Her new relationship with Philip reminded her in so many ways of her first crush. But this time there were no media or stubborn dads.

"I can see that you're not ready to give me up yet...?" she teased. He smiled.

Then just as before, he was quiet again. There was definitely something on his mind and Natalie wasn't giving up until he'd spilt the beans. She continued looking at the magazine, then as they dined.

"Have you thought of staying in the U.S. permanently?"

She was enjoying her time with him and didn't want to be reminded that she was on vacation.

"Could we discuss it later? I still have lots of time to think about it. Yet, even if I choose to stay permanently, is it even possible?"

"You're absolutely right, let's enjoy our evening," he said, patting her hands.

As they ate dinner, the two new found friends knew that what was happening between them was a lot more than friendship. This was only their second date, and they already felt like they couldn't be apart from each other. Were they moving too fast...? The three day weekend flew by, and after Philip drove her home, Natalie thought long and hard about what Phil had asked her. She never really thought about it until now. While on her flight to California, she remembered wondering what it would be like if she happens to meet someone while visiting California. However, she doubted the possibility of it because her plan was to visit for only six weeks. She thought of her previous relationship in London to her High School sweetheart Bient Attaway, and it made her cringe. How could he have betrayed her like that; and with her cousin no less. It's been three years and the last she's heard; they were getting married. She knew it was time to move on.

As she ate dinner, for the first time in a while, Natalie thought of her mom on the Island, who would want nothing more, than for her daughter to fall in love and marry someone that could fill her heart's desires. Having five older siblings, Natalie being the youngest, she was a lot closer to her mom and mostly a stranger to her other siblings, who was much older than she was. As the only daughter of a Royal Guard, there were rules that prevented her from seeing her mother as much as she would like. However, that didn't prevent her from having dreams for her. As a child she always had this secret desire that her parents would get back together. But, of course this was only a child's desire.

She was having a remarkable time with Philip and could hardly wait to see him again. They had made plans to have a BBQ with her cousin Belle and her friend from San Francisco, but they had cancelled. They were going on a cruise instead and her and Phil hadn't yet made plans for the upcoming weekend. She simply wanted to enjoy some quiet time with Philip, and was open to whatever he planned.

It was Friday morning and her cousin had already left for their cruise to the Bahamas. Suddenly alone for the first time in a few days, Natalie laid in bed thinking about her mother who'd become her newest best friend. Natalie knows that her mother still worries about her, the fact that she was so picky about men and dates. Her mother had advised her to keep her options open because she always believed that her future was in England. Having been brought up mostly by her father, she'd often missed her mum terribly. It's only been a few months since she'd seen her mother, but it felt a lot longer. They'd grown very close the last three years she had spent with her in the Caribbean. She had left England a few weeks after her eighteenth birthday, fleeing the pain of her fiancé's betrayal. After all, she wanted change and this was beyond what she'd expected.

Her father Richard, a Royal Guard to the Prince of Edinburg didn't know that she was in America and she wasn't about to do him the honor of informing him of her plans. She was still very upset with what he'd done and the fact that he still treats her like a child was beyond her. Her father's occupation as a Royal Guard was very demanding and growing up she saw very little of him. He's a beloved guard and close friend of Baroness Ester and her Grandson Prince Ethan; the late Princess Annie's son. Being the daughter of London's most popular Royal Guard, she was constantly pursued by the London paparazzi. Being in the U.S. will protect them both from further publicity by the London Press. She felt a sense of freedom here, one she'd always yearned for. Then suddenly, she realized that she wanted to remain in the U.S. She beamed with excitement, because she now has an answer for Philip.

Chapter 4

It's been a week since she had seen Philip. They'd spoken briefly on the phone and she realized that they hadn't made any plans for the weekend. Was he slowing things down? What was it? She thought, sitting up in bed. She thought that Phil might have realized that after all, she was only visiting and sooner or later she would have to go home. She knew he needed answers, at least some assurance, but even with her new decision to stay, she wasn't certain whether it was possible. Were they chasing the impossible...? Two weeks had gone by since she last visited with Philip and he hadn't returned any of her calls. She knew something was wrong and she wasn't going to wait; she had to see him. After packing some cold drinks in her backpack she slipped on some tennis shoes and began a three mile walk to Phil's Condominium. She wanted to call a cab but changed her mind. God knows that she's had that luxury her entire life.

Her time spent away from her home in London has been remarkably rewarding. Not to mention her Island paradise where she lived only a stroll from the beach and whose sunrise and sunsets leaves magical memories on her mind, the place she called home for the past three years needed some deep thought. Truly, she has the best of both worlds, a life that many would envy. Less than an hour later, exhausted she sat on the stairwell of Philip's Condominium. As she reached for Phil's doorbell, her phone rang. It was her cousin Belle. She was now onboard the Carnival Cruise lines with her friend and was checking in on her. It was something they always did.

"Hey sweetheart, what have you been up to honey?"

"Cuz, you won't believe this. I just walked three miles to Phil's place."

"You did what? Sweetie, how's everything with Philip?"

"You're not supposed to be thinking about me cuz, you should be having a lovely time with John."

"You're right darling. Are you sure you're okay?"

"Yes my love, now get back to your cruise."

"Love you."

Love you too, Hun."

After getting off the phone, she dialed Philip's mobile. The sound of a mobile ringing close by startled her.

"Nat, when did you get here?" He asked.

"Philip darling, how long have you been standing there?"

"I wasn't sure but I knew I heard a British accent in front of my house, and sure it was," he said. He was happy to see her and she was relieved. When they were inside she apologized for showing up unannounced and explained how afraid she was that she hadn't heard from him.

"Come honey, I need to show you something." The sight of him, the sound of his voice made her nervous. She knew she had more questions for him but all she wanted was for him to take her in his arms. As if reading her mind, without saying another word he reached forward and kissed her passionately. He wanted to remove her blouse, but he respected her customs. She rested in his arms as he kissed her lovingly.

They were happy to have each other. He kissed her endlessly.

"I love you," he exhaled. Joyful tears filled her eyes as she kisses him passionately. Their bodies became one as fires kindled bringing waves of passion, unfolding something neither of them had ever felt before.

"I love you Natalie."

"What a relief, because I love you too."

With these words he kisses her face lovingly. He then lifted her up and carried her to his room. After gazing at her beauty he kisses her face all over and touched his lips over her pretty nose.

"*You are so lovely,*" he whispered. Still respecting her traditions and beliefs, he did not make love to her. He then embraced her so tightly, she felt like a Dove in the hands of her maker. They stayed in bed the rest of the day, nothing else mattered. When they awoke, it was already dark out. They had spent the entire day in bed.

"*I'm starved,*" Philip whispered. Natalie rolled over lazily…

"What time is it?" she asked.

"Almost seven" he said, yawning. They both laughed.

"Dinner?" he asked. She nods excitedly.

"I'll order in," he said, reaching for the handset. After a very late dinner, the two slipped into Philip's oval tub. Natalie reached over to massage soap over Phil's shoulders but instead he took it playfully out of her hands and massaged it over her instead.

"Please give me the honor," he whispered. He washed her thoroughly, from head to feet and from feet, slowly caressing her. Every bit of touch instilled a fire within her. She leaned forward, kissing him. Yet again, he resisted her. He reached for her hands and pulled her close to him...

"You are a stunning beauty, something about you drives me wild...yet I will not touch what is not yet mine."

The next morning, Natalie was surprised that Philip wasn't next to her. She looked up and met his blue eyes staring at her. She sat up startled. He winked at her. He was sitting on a sofa next to his bed and was holding a pencil and drawing pad in his hand. A cup of coffee sat on the end table next to him.

"Good morning," she said with barely opened eyes.

"What are you up too?"

Then he showed her a beautiful drawing of herself as she lay sleeping.

"You're amazing, this is remarkable," she said excitedly.

"Can I have it?"

"Nope," he said eyes narrowed.

"This one's for me."

She pretended to be sad. He smiled.

"Do you drink coffee?"

"I'm kind of a tea person, however, I'm in your country so I'll give it a try," she said, sounding unsure.

He handed her a small cup almost filled with coffee. She took a sip and her face transformed into a comical expression of disgust.

"Yuck, that's coffee."

Philip laughed hysterically.

"Come on, you have to give it another try. I've heard that first timers have to take a couple of swigs to develop a taste for it."

"Nope, no way, never," she refused and replaced the cup on the nightstand. He reached over and scooped her up. He tickles her, she screams. She was terrified of tickles. She struggled to get away from him. He had stopped tickling her but she was still tussling across the bed as though she was still being tickled. Then suddenly she realized

19

that he had stopped, and she laid there with a silly girlish expression on her face. She looks beautiful and he wanted to make love to her, but he would wait. She was a timeless woman and in due season, maybe soon, yet however long it takes, she would be his masterpiece. He kissed her passionately, before releasing her.

"Darling, I have to get ready for work," he said.

"Please take the day off," she suggested.

"I wish I could, but I can't," he said regretfully.

"I had a day off last week. Maybe I can bring it up with my Partner; after all I am the owner. Nat, please stay here, and wait for me," he said boyishly. It would be a dream to come home to you."

She smiled broadly in response.

"Please babe," he pleaded. He then kissed her on the forehead and hurried out the door.

After Philip left for work, Natalie tidied up a bit. She smiled as she observed Philip's taste in decor' and Art. She reflects back on the previous day and realized that her life was being dramatically transformed. She was falling in love, and with an American. Her father has always quoted these words... "Neither place nor time decide the matters of the heart." She wanted the day to go by quickly, so she kept herself busy. Since she couldn't do much to his already tidy home, she decided to surprise him by rearranging some furniture, and filling his empty picture frames with family photos that were sitting on the coffee table. There were two attractive women in one of the photos who shared a strong resemblance of each other, and she thought that this must be his mom and aunt when they were younger.

It took her almost two hours to finally frame the photos and there were still some sitting in a box under the coffee table. She had finally run out of frames. Natalie dug through the photos in the box and noticed that a lot of the photos were of Italy and some she recognizes as parts of London. Looking at the photos made her think of her father. There's no denying that a large part of her misses him. As angry as she was with him, she knew that she wasn't ready to give up on London's favorite Royal Guard. Other than chasing away her fiancé, he's been a wonderful father. She was only five when she had learned his contact information in London and had never forgotten what they were. She thought that maybe it was time to put the past behind her and put in a call to him. But she resisted, she had promised that she would never phone him again. Whether he realizes it or not, he'd cross the line, at least that's how she felt. He always said that she was very fortunate to have been born on a beautiful Island and even more fortunate to have received a proper upbringing. Richard always spoke to her as though she was responsible for the outcome of the entire world. Yet, life as she is learning cannot always be planned; as time and treasure wait on no man.

Philip came home to find her fast asleep on his sofa, curled up into a ball. She was wearing nothing but his dress shirt and shorts. She lay there peacefully and he didn't want to wake her so he grabbed a blanket from his closet and covered her waist down. Then he notices there was something different about his home. Hmm, someone's been busy, he thought. She has beautiful taste too. With all that she had done, he wondered if she had anything to eat. He looked through the refrigerator and noticed that the sandwich and salad he'd made her was gone. He looked around his home and was surprised by how different it looked. He's usually not friendly about changes made to his place, especially when his Aunt Becky visits and makes changes, but something about this was different and he liked it. Maybe, she was the change he needed, he thought.

Suddenly, he heard an adorable yawn, and a short time later he heard footsteps approaching. He hid himself and watches as she steps into the bathroom. He didn't want to scare her so he sneaked his way across the living room and out the front door. As Natalie heads back into the living room and sat on the couch, Philip entered through the door pretending that he had just arrived.

"Hello beautiful," he said.

"Hi there," she said smiling broadly.

"Hi there handsome, I knew you were home because I was covered when I awoke, Gotha!" He laughed

"Good one," he said, kissing her on the lips.

"You look quite fetching in that shirt that I had to peel away from you to allow you to sleep."

"You are so knotty," she laughed, looking at him slyly.

"I'm headed out for a walk on the trails, want to join me?"

"Sure, let me get changed," she replied.

"Hope you're up for a little race," she challenges him.

"Hmm, someone's making promises they can't keep."

"We'll see," she laughs. Natalie ran ahead of him.

"No fair, wait up," he called pretending. She stood on the trail behind his Townhouse and as he came closer, she took off running.

"Ahh, so that's how you play?"

He watches as she disappears over the small foot hill ahead.

"Awesome view," she called. He pretended for a while that he wasn't going to race her, then like a speed boat he took off and left her hundreds of yards behind.

"Alright, if we keep this up we'll exhaust ourselves, and that would easily ruin what could be an enjoyable stroll," she replied.

"Hmm, somebody doesn't like to lose," he laughed.

She clenched her tiny fist.

"I'm going to get you," she called.

"What are you going to do with those?" He laughed. He gazes at her as she strolls towards him. She looks cute in her pink tennis shoes and matching visor.

"Oh well, I guess I've met my match."

"You think?" he says taking her hands.

As they walked on the rugged terrain, Philip shared with her the reasons he came to California. One of his main reasons was to attend University and obtain a degree in 3D Character Modeling and Animation. It has been his dream to open his own video game studio which after many setbacks became a major success. He boasted the twenty-five people which he employs and the success they've brought him. Then he paused as though hesitating. He then told her about an accident he'd endured when he was only sixteen. He and his cousin Aaron were riding their new ten speed bikes when he was hit by a small tow truck going around sixty miles an hour. No one believed that he would have survived. He told her that he'd sustain a minor injury, and had spent a little over a week in a coma. He told her that in the midst of doubt, he'd made a complete recovery; some called a modern day miracle. Natalie couldn't believe it. Despite his traumatic experience, she could tell that it would be difficult for anyone to believe that he had endured something of the magnitude. He's a survivor; a handsome one too. He told her that he'd promised himself that he would make each day count. He believes that the year 1998 defined his entire life. It is a time he would always reflect on throughout his life to keep the promise he had made to himself to make the rest of his life an adventure, a wonderful adventure.

Since his accident, Philip has traveled to the 'British Isles' as well as Italy. Of all the places he'd visited, Italy was his favorite. He named it a place filled with Art, Love and passionate expressive people; a people who keep their city's name alive by their genuine public displays of affection. It's a place any Artist like him dreams of. Natalie enjoys listening to Philip; it was like a version of the Indiana Jones movie and she felt like she was a part of it.

"Tell me more about Italy," she said excitedly.

"After getting through customs, I was truly convinced that Italy has the busiest Airport of all the European countries I've visited. It wasn't just the airport. The streets of Italy are always very busy, with people from many different countries and all different walks of life. It was the most involved place I've ever seen, with artists from many different backgrounds. There were those who lined the streets like in San Francisco, offering to sketch anything of one's liking. Some people refused but still would drop coins in their money pans-it was a glorious sight to see.

Silly me, I really should have made better travel arrangements. I remembered how difficult it was for me to find a hotel room. Every place I had enquired was fully booked. I eventually ran into a nice couple who pointed me to Camp Alpi Doro. I was very surprised by the Amount of Americans and Brits I ran into there.

"Yes, Italy is quite beautiful; my grandmother Annabelle enjoys visiting in the summer."

"I see," he replied. "I went from being a lost, confused American in what appears to be the busiest city in the world, to finding home. After a nice camp shower, and a hearty meal, I pulled out my coffin shaped tent and called it a night." He paused and shook his head. "Suddenly, I felt like my favorite TV star, Indiana Jones." Philip busted out laughing. Natalie grinned.

"What happened?" she asked.

"I awoke the next morning staring in the faces of over a dozen Italians standing next to me holding up small crosses. It was the perfect movie scene."

Natalie laughed uncontrollably.

Philip then knew that coffin shaped tents were no longer welcomed in Italy, at least not at camp Alpi Doro.

Philip continued...

"I swore that it was pure luck when I ran into Stephen and his wife Pricilla, who was cutting their trip short to return to England. Stephen offered me to stay at his 'Shi Lai Lai' which we Americans would call a hotel on wheels. It was the perfect setup with a nice warm bed, television and a refrigerator filled with food. Not forgetting the finest collection of wine any wine lover could dream of. Before leaving, Stephen warned me that all this food had better be completely gone before I return to the States. He also told me that I can have all the wine that I can manage, but, if upon his return he finds any of his other personal possessions missing, he will personally hunt me down." Then they both engulfed in laughter, catching the attention of other joggers on the trail.

"Stephen thanked me for being his guest and bid me farewell. For a trip I hardly planned, it turned out to be the ideal vacation.

"That was bloody fantastic Phil and I love the way you told it; I think you should write about it," Natalie said.

"I just might," he said, taking her hands.

After they returned, the two enjoyed a homemade dinner and later they watched one of the movies that they bought the day before, "Something's Gotta Give," on DVD. They both enjoyed the film. As a matter of fact, it became their personal favorite. Later Natalie teased him that he had a crush on one of the women in the film.

"Nope," he blushed. "I think it was really cute the way she did that little dance; it was real free flowing."

Natalie winked at him. "Yep, you have a crush."

They both laughed and cuddled up together on the sofa. They gazed at each other... Natalie ruffled his hair and tugged at his ear. He leaned forward and kisses her softly. She could tell that he was very patient. The perfect gentleman who treasured her traditions and beliefs. There was definitely something on his mind... He then kissed her on the forehead like a child, and gazing into her eyes, he said "I love you." He then reached into his shirt pocket and removed a little black box and submitted to his knees...

"Natalie, my lady in waiting, I understand the short timing of this, would you marry me?"

Overcome by the moment, tears filled her eyes, and almost lost for words, she said "Yes, yes I'll marry you," she said beaming with excitement as he slowly slipped a gorgeous Diamond ring onto her finger. At the sound of the most beautiful woman he's ever known agreeing to marry him; he kissed her lovingly, holding her snuggly in his arms, cherishing her presence like never before.

Chapter 5

It's been a week since Philip's proposal. Natalie wasted no time informing her relatives of the amazing news. Word of her engagement had reached relatives far and wide, the heart of London and the furthest corners of West Croydon, England. As she reflected back on the past few weeks, she knew that the day that she had waited for her entire life had finally arrived. As all of her dreams are coming true, Natalie reflected on her life in England, she realizes how very random it was to meet the one she loves in a country that never once crossed her mind. Maybe, she thought that not everyone finds their soul mate in their backyard. But one thing is certain, that rivers, nor lakes or oceans, can keep true love apart.

As she thought of the criticism she's received from her Caribbean friends; to them she was fortunate to be British and the daughter of a Royal Guard. To some she was an oddball; the fact that she was so attractive and in her early twenties, but wasn't in a relationship. Unknown to them, Natalie was previously engaged, but had kept this information to herself and was single by choice. It was not common for a lady of her upbringing to be in a relationship shortly after a previously failed engagement. Something she realized was foreign to most. Natalie knew that news of her engagement may only rest well with some of her relatives, the fact that Philip is American. However, the only opinion that matters was that of hers. Although she would love her Grandma's opinion, she didn't depend on it. Yet, despite her straight forwardness, she is someone Natalie always secretly admired.

The phones over at her cousin's house and at Philip's rang constantly from relatives all over; some seeking information on dates, while others sought information regarding location and others that were downright nosy. The phones rang nonstop at all hours of the night as some folks were hardly aware of the major time differences.

Philip watched as Natalie patiently listened to the hundreds of messages that were on her voicemail; this made him love her all the more. How was she this patient, listening and making her best attempt to return each phone call by the end of each week? It was becoming a daunting task, more so a fulltime job with overtime. It seemed that all her time the past few weeks were consumed with phone calls. Philip didn't want the most amazing days of their lives to become consumed by unnecessary distractions. He reached out to his fiancé with a suggestion. ~" *Hey babe* " ~ he said lovingly with a slightly wicked expression on his face. Then he reached for the answer machine and switched it off. They both laughed.

"Hunny, I'm marrying you, not them," he said.

Suddenly she only wanted a small wedding with only the people that really mattered to her. Then she stared at her fiancé as though she'd seen a ghost.

"What's wrong Hun?"

"My dad, I want my dad to be there."

"Well, call and invite him."

"It's not that easy, I haven't spoken to him in over three years."

"Wow, umm, why not?" Phil asked, scratching his head.

"Long story," she replied looking embarrassed.

"I don't think I'm mad enough to not invite my dad to my wedding."

"Then phone him in the morning."

"He doesn't even know I'm in America. This alone would make him *pitch a fit,* much more for the fact that I'm getting married."

She looked really concerned which made her appear even more beautiful. He was beginning to worry how important this was to her. Will she call off the engagement without her father's approval? Philip didn't fall asleep until after four that morning thinking of ways in which to talk Natalie out wanting her father's approval. Natalie woke up earlier than usual, since England was seven hours ahead of California, she didn't want to phone her father too close to his dinner time, which her entire life, she knew was improper. Since it was only a little after seven in the morning in California she knew it was after two in the evening her dad's time.

"Phil," she called. "Wake up, I'm getting ready to phone dad, would you please sit with me for support."

Philip giggled at how nervous she was about phoning her dad.

27

"Oh Hun, I'm beat, you can do it, after all he's your dad," he replied.

Natalie finally brought herself to dialing her father's number; the 01144 number she found in her mother's journal when she was only five and had never forgotten. The phone rang several times, the familiar sound of that ring made her nervous. Then after the fourth ring, a female British voice answered,

"Hello!" It was Maureen.

"Hello, hi Maureen," she said nervously.

"Is dad home?"

"Who's this?"

"It's me, Natalie, I would like to speak with my father, it's rather urgent."

"Oh my goodness, I can't believe this. Natalie, how are you, and where in the world have you been?"

"I'm sorry I haven't been in touch, Maureen. You know what he did was unforgivable."

"Are you coming home?" Maureen asked excitedly.

"I'm not sure. I'm in the States and I'm getting married, I would love it if you can come."

"Oh my God, you're getting married, my goodness. That's wonderful Nat, is he an American?"

"Umm, yes he is."

"It doesn't matter to me, I'm just so happy for you, my love."

"Okay sweetie, I'll put you on with your dad, and then we'll talk some more afterwards, alright."

"Okay, I love you sweetheart."

"Love you too, Maureen." Natalie could hear the conversation on the other side of the Phone.

"Richard, could you please pick up the phone, it's your daughter."

"Natalie?"

"Yes," she replied.

"Please tell Natalie I'm occupied at the moment and will return her call momentarily."

A short while later Maureen returns to the phone.

"Are you there love?"

"Yes I'm here."

"He's not available at the moment, and would phone you back momentarily."

"Ok then, thank you Maureen.

"Come home Nat and get married here, at the Manor. Please try and make things right with your dad, we all miss you."

"I'll think about it."

"Please Nat, you know how this will look if the press picks up news of your marriage in the Americas; it wouldn't look good for your father."

"I know, but that's all the more reason I should get married away from there. It's one of the reasons I left."

"Come on Nat, please listen to me. Remember you only have one father and you might live to regret it."

"Okay Maureen, I'll give it some thought."

"That's a girl. Alright, bye for now sweetie."

"Bye, Maureen." Natalie returned the phone to the handset.

Philip was no longer in bed and the smell of coffee was coming from the kitchen. Her fiancé was right, after her second dreadful cup of coffee, she was now a fan. She walked toward the kitchen and joined him at the table.

"You look happy, I suppose it went well," Philip said.

"Can't promise, but he was occupied and said that he would return my call momentarily."

"He will darling, you'll see."

About two hours later the phone rang. Philip peeked at the caller ID.

"It's an 044 area code, looks international," he said.

Natalie hurried to the phone and answered with a cheerful...

"Hi dad." It wasn't her dad, it was her grandmother calling to congratulate her on her engagement and to get wedding details.

"I suppose that you were expecting to hear from your father?"

"Yes Gram," Natalie replied.

She was pleased that Natalie is making an effort to reach out to her father, as it displeased her greatly when she learned that the two hadn't spoken in several years. Philip observed Natalie's posture as she spoke to her Grandmother. It was as though she was speaking to the Queen of England, addressing her with the utmost respect. After their conversation, Natalie turned around and looked at Philip.

"This was my Grandma; she is thrilled for me and would be attending my wedding," she said with a broad grin.

"That's awesome!" Philip cheered. Then he watched as her face became sad and unexpressive. He didn't like seeing her like this. *"Why hasn't her father phoned yet?"* he thought. It was the weekend so Philip suggested that they give him more time. Despite having drunk two cups of coffee, they returned to bed and fell asleep. She awoke around late afternoon and after checking her caller ID, she realized that her father hadn't returned her call. It was now after nine in the evening in London and she knew that the chances that her father would phone were slim to none.

That evening, she skipped out on her walk with Philip and waited by the phone; she couldn't risk missing his call. Philip returned from his walk and she was still sitting by the phone. He didn't have to ask whether her dad had called. He can tell by her girlish expression, waiting patiently by the phone that he hadn't. It was now a little past midnight in England and she had given up all expectations of hearing from Richard. As she was about to sit down to dinner, the phone rang. She answered and it was him.

"Natalie, you're in America."

"Umm, hi dad, yes, how did you know?"

"An hour after you called, I tried pulling up your number from the caller ID to phone you back and I realized it was an American area code. Young lady, couldn't you inform me that you were traveling to the States? How could you have done this to me?"

Natalie tried to break the conversation to tell her dad that she was getting married, but she realized that it would only make matters worse. He continued on for almost an hour, he was more upset than she had anticipated. She didn't want to speak in her defense because she knew that would do no good. He was wrong, but she didn't interrupt. She did phone him to inform him of her plans, but he did not return her call. She thought that maybe she should have put it in writing. Learning how hurt her father was almost broke her heart. The least she expected was that he would decline her wedding invitation, then at least she would have an answer. But he didn't give her that opportunity. She didn't get to tell him why she had phoned. She realized that leaving England had hurt him more than she realized.

About an hour later, Philip heard the receiver return to the phone, and by the way she looked, he knew it didn't go well. As a matter of fact, he didn't hear his fiancé say a word. He walked toward her, embraced and kissed her on her forehead.

"You don't have to talk about it now if you don't want to," He said. He then drew her a warm bath which he sprinkled with strawberry bath salts and lavender. After turning on her favorite music, he scattered rose petals around the bathtub. At the sound of her favorite Artist's voice, she felt an inviting sense of relief. As her fiancé hung her bathrobe she walked toward him and embraced him from behind. He turned to face her and the look of sadness in her eyes begged him to make love to her but he remained a perfect gentleman. As she got into the tub, Philip left the room and returned momentarily holding a bottle of Cabernet Sauvignon; his favorite red wine. He poured them both a glass, and after placing hers within reach, he sat back and enjoyed the view he had created.

She sparkled in the softness of the candlelight. He wanted nothing more than to join her, but he respected her too much to take away that precious opportunity she needed, to break her silence. When she had finished her glass of wine, she spoke in a tearful voice.

"Phil, he made me feel like I was an infant."
And before she could say another word, she was reduced to tears.

"I didn't even get to tell him that I was getting married. I didn't even get a word in."

Philip couldn't watch the woman he has come to love continue in sadness any longer. He had to do something. If he loves her, he must find a way, and soon. He wasted no time in devising a plan to make her the happiest woman alive. Suddenly, he had the wildest idea ever. *No way, he thought.* But it was the only way. Philip spent half the night surfing the web. He wanted this problem to be solved by morning.

At around 2:00am, exhausted, as he was about to get into bed, he realized that his fiancé was not in bed. Suddenly, he had a horrifying thought. He hurried toward the master bath and his fears were confirmed. There she was, fast asleep in the tub and the bottle of wine was almost gone. The water must have gotten cold by now. He panicked as he reached into the tub and lifted her out.

"Honey, are you okay."

He placed her on the bed and wrapped blankets around her. As he wraps the blankets around her, she awakes.

"What happened?" she asked.

He giggled at the clueless expression on her face.

"I'm freezing, what happened?" she said looking puzzled.

"I think you had a little bit too much to drink, but you're going to be okay. Let me get you some water, it works wonders."

She drank the entire glass and then rolled over to sleep. She was shivering and Philip dug through her bags to find her something to wear. He removed the blankets and helped her into a very enticing pair of sleepwear. Her soft skin smell of lavender and as he climbs into bed next to her, they cuddled. He resisted as she turns to face him. He yearned to fill her desires, but she was still drowsy from too much wine. He kisses her and watches as she fell asleep. In a matter of weeks, he'd fallen helplessly in love with a British, Princess. It was almost impossible to believe that someone so beautiful could be found dining at a local Mall.

The following morning, Phil presented Natalie with two printouts. As she observed them her eyes widened in disbelief...

"This cannot be? No way, are we going home to London?"

"Darling, we are going to fetch your dad and I'm not taking no for an answer," he said in a very convincing British Accent.

"Well, for how long?"

"Three weeks, I want to give us sufficient time, in case your old man turns out to be as stubborn as you."

"Oh, be warned, he is," she said somberly.

Philip watch as the woman he loves transforms into the happiest person he could remember.

"Now that's the young lady I remembered," he said, pouring her more tea. He learned something from this. That in order to win a woman's heart, one must be certain that part of her heart is not missing. They had exactly one week to prepare for their trip and exactly two months to the day to get Natalie's father to attend her wedding.

"Cousin Belle would be home from her cruise tomorrow. I'm going to stop by for a minute before she gets home. I think she would appreciate the quiet time alone with her new guy."

"Great idea. Let's head over there after breakfast."

Then Phil paused for a moment.

"I have an idea babe."

"Guess what, I have one too."

"You first," he said.

She smiled. "Umm, let's move in together."

He approached her and kissed her on the lips. "Exactly what I had in mind," he said.

"Technically, I think I already did." They both laughed and kissed each other affectionately. After breakfast the happy couple headed over to Belle's. After a few hours and three trips back and forth, Natalie has officially moved in with her fiancé. Later that day her mobile rang. It was her cousin checking in on her.

"How're you hunny? Got cold feet yet?" She joked. "I still can't believe that you're going to be married. I cannot say that I'm surprised. You are very beautiful."

"Well thank you my darling cousin, is that your approval?"

"You've got yourself a real catch," Belle raved.

"Don't worry Cuz, I promise to keep him away from you."

They both chuckled.

"I have another surprise for you... I moved out. I figure you'll need your space."

"No you didn't!" she cried. "Babe, that was way too fast. What if it doesn't work out? And who's going to look out for me, and give me the will to live when I'm going through one of my girly days?" Belle cried.

"I'm only three miles away sweetheart. Plus, you don't like living with me all that much."

"Don't say that, you know I'm crazy about you silly."

"Alright then, I'll come over in a few days to meet your friend from San Francisco."

"Okay babe, say hi to Philip for me."

"I sure will cuz, I'll see you later."

"Okay honey, bye."

By the great smell coming from the kitchen, she knew that Phil had started lunch.

"How's your cousin, is she enjoying her cruise?"

"Not after our conversation. She can't believe that I moved out."

"She'll be okay darling."

"You love her don't you?"

Natalie smiled. "I do; she can be lovely. However, I think that this new boyfriend will do her some good." Philip agreed.

Later that day, Natalie phoned the Embassy to inquire about an extension to her visa. She informed them of her pending marriage to an American Citizen and she was told that she is now eligible for a K1 Visa which allows re-entry into the U.S. Philip then mailed documents to immigration to confirm his title of citizenship. Within five days his fiancé received an appointment with a local Immigration Consulate. While at the Embassy, she learned that because of her British status, that she didn't need a Visa or an extension. Philip couldn't believe it.

"I should have known that," he fretted.

Natalie smiled.

"Truth is, when you're born here there's no need to be up to speed with immigration laws."

Later that same day Philip took his fiancé to dinner to celebrate. They were both excited and were looking forward to their trip to London. They discussed their plans over dinner.

"Do you think they have GPS in merry ole London?"

"They didn't when I was growing up, but I doubt it," she giggled.

"It's been three years since I left and of course, a lot can happen in three years," she reminded him.

"You're a good woman Natalie. Some women wouldn't care whether or not their father came to their wedding. Truth is, after losing my parents at a young age, I am happy to help you make amends with your dad, because you only have one, and they don't live forever," he said.

"Philip, this really means a lot to me. Not only are you handsome, but also very wise. I'm a very lucky woman."

"I'm the lucky one," he said, reaching across the table and taking her hands.

After dinner, Philip and Natalie visited Belle to inform her of their plans to return to England for a few weeks. She was surprised by the suddenness, but agreed that it was a great time for her to visit her father. As the three sat discussing England, Belle's friend entered the room.

"Hi you must be Natalie, I've heard a lot," he said reaching out his hand to hers.

Belle smiled broadly as her friend joined them at the table.

"Philip and Natalie, I would like you to meet my friend John," she said. There was excitement in her voice.

"Hello John, it's a pleasure!" They said simultaneously. He shook both their hands and congratulated them on their engagement. John

34

is a tall blue eyed brunette and recently retired firefighter. Phil and Natalie thought he seemed very genuine and appears to be very fond of Belle, as confirmed by their occasional open displays of affection. After visiting with her cousin, they headed home to prepare for their trip.

Chapter 6

The next few days flew by and before long, the happy couple were aboard British Airways to London. Philip would have chosen first class but decided against it when he learned that their flight was going to be lightly booked. There were two empty seats next to them and a few empty seats elsewhere on the flight. Economy has always bothered him but he wanted to be humbled for his fiancé, who's apparently very well off but doesn't mind walking for miles or even spending years away from her posh English lifestyle. She was a rare beauty; the type most men would search for their entire life.

The pilot announced that their flight would be departing shortly. The stewardess was a tall attractive blond who appeared in her mid-thirties. She was dressed comfortably in a navy-blue pants suit, white blouse with a matching navy-blue scarf, tied neatly around her collar.

"I love the extra space on this flight. Maybe we can ask the stewardess if we can make use of the extra seats," Philip suggested.

"Good here's our opportunity, she's headed in our direction."

"Excuse me ma'am. Is it okay if we occupy the other seats?" Philip asked.

"Absolutely, we should be departing shortly," she replied, in a soft British accent.

"Thank you," Philip replied.

"You're most welcome."

Then surprisingly as she turns to leave, she glances over at Natalie.

"Ma'am, if you don't mind me saying, you look very familiar. It can't be, or you'd be flying your own private jet to London," she said now smiling. Philip glanced back and forth at the stewardess and Natalie.

"I'm aware of whom you're referring to, however, I have no comment at this time," Natalie said smiling. The stewardess knew that "no comment" meant that she should keep her discovery a secret. Thrilled, she took Natalie's hands and shook it gently.

"May I say, it is truly an honor. Thank you for choosing British Airways."

After she left, Philip looks at his fiancé.

"*Who are you?*" he asks in a quieted voice.

She made a comical face at him and said...

"Just your fiancé darling, the one who buried her servants in a shallow grave in her backyard."

"Oh that one," he laughs. Glad we finally meet, darling."

Philip was still curious and thought that maybe she might have recognized Natalie from flying with them before. A few moments later, after the stewardess did her final rounds, the Pilot announced that the flight was now ready for departure. All passengers were instructed to take their seats and fasten their seatbelts.

"Don't you just love the way the stewardess performs her demonstration. It's perfect."

Philip glanced at her and smiled. After what seemed like hours later, Natalie had fallen asleep and was awakened by the sound of a moving cart. Her Fiancé had also dozed off. She patted him gently.

"Honey, would you like something to drink?"

"What time is it?" he asks half awake.

"It's exactly five in the evening," the stewardess responded.

"What would you two like to drink?"

"We'll take two glasses of your finest champagne," Philip said, stretching his arms.

"Most certainly sir," she responded. "You can also purchase an additional bottle if that is of any interest to you sir."

"Please do, thank you," he replied.

For lunch, they each had salmon steaks, with a side of garlic herb rice and assorted vegetables.

"Yummy, this looks awesome, bon appétit," Philip said, folding her napkin on her lap.

After a filling dinner they enjoyed their Champagne. And despite having had dinner, after only two glasses of champagne Natalie became drowsy and blew kisses at Philip.

"Come here babe," she said. There was that expression in her eyes.

"Oh, sweetie," he said. She then leaned toward him and he kissed her gently on the lips.

"In only a few more hours, we'll have a nice warm room all to ourselves."

Philip lifted up the arms of the two empty seats next to them and sat in the next seat over. Natalie was now able to stretch her legs. She placed her head on his shoulders and he held her lovingly. He then requested two extra blankets from the stewardess. He made one into a pillow and covered her with the other. Philip gazed at her as she drifted off to sleep. Her angelic face and full lips begged for affection.

The next six hours drifted by slowly. Philip was awakened by the sound of the pilot over the intercom announcing that they were roughly forty-five minutes away from landing at London Heathrow. Philip had booked a three week stay at the Palace Hotel which is located only a quarter of a mile from the Airport. Nearly an hour later, their flight landed gracefully on schedule at the world renowned, London Heathrow International Airport.

The lines were moving slower than usual and an hour later they still hadn't clear customs. Finally, it was their turn and an airport personnel motioned for them to come forward. She's an attractive African woman who appears to be in her mid-fifties.

"She doesn't look very friendly," Philip whispered.

"Are you visiting England for business or pleasure?" she asked sternly.

"We are visiting family madam," Philip answered warmly.

She then appeared a bit friendlier.

"Oh, you have family in England?"

"Yes, Madam, this is Philip Lane, my fiancé. My name is Natalie, the daughter of Richard Baldwin; a Royal Guard. We are here to get my father's approval to marry."

Natalie then presented her with her Passport. By then the attendant appeared much friendlier.

"How wonderful. Since you are a British Citizen, it is required that your fiancé obtain a visa to enter the United Kingdom. Would a six month stay allow sufficient time?" She asked warmly.

"Absolutely madam," Philip replied enthusiastically. Although they didn't need this much time, the couple was ecstatic and thanked the officer for her generosity. Luckily their luggage was ready to be claimed. They grabbed their belongings and prepared to flag down the first available taxi to the Palace Hotel.

It seemed that every passenger was waiting outside the airport for the same purpose. They were thankful for two things; they had arrived safely and the city of London was not as cold as they had anticipated. It was almost a half an hour wait, but they finally got into a taxi. When they arrived at the hotel lobby, they were surprised that there were only two people ahead of them.

"Thank goodness, I was beginning to get sick of lines," Natalie said in relief. The couple standing in front of them looked over and smiled as though agreeing with her statement.

"That's hilarious darling, but I have to agree," he said with a chuckle. When they got into their room it was cold, yet cozy. After turning on the fireplace, they both took hot showers. Moments later, despite having slept almost the entire trip, they both fell fast asleep.

The following morning, Natalie awoke to the smell of freshly brewed tea and the flaming sound of the fireplace as it warms their room. Philip was peeking through the window. She glances at the clock on the wall and it was only a little after six in the morning.

"Ugh, it's very early, please come back to bed love," she called. Philip turns to face her. Her messy hair and half opened eyes were more inviting than the busy London streets below.

"We made it babe. We are in the largest little city in the world."

"I'm home. Yikes!" she said and buried her head under a pillow.

"Come have tea with me babe." Before he said another word, he heard soft snores coming from below the blankets. He shook his head and smiled...

"I thought she would be more thrilled about being home, oh well," he sighed. A short while later, he returned to bed. Somehow he just wasn't tired and was a little jealous that his fiancé was completely passed out. He slowly removed the blankets revealing her silky nightwear. He ran his fingers over her perfectly sculpted abs. He thought she looked quite becoming. He kissed her gently and she wrapped her arms around him. She opened her eyes slowly revealing her large green eyes which almost appeared frightened. She then pulled her long legs up to her chest, cuddling a pillow into the fetal position. Surprised and unsure, he brushed her hair out of her face, surprised that she has resisted him.

It was almost noon when she finally awoke and noticed that Philip was not next to her. She searched around the room and peeked into the bathroom, but he was nowhere to be found. Then she notices a piece of paper on the floor next to the bed. As she got closer, she realized that it was a note that Phil had left which must have fallen on the floor, when she got out of bed.

It read...

"Hey Hun, I went to pick up our rental. You were sleeping so beautifully; I didn't want to wake you. I will return within the hour-xx Philip." After breakfast and a hot bath, Philip still hadn't return. She pulled the curtains and peeked out of the window. There's a major advantage being on the fifth floor and having a soundproof room. The view was spectacular; and despite being in the heart of the city, she couldn't hear a sound from all the commotion taking place in the busy streets below. As she was about to go through her luggage, Philip came through the door.

"Hey babe, ready for a little adventure. The weather forecast this morning said that we'll have a few hours of sunshine. I also GPS your dad's address this morning; he's roughly an hour's drive outside of the city."

Natalie yawned. "Yes, about that," she paused.

"It's a good thing we're here for a few weeks; I think it will take me at least a week to get over this jetlag," she said exhaustedly.

"So what did we rent?"

"It's a surprise, but rugged enough to get around the toughest terrain," he boasted.

"What's that you're holding?" she asked.

"Oh it's a city guide I got from the front desk; we are only a short drive from all of London's major attractions."

"Sorry babe, but we won't be needing that, forgot?" she giggled.

"Sure we do," he said, unfolding the guide.

Finally realizing he said...

"Oh silly me, that's right, this is your old stomping ground," he laughed.

"Bet I can tell you exactly what's in that tour guide," she said sitting on the sofa next to the fireplace.

"Edinburg Clock is only twenty miles away and the Palace Manor is only a half an hour's drive from here. Thorpe Park, one of

London's most popular theme parks is only a twenty-minute drive from here."

"Oh really, how exciting," he said pretentiously. Want to hear something even more exciting; Windsor Castle is only about a ten-minute drive from here and they conduct tours every hour. They conduct tours all week except for the weekends. The final tour occurs right at six thirty this evening."

"That's awesome; maybe we can make that one. That's the only Castle I didn't visit on my tour of Europe," he replied.

Then suddenly Natalie appeared withdrawn. He sat beside her.

"Are you okay babe?"

"Umm, maybe I should call my father," she said looking up at him.

"Perhaps you should wait till after we get back, by then you might feel better about it," he suggested.

"You're right, but I must remain as discreet as possible," she warned. Philip was already dressed, so she slipped on some casuals, a visor and matching white tennis shoes. After looping a cardigan around her hips, they were off.

Chapter 7

Phillip pointed the key fob toward the Jeep, unlocking the doors to their rental.

"A Jeep Wrangler, that's perfect!" she beamed. "How long do we have it for?"

"The entire trip," he said excitedly.

"Awesome!" They both scrambled into the vehicle and sped out of the lot onto the busy Southgate Ave.

"Look out, you're driving against traffic!" someone shouted. Philip maneuvered and aligned himself over a solid double yellow line, making an illegal U-turn in time, avoiding a head on collision with an incoming taxi.

"Wow that was a rude awakening. Not only do they drive on the wrong side of the road, the driver seat is on the wrong side of the car," Philip laughed.

"I think it was your fault Fluff." she teased

"Fluff, is this my new name?" It's what Maureen calls me when I make a mistake," she giggled.

"But Fluff!" He laughs hysterically.

"There's Windsor Castle coming up on our right," Natalie said pointing excitedly.

As they entered the visitors parking, Philip couldn't believe his eyes.

"This place is fantastic. The structure looks brand new, have they recently upgraded the architecture?"

"Not that I know of. I've seen it over a dozen times but it never gets old."

"Look honey, I think they are getting ready for the next tour. Is there a fee to get in?"

"The last time I was here with Maureen, we bought our passes inside this building over there," she said pointing. A husky bearded male in green uniform approached them from behind. He cleared his throat to get their attention.

"Welcome to Windsor Castle, here for the next tour, folks?"

"Yes sir!" Philip said enthusiastically, placing his hands in his pockets.

"The next tour begins in ten minutes; you may obtain your passes over there at the booth, unless you've already purchased them at an alternative location. Passes are thirty-four pounds per adult. Persons under eighteen are free," the tour guide said in a welcoming voice.

The couple bought their passes and joined the evening group.

"This is a small group compared to what I've seen in the past," Natalie said. Philip looked on in amazement at the high towers and magnificent arches of the Castle. He reached into his backpack and pulled out his Camera.

"Sorry Hun, cameras aren't allowed," Natalie whispered. She was only five when she first saw Windsor Castle. Her father used to often tease her about her first reaction from being in the home of royalty. According to her father, on her first visit she asked whether she could stay here with the Queen and created quite a fuss when it was time to leave. Of course her reaction had won the affection of the group, who all pitched in to comfort her.

Before they began entering the castle, the group was given the opportunity to purchase items at the shop in the castle's courtyard. Then the visitors were asked to place all food items in sealed bags before entrance. Before being admitted to the castle, a process similar to that of airport security occurs. They were then taken through security where all bags are checked for suspicious items. After everyone completed security, the Tour Guide gave the group a short introduction of the castle. He then took them through the entrance to Queen Mary's Doll House. The group gasped in amazement, and quiet murmurings could be heard.

"Welcome to Queen Mary's Dollhouse at Windsor Castle. This was one of Queen Annie's favorite rooms," the tour guide announced. "One cannot begin to describe the magnificent craftsmanship that went into this room, truly amazing," the Guide said enthusiastically. After their visit to Queen Mary's Doll House, they were introduced to Windsor Castle State Apartments. Philip placed his arms around Natalie's shoulders.

"This would have been part of the perfect honeymoon. I think we did things a bit differently."

"There's nothing wrong with changing tradition," she said joyfully. As they walked around the Tower to get to the Apartments, loud murmurings could be heard as the visitors looked down upon the lush countryside views of Windsor. The State Apartments were an even greater work of art.

"I still can't believe that Windsor Castle is over nine hundred years old," Philip whispered.

"If we'd come earlier, we would have seen the changing of the guards," someone whispered. After their visit to the Apartments, they were guided to the St. George's Chapel.

"One cannot deny the beauty of this ancient structure. From roof to foundation, this medieval arc portrays some of the finest artistry of modern England," the tour guide said proudly, leading on.

"Is this chapel open to the public?" a member of the group asks.

"As a matter of fact, it is. However, although open to the public, membership is limited only to members of the Royal family," the guide replied.

"As some of you may know, that this chapel has a distinct difference from the other chapels around London, due to the fact that within its walls are the resting places of some of the former monarchs of England."

"Yikes, that's rather creepy," said a little boy who appears to be no more than six. The members of the group including the Tour Guide erupted in laughter. At the end of this statement, the Guide announced...

"This brings us to the conclusion of our Tour. Thank you for your genuine interest and continued support of the Tour of London." This was followed by a round of applause followed by a familiar chant... "Long Live the Queen." All visitors were then escorted toward the entrance of the Castle, where some members retrieved their electronic devices from the security desk.

"That was quite the treat," Philip said exhausted. "Think we have time for another tour?" he asked.

"Not today darling."

"Okay sweetheart, let's head back and catch up on some sleep, tomorrow, we'll go look for your dad. How does that sound?"

"Sounds marvelous, darling," she replied, as they searched the crowded parking lot for their vehicle...

"I can't wait to marry you," Philip said.

"Me too darling."

After locating their Jeep, the couple sped into London.

The following day, after coffee, feeling a little bit daring, Natalie picked up the phone and dialed her father directly. A male voice answered... "Hello." It was Richard.

"Hello father, how are you?"

"Natalie I do not wish to speak with you at the moment."

"Dad, this is ridiculous, you can't avoid me forever. I really don't understand why you're so upset."

"Well after all, the last time I checked, I was still your father. You wanted to go to America; you should have informed me first."

"Dad, I'm a grown woman, I do not need your permission for each time I need to cough." Philip laughed out loud.

"This is not what I mean and you know it!" he yelled.

"Well I'm here in London and I need to see you."

"Well don't bother; you're just wasting your time," he shouted.

"Father, I'm engaged to be married and I need you to be there," she said, cutting him off.

Richard exhale deeply and then the line went silent.

"Dad, dad, darn it," she fretted. Then she felt Philip's hand on her shoulder.

"Come here love, don't fret. Maybe he's just not ready to give up his only daughter."

She turns to face him and he embraces her.

"I love you," she said.

"I love you too, doll."

"But Philip, do you really believe that three weeks is sufficient."

"Hey there, you worry too much," he teased. She laughs in agreement.

Later, the couple got into the Jeep. They were going to pay Richard a little surprise visit.

"I don't think that we should bother, he's being so stubborn," she cried.

"He'll have to get used to his American son-in-Law because, as he would learn, we do not take no for an answer, especially when it comes to the ones we love," Phil said in a half daring, half entitled tone. Natalie laughed. When they arrived on the outskirts of London, Philip reached into the glove compartment and pulled out the hand written directions he wrote the previous morning.

"It looks like we have to head toward West Croydon. He lives in Surrey, correct?"

"Darling, you made a wrong turn back there."

"No Hun, I got this," Philip replied.

"Alright then, be warned. I'll only be here to enjoy the ride," she kidded. She wonders why Philip kept forgetting that this is her hometown and that they didn't need written directions. After about a half an hour's drive, the two found themselves on a quiet road in a very rural part of town.

"It's so quiet and beautiful out here, nice break from the busy city," Phil said.

They kept driving for another few miles.

"I think we might have made a wrong turn somewhere," he finally admitted.

"We shouldn't be too far off now," she teased.

"What's that sound?" Philip asked.

As they turned a corner, Philip swerved just in time to avoid a large herd of sheep and landed the Jeep in a muddy ditch.

"Darn it, where did they all come from?" he fretted.

Natalie reached for her camera and took photos of the herd.

"Honey, this is one of the highlights of the English Countryside," She said in an entertaining way.

"Well my love, this is one highlight that absolutely sucks!" he ranted. As she got out of the car to take more photos, she landed flat on her butt in the muddy ditch.

"Oh, just perfect!" she yelled.

It was Philip's turn to make fun of her.

"I'm starting to love this highlight, quite a lovely highlight," he laughed.

"Not funny!" she beamed.

"Nor is our rented four-wheeler in a ditch while you take photos of sheep," he laughed.

"Need a hand their folks?" asked the Sheepherder who's been observing them the entire time.

"Umm, yes please sir," Philip replied a little embarrassed.

"I guess you folks aren't from around here," he said in a rusty tone, a pipe sticking from one side of his mouth.

"I'm from America, but my fiancé is English. We're here visiting her family."

"I see, gullible Yankees, alright, let's see if we can get you out of that ditch ladies."

"What did he say?" she asked, growing more upset.

"It's alright honey. We need his help," Philip said.

"That's a four-wheeler you got there, with the right amount of sass, you can swerve right out of that ditch," the herder barked. Philip got into the Jeep and stepped on the gas.

"Keep it up, she's moving," the herder assured while walking closer to the Jeep.

"Get in Honey, unless you want to stay here with grumpy over there."

Natalie got into the Jeep and Philip stepped on the gas pedals, furiously. The vehicle sped out of the ditch spraying wet mud all over the herder's face and clothing. As the herder stood in shock, Philip shouted...

"That's what you get for calling us gullible Yankees."

They laughed and sped off. After a few miles they realized that they had made a complete circle.

"Phil, we're back at the fork where we made the wrong turn," she said.

"We should call it a day sweetheart. I don't think a muddy behind is very convincing," he giggled as she tried dusting off the dirt on her backside. As they headed back into London, Philip toyed about his London experiences so far.

"Can't imagine that this herder thinks that we are all Yankees now," he said sarcastically.

"I bet he's learned his lesson, the grumpy stereotypical jerk," she said attempting to sound ill mannered.

"I don't remember thanking him for his help," Philip said remembering.

They laughed heartily and headed back into town.

The couple spent the rest of the evening indoors. The temperature outside had suddenly dropped and grey rain clouds began to form over the city, cancelling all plans for further sightseeing. Philip pulled his laptop computer from his backpack.

"Hey babe, maybe we can try catching up with your dad at his job?" Natalie looked up from her computer.

"Honey' there's something I never told you."

"And what's that?" Phil asked, looking slightly curious.

47

"My father is one of the *Royal Guards at the Palace Manor,*" she said her voice fading.

Philip glances in her direction with narrowed eyes.

"He's what? You're kidding right?"

Natalie took her gaze away from him and stared at her computer, smiling.

"You're not kidding are you?"

"Does this mean you're Royalty?"

"No silly," she laughed. "It means that the media…" She paused.

"The media…? You mean The Media?"

"Yes darling, if the press learns that I've returned to London to get permission to marry, they would follow us around. They would also be heading over to my dad's house and that's not very good for his position."

"Are you sure that this can alert the media?"

Natalie sat on the sofa with her legs crossed.

"I'll tell you a little story," she said.

"For five years, Richard didn't know that he was a father. You see, my dad was on vacation in Grenada, the same year he met my mum. The two spent the entire summer together. Before he went back to England, he and my mum had a fight and they broke things off. She never told him that she was pregnant."

"You're kidding. How did he learn about you?"

"You won't believe this," she smiled.

"Try me," he said.

"I was about five years old when I learned from my older siblings that my dad lived in England, and that his name is Richard Baldwin. They didn't realize that my mum didn't want me to know this information. One evening, I went up to her and asked...

"Mommy, when can I go to England to visit my dad?" Mom looked at me as though she'd seen a ghost.

"*My goodness, sweetheart, who told you this?*" she said in shock. Seeing that my mom was upset, I ran into my bedroom and hid under the covers. After giving my siblings a good telling off, she came into my bedroom and told me how she met my father. Of course when they met, he was not yet a Royal Guard. It was shortly after returning to England that he had joined the British Military and enlisted in the Household Division Infantry. These are known as Royal Guards or Foot Guards. Of the five units of the Royal Guard, my father belongs to the highest unit known as the First Battalion. Having learned of my father's new occupation, she feared that he would have no time for me. She warned me specifically that she would inform my father in her own time. Despite her stern request, I went into her room and looked through her telephone Journal. I found a telephone number next to the initials R.B. This was the longest telephone number I'd ever seen. This must be it I thought. Not being certain, I picked up the phone and dialed all fifteen digits. The phone rang, and a person with a very proper English accent answered.

"Baldwin residence, how may I help you?"

Ecstatic I shouted, "Daddy, daddy it's me Natalie. I'm your little girl, from Grenada." The line was silent for a moment, and then he said,

"Sweetheart, I don't know who you are, but you must have the wrong number."

"No, no, you are my daddy; your name is Richard, aren't you?"

"I don't know how you got my name and number, but this has to be a misunderstanding," he said.

Then I finally said…

"My mommy's name is Lisa." The line went silent again.

"This can't be," he said. "Are you Lisa's little girl?"

"Yes I am," I said excitedly.

"May I ask, how old are you?" he asked.

"I've just turned five on July twenty-first," I answered.

"Is your mummy home now?" he asked.

"Yes, she is, would you like to speak with her?"

"Yes please sweetheart," he answered, sounding a little bit friendlier.

"Mommy, mommy, please take the phone," I said excitedly.

"Who is it?" she asked.

"Umm," I said, looking at her nervously. My mum took the handset and went into her bedroom. I couldn't hear what she was saying to him, so I went into the kitchen and took a red plastic glass and placed the open end onto the wall and the bottom of the cup covering my ear. It was something I had learned from my older brother Jack. I was able to hear everything she was saying. They spoke for a long time and I could hear my mum arguing.

"Would you have cared about her, if I had told you the truth?" After a while my mum came out of her room. She glared at me. For a while she said nothing. Then she started laughing hysterically.

"Natalie, what have you done?" she said, trying to sound upset. On that note, Philip began laughing uncontrollably, bending forward grabbing his tummy.

"You were probably the smartest, nosiest five-year old I've ever heard off," he laughed.

Natalie smiled at his reaction.

"Soon after learning of my existence, my father came to Grenada. He and my mum agreed on a custody arrangement outside of the courts. Then a few short months later, he took me back to England where I lived with him continuously until my eighteenth birthday; other than when I was seven and had visited with my mum. After moving to London, news of a Royal Guard having a daughter out of wedlock had reached the press. The months following were a complete nightmare-with the press following us around. They even visited our private home and that was no picnic." Natalie paused for a moment, and then continued.

"As a Royal Guard in the first Battalion, one needs to be of well-polished character. My father later told me he always wanted to be a father, but his busy life never allowed it. This is why he didn't care how he looked to the media; it just wasn't worth missing out on being a father. Of course, news of him being a father to an illegitimate child did finally reach his superiors. Their only concern was whether I would be a distraction to his commitment to the Royal family. By then, my father had already had his priorities lined up before I arrived in England. There was a bit of public disapproval that my father continues as the lead Guard to the Royal family, but that was because of the press, blowing this way out of proportion. I was about seven when I saw my mum again. I spent about eight weeks with her and I began missing my father and my nanny. I loved being with my mum, but because of her Nursing schedule, she was always very busy, and my older siblings were all working and attending college. Therefore, my mother agreed to have me return to my father, with whom I've lived continuously until my eighteenth birthday. By then, the warm Caribbean sunshine was much more attractive and more appealing to me than the London gloom."

"I was also a typical teenager and was giving my father a difficult time. After he prevented me from marrying my boyfriend Bient, I thought it was the end of the world and so I decided to return to Grenada. Of course, after returning to the Caribbean, my father and I barely spoke." Philip stared at his Fiancé in utter shock and disbelief.

"Oh, by the way who looked after you while your dad was on the job?"

"Edna, Sofia and Lily." she answered.

"Lily was my favorite, then Edna, then Sofia," she said as she stepped off the sofa and threaded around the room in a somewhat dancing rhythm.

"Edna cared for me for the first two years. Edna had very little to say. She was all business and stuck strictly to the schedule she was given. After I return to England, Edna had found another job and was not available for rehire, so my father hired Sofia. Sofia stayed with us for a little over two years and later started developing an unusual attraction toward my father. Angered by my father's lack of interest in her, she quit her job and sold a bunch of lies about our family to the press that my father had behaved untidy toward her; none of which were true-as they later found out. Lily was my favorite; she stayed with us until I was seventeen. She was the preferred Nanny with an excellent track record as my father would say. Although she had no children and was never married, I always thought that she would have made the perfect mum; because that's what she was to me. Lily loved to sing and she has the most beautiful voice you've ever heard. She would sing for me every night until I fell asleep. Despite the unwanted attention from the press, she never kept me locked up indoors. Every evening, we would have picnics by my garden pond and take long walks out on the moors, especially in the spring when everything's a bloom. Another favorite of ours was Tadworth Park; where we enjoyed the purest of nature and our favorite refreshments from the Servery. Natalie paused for a moment...

"I wonder if it's still operating" she said putting her hair up in a pony. Philip stared at her in amazement.

"I wished you'd told me that I was marrying royalty," he joked.

"Royalty? No, Philip Lane, I'm not Royalty."

"You are to me darling, everything about you screams royalty."

"I'm a down to earth fun loving girl that simply enjoys the best of both worlds," she said, with a sense of entitlement.

"Oh well, la de da," he mocked.

"I'll get you!" she warned, while tossing a pillow at him.

"You know, my father will flip when he finds out that I'm marrying an American," she said while walking toward the restroom.

"What's that?" Phil asked. She said something from behind the door but it was too muffled for him to hear.

"Darling, are you having second thoughts?"

A little while later, she still hadn't returned from the restroom. He opened the door and found her on the floor. Having had CPR training he quickly reached down and placed his index and middle fingers on her upper neck.

"Natalie, hunny," he called and shook her. No response. He called her name several times but still no response. After verifying that she had a pulse and was breathing, he reached for the phone and frantically dialed 999."

"This is 999, what's your emergency? Please send an ambulance to the Palace Hotel, my fiancé has fainted in the restroom. We are in room 504." Philip hung up the telephone while the operator was still asking questions. He returned to his fiancé and began mouth to mouth resuscitation. After several minutes, Natalie coughed and sat up.

"What happened?" she asked, appearing confused.

"Honey you must have fainted. You scared the living daylights out of me."

"I'm sorry," she said. Despite having regained consciousness, she seemed tired and a little disoriented. Suddenly there was a loud bang on the door of their hotel room.

"It's Paramedics," they called.

Philip reached for the door quickly.

"My fiancé is over here, she's regained consciousness."

"Thank you sir, we'll take it from here," they responded. One of the medics recognized her.

"It's Richard's daughter," he whispered to his partner. After evaluating Natalie, they told her that she seemed to be okay, but that they still need to take her to the hospital for observations.

Thinking of her father learning of this, at first she disagreed...

"I'm feeling okay. I don't want this to get out."

"It's okay honey, I think it's a good idea to go get checked out," Philip assured.

She stood up reluctantly and the men helped her onto the gurney and placed an oxygen mask on her face. Less than five minutes later they arrived at Middlesex University Hospital. Philip insisted that he accompany her but was asked to wait in the visiting area.

"But she's my fiancée!" he yelled.

"Please wait here sir, we will call on you shortly," the head nurse responded.

About a half an hour later, Philip was called into Natalie's room.

"Have they figured out what caused my fiancé to faint?" he asked anxiously.

"We are awaiting her test results, sir. We should have them in a little while, but you can see her now," the nurse responded politely. The nurse then asked Philip a series of questions about their activities leading up to the moments before his fiancé' fainted. After giving her a detailed account, the nurse assured him to phone Richard.

"Richard, you know her father?"

She nodded yes and left the room. After the Nurse left the room, he reached for Natalie's hand.

"Hey there, how are you feeling sweetie?"

"I feel great, let's get out of here," she laughed.

"I like that idea, but I think we should wait for the results," he giggled. A few moments later, the doctor came into Natalie's room.

"Hello there," he said cheerfully.

"It's good to see that you are fully alert, that's always a good sign, and won't you agree?" he asked looking at Philip.

"I quite agree," Philip said. And on that note, his smiling face became serious.

"Miss Baldwin, after careful examination, I am happy to say that you're in excellent health."

"But what cause her to faint?" Philip asked, this time more anxiously. The doctor looked at Philip then at Natalie.

"It appears that… then he paused.

"By the way, I almost forgot. If you don't mind me asking, who in the world are you?"

"He's family, we'll soon be married," she said.

"Is that so?"

"Yes sir," Philip said standing and folding his toned arms.

"Shall we continue?" asked Natalie, squaring her forehead.

"Certainly, now where was I...? It appears that you've suffered an allergic reaction, but it's difficult to say what triggered it. This also explained the mild stomach cramps and temporary loss of consciousness?"

Natalie and Philip looked at each other.

"I've never been allergic to anything, ever," she said.

"Thanks Doctor," Philip said.

"You're both quite welcome. I will return shortly. We are waiting for one more test to determine what triggered the reaction."

"Don't worry about a thing babe, you will be okay," Philip assured her.

"Hon, I think we should phone your dad, before you make headlines."

Philip removed his mobile and boldly dialed his fiancés father.

"Hello, this is Richard."

"Hello Mr. Baldwin, my name is Philip, your daughter's fiancé." There was silence on the other end, and then the sound of beeping followed. A little surprised, Philip dialed Richard again.

"This time Richard answers on the first ring.

"You did not get my permission to marry my daughter." Then he hung the phone up once more.

At this point Philip became annoyed and he dialed Richard's number a third time. After the fifth ring he answered.

"Whether you realize it or not, I have very little time for gullible yanks like yourself!" he said. This time, without saying another word, Philip blotted out...

"Sir, your daughter is here in London and she's at the Middlesex University Hospital!"

"She's what? When did she get here and why is she at the hospital?" Before getting a chance to speak Richard scolded him.

"Why didn't you say something? What have you done to my daughter?"

"Sir, she's fine!" Philip said, rolling his eyes. He then hung up on Richard without saying another word.

Chapter 8

Less than an hour later, Mr. Baldwin arrived at the hospital. After confirming whether his daughter was being given top priority, he walks briskly into her unit. Seeing his beloved daughter, all feelings of anger had left him.

"Sweetheart, are you all right," he asked anxiously.

"Hi Daddy!" she said smiling broadly.

"I'm alright, just a bit exhausted."

"Where's your fiancé?" Just then Philip walked into the room carrying a food tray with two cold drinks and light snacks.

"You must be Mr. Baldwin, I'm Philip, and it's a pleasure to finally meet you," Philip said reaching out his hand. Richard stared at Philip, then slowly reached and shook his hands. Richard; a tall Caucasian male who appears in his early 50's seems a lot friendlier in person. After filling him in on all the details of their trip, Philip asked to be excused.

"He seems like a nice fellow, a lot friendlier in person," Richard admitted.

"He's been very good to me dad. He's unlike anyone I've ever met."

"What about your old dad?" asked Richard.

"You let me go dad. I also heard you've been seeing someone behind my back." They both laughed.

A few minutes later Dr. Jefferies walked into Natalie's room with Philip following closely behind. He looked directly at her.

"We're all ready for you young lady," he said. Natalie's father stood up.

"Dr. Jeff," it's good to see you. It's been a little while," Richard said, shaking the doctor's hand.

"Richard, I noticed that you missed your last few checkups. I know that you won't be forgetting now that Natalie's home," said Dr. Jefferies.

Richard laughs.

"You're a good man Richard, and a good father," Dr. Jefferies said leaving.

Two Nurses came in and wheeled Natalie's bed out of the room.

"Please gentlemen have a seat in the waiting room, we would call on you shortly," they said, hurrying off.

Both men grabbed a magazine and sat on opposite sides of the room. Richard looked up from his magazine.

"How and where in the world did you meet my daughter?" he asked, appearing more seriously. As Philip was about to respond, both men were called into Natalie's room. Philip stood at the foot of the bed and watched as his fiancé's father ran to her side.

"Hi sweetheart, how are you feeling?" he asked.

"I feel great and I'm ready to get out of here," she said munching on the sandwich that Philip had bought her earlier.

Philip came closer and sat next to her on the other side of the bed. Dr. Jefferies walked into the room.

"Hello, I'm happy that you are all here.

"Natalie, I have some great news, everything came back normal, except you're mildly anemic. I've prescribed a few weeks' worth of supplements. The nurse forwarded your electronic prescription to Royal Medical. They should arrive in the morning. The hemorrhaging would continue until the shrimp serum leaves your system. Richard, we were unsure of what caused Natalie's allergic reaction, so we administered two of the most common types of serums; shrimp and peanuts into her system. Two nurses were prepared to administer an epipen the moment the reaction begins. We've confirmed that she's highly sensitive to shrimp. She needs to avoid it, not even a small amount is safe for her."

"Thank you, Jeff," Richard said and left the room. He was suspicious of Philip and assumed that the doctor was covering up the real reason his daughter was in the hospital.

"You'll be alright honey," Philip said, kissing her hands."

"How about you two come over and try some of my homemade wine sometime," Dr. Jefferies said to Philip with a wink.

"When can I get out of here?" Natalie said, removing the oxygen mask from her face.

The men laughed because she's been asking this question all evening.

"I usually recommend an overnight stay for observation," the Doctor replied. It's a mandatory requirement after this type of allergic reaction. It wouldn't be safe to send you home today," he said smiling warmly.

"How long do I have to stay here?" she asked annoyed.

"Usually one day, but since you're feeling well, and everything else looks good, I'm allowing you to go home," he smiled.

"Thank you Dr. Jeff," she said, embracing him.

"You're welcome sweetie, promise me you'll get some rest," he said.

"I promise," she smiled.

"Honey, please find my dad."

"But I thought he left," Philip said.

"I know him only too well, he's somewhere out there, you'll find him, don't worry," she assured.

Natalie was right. Richard was standing right outside her door pacing back and forth.

"Mr. Baldwin sir, your daughter is asking for you," Philip said firmly.

Natalie's father reentered the room.

"Since everything else looks good, Richard I am allowing Natalie to go home," Dr. Jefferies said.

"However, I recommend three days of rest. This means no rigorous activities for the next three days."

"It was a pleasure meeting you Mr. Lane. Good night Gentlemen. Richard, I'll see you next week," he called.

"O thank goodness," she said in relief. It was already midnight when they finally left the Hospital. The nurse wheeled Natalie down to the main entrance.

"Here you are Lady Baldwin, it's always a pleasure," she said while embracing her.

"Soon to be Mrs. Lane," Philip reminded.

"How wonderful," she said, smiling warmly at Philip. She was a friendly Nurse with short, shoulder length hair and huge glasses. After thanking the Nurse, Philip lifted Natalie out of the wheelchair.

"Oh, I could have carried her," Richard said sounding entitled.

"That's okay daddy, I'm much heavier now than when I was seven." They all laughed.

"That was quite a scare, you gave us there sweetheart," Richard remarked. Natalie's father was suddenly silent. Then he broke his silence.

"You two don't need to go back to the hotel tonight; there's more than enough room to accommodate you and besides Natalie would be much more comfortable in her own home."

"Are you sure it won't be too much trouble?" asked Philip.

"Not at all, and besides sweetheart it's your home," he reminded her.

"But dad we're paid up for the next three weeks."

"How many days did you arrange?" Richard asked looking over at Philip.

"We had reserve a three week stay."

"Natalie didn't you remember that one of the perks of being the daughter of a Royal Guard, means that you can stay at this particular Hotel free of cost for up to four months out of the year? I'll make arrangements tomorrow to have you properly reimbursed," he said.

"No it's alright, it was my treat for us," Philip said.

"Oh no I insist, I'll have you properly reimbursed shortly," he said arguably.

Philip shook his head. He realizes there was no winning an argument with Richard and so he simply thanks him. Then Philip realizes...

"It's a good thing you came, Richard. I just remembered we had taken the ambulance here."

"That's right, wait here," he said.

"Philip darling, I love you but you can let me down now," Natalie reminded him.

"No babe, you are supposed to take it easy, and besides, you're Royalty," he teased. She laughed and tugged his ear playfully.

"Nope I'm not."

Then Richard strolled up in what looks like a black Rolls-Royce.

"Wow, nice ride Richard."

"Thanks, that's Princess Elle, she's one of my little darlings."

About an hour later, they drove up into the driveway of what looks like an English Manor and were greeted by blinding lights.

"Sorry about the brightness, it's one of our security features," Richard said, sounding exhausted. Natalie had fallen asleep on the way. Philip lifted her out of the car and laid her over his shoulders.

"Come on in, I'll show you where you can lay her," Richard said leading the way up the stairs and down a long hallway on the second floor. Richard pointed Philip into a beautiful bedroom; fully furnished with a large king size white canopy bed nestled in the center of the room. On the walls were framed photographs of Windsor Castle and wall Posters of the Princess of Edinburg. Around each poster frame hung pink and white decorative Roses and Lilies. On the wall straight ahead hung a Roman Clock with the name Edinburgh Clockworks written in small letters on the lower front. There's one major detail Philip couldn't ignore; a large painting of Natalie. She appears to be in her early teen's, wearing a flowing white gown sitting on a swing in what looks like a garden surrounded by an array of flowers in full bloom. Her long wavy hair lay softly on her shoulders, causing her eyes to sparkle. There's a garden bench near the edge of a pond and the sun's soft golden reflection in the background fell on her hair, causing her to appear angelic.

"Philip," Richard called.

Phil turned around startled.

"You can lay her here," Richard says pointing to her bed.

"Yes sir, this certainly is an exquisite bedroom."

"Yes, this has been her room since she was five," Richard said, sounding slightly emotional. The furnishings and paintings are her ideas. She's always had a slight fetish for Princess Annie. She admires her a great deal. Alright then, I will leave you two alone, there's a refrigerator down the hallway, please help yourself. William our Butler has already left for the day. But Maureen, our family chauffeur lives here; her room is further down the hall. I'll see you both tomorrow. I have company waiting for me over at my house in Purley," he says with a nod, and heads down the stairs.

Philip could hardly believe that this was the same individual he'd spoken to earlier. He wondered why his attitude toward him had suddenly changed.

"He's turned out to be an alright chap after all," Philip said in a convincing British accent. Before this thought had left his mind, there was a knock on the door.

"Come on in," he called.

"Philip, since you are only engaged to my daughter, I think it's proper that you sleep in separate quarters, well at least until you marry," he said, trying not to sound too harsh.

"Not a problem," Philip said.

"There's a guest bedroom across from Natalie's," he said pointing. "It should have everything you'll need. I had Maureen arrange the closets with proper linen and attire to accommodate our guests. I'm sure you will find it most comfortable and to your liking." Philip was tempted to sneak out of the guest room, but he chose to respect Mr. Baldwin's house rules. He loves Natalie and he wouldn't want her father to think otherwise.

Natalie awoke to the smell of Coffee and a hint of Chamomile. She couldn't remember anything and wondered if Philip and her father might have had an argument. She wondered why she was in her bedroom and not at the Hotel with Philip...

"Phil, where are you?" She called. Then she heard footsteps and her door opened slowly.

"How was your tea?" Philip asked, sounding cheerful.

"Phil!" she said jumping out of bed and running into his arms, spilling tea on his shirt.

"Ouch," he said.

"I thought something had happened and you left. Where were you?" She said excitedly.

"Your dad had me sleep in the other room. He said that's how it will be until we marry."

"Oh don't be silly, you listened to my dad? Wait a minute, he must be pleased with you. Did he say until we marry? Sounds like an approval. Philip we can marry!" She shouted. Philip stood watching his fiancé bounce around the room like a Rabbit.

"I'll go get you some more tea," he called, shaking his head as he walks away. Natalie hurried into the shower and a few moments later, she slipped into some of her teenage years' undergarments, a silk robe and ran down the hallway.

"Philip, we are going to be married. I still can't believe that my dad, of all people, has been this cool," she beamed.

"Not so fast, maybe he just said so hypothetically," Philip said sipping on his coffee.

"Come on, if that's not a yes then what is?" she said refusing to accept a potential alternative outcome. Phil handed her a cup of tea...

"Here you go love, and this time don't spill it," he said with narrowed eyebrows.

"I thought Richard was going to be here this morning," Philip said.

"He hardly ever stays here. Dad spends most of his time at his other home in Purley, because it's closer to his employment.

"I see," Philip said, trying to not appear relieved.

"William, my dad's Butler should be here shortly. What time is it?" She asked. Philip looked at the watch on his wrist.

"I'm still on American time," he called. He then glanced at the clock on the kitchen wall.

"It's almost eight thirty."

"William won't be here for another hour," she replied.

"What are you wearing?"

"Oh, how about that," she said, dropping her silk robe on the kitchen floor revealing her sexy undergarments. At the sight of her, Philip's eyes widened.

"Wow, you look amazing," he said, kissing her adorable face, and slipping her robe back on. She laughed as he tied her robe in an impossible knot, as though assuming she wouldn't get them loose. He then threw her over his shoulders and carried her up the stairs, and down the hallway. As they entered her bedroom, Philip remembered…

"Honey, we're forgetting something," he said, returning her to her feet appearing regretful.

"You have to take it easy, remember your trip to the hospital last night? Dr. Jefferies orders?" he said, stroking her hair.

"Philip Lane, do you always follow the rules," she said, appearing slightly frustrated. "I had an allergic reaction, it's not a big deal," she said, growing upset.

"Do you realize that we've never made love?"

"Um, yes," he responded nervously.

"*Philip, do you love me?*" she asked in a whisper. Philip stood silent for a moment then he said…

"Honey, you should get some rest. I'll bring you breakfast. How does that sound."

"Rest! Philip, what in God's name are you talking about?!" she yelled

"Natalie, you are a lovely woman, and in due time, all will be well. After all, we've just met, and we're not even married," he said modestly. Suspicious of his demeanor, Natalie kicked him out of the bedroom and locked the door. For the first time since they met, he had upset her. Surprised, and a little worried, he headed toward the kitchen to make her breakfast.

A little while later, he knocked on her bedroom door.

"Honey, please open the door, I have your breakfast, you really should eat something," he called. He tried for the longest while, but she refuses to answer. He then heads toward the kitchen and almost bumped into William.

"My goodness, you must be Philip the American fiancé?" the Butler said with a broad grin.

"And you must be William, the Butler, nice to finally meet you."

"Likewise, please call me Will," he said warmly. The Butler; a tall African British man appearing in his early fifties and reminds Philip a bit of Morgan Freeman.

"Richard told me that you too were here and left specific instructions for me to ensure you two are properly cared for," he said with a genuine smile.

"What's that you're holding?"

"It's my fiancé's breakfast," Philip said, sounding slightly exhausted.

"Don't you worry, I'll get this to her," he said, taking the tray from Philip's hands. Philip watched as the Butler knocked on the door.

"Madam, may I come in?" he called in respectful resonance. Philip heard the muffled sound of his fiancé voice and watched as William entered her bedroom. Relieved, he went into his guest bedroom to prepare for a trip into London. Before he left, he knocked on his fiancé's bedroom door...

"Honey, I'm going into town to pick up our Jeep and check out of the hotel. Would you like to accompany me?"

"There was no response, so he opened the door slightly and peeked inside. She was sound asleep. He walked into the bedroom to be sure she was okay. He noticed that she had only eaten a little of her breakfast and he was beginning to worry about her. She hasn't been herself all morning but she still looked beautiful, and he yearned for her. He couldn't begin to imagine his life without her.

"I've informed Maureen to take you into town, she's our family chauffeur," William called.

"You did. But William, how did you know I was going into town?"

"Because I'm the Butler," William said, folding his hands on his chest.

"I owe you one Master William. I was beginning to forget."

"Not a problem at all, she's waiting out front by the gate. I have a feeling you'll enjoy her company."

"We'll have to wait and see," Philip said smiling. Before turning to leave…

"William if you may, when she awakes, please inform her that I will be back within the hour."

"I certainly will," he replied

"Thank you kindly Master Will, if I may."

You are quite welcome, sir, and yes you may."

Philip nods at the Butler before heading toward the courtyard where the chauffeur awaits.

Chapter 9

Maureen was waiting in the courtyard as William had mentioned. She's a tall redhead who appears in her late forties. She was dressed quite studiously; in a grey pants suit, and low-heeled black dress shoes. She also wore a white vest and grey neck tie over her long-sleeved pink blouse. Philip thought her dress code was strange, yet appropriately becoming. He smiles as he approaches her. She was standing on the passenger side of the car and held her hand out as he approaches.

"Hello, you must be Philip. I understand that I'm taking you into London.

"Yes ma'am," Philip replied, shaking her hands firmly. As they drove, Philip broke the silence.

"I must say that this is the first time someone has ever opened the door to a car for me," Philip laughed.

Maureen chuckled at his coy humor.

"Well Mr. Lane, you'd better get used to it, because all of Mr. Baldwin's family gets treated like Royalty; we leave the rest to the Commoners, " she said with a serious scowl.

"Commoners? Did you say, Commoners?" he repeated holding back a laugh.

"You heard correctly." she said with an even more serious scowl.

As they continued into town, Maureen shared with Philip a little about Natalie's childhood.

"I remembered how afraid she was when I dropped her off at St. Mary's Catholic Infant Girls School. She was only five and had just moved to England. This was her very first day of School. I shall never forget how pretty she looked in her uniform; black shoes with tall white socks, green pleated skirt and white blouse. Her beautiful hair was in two adorable pigtails; held together by two white bows. She has warmed the heart of everyone who's ever laid eyes on her."

Philip smiled at how well Maureen remembered that day.

"You've been the family Chauffeur this long?" Maureen nods.

"I promised her that I would wait for her until school lets out, and that's just what I did," she said with a smile. Philip was about to say something and Maureen placed her right index finger over her mouth to request his silence. He chuckled at the expression. She must love telling Natalie's story, he thought.

"I always knew that there was something special about our little Natalie," she said with a pause and eyes narrowed. "She was always so drawn to nature and the less fortunate. Did you know that she always wanted to stop off at the park after school to feed the swans there?"

"Interesting?" Philip replied, trying his best to not interrupt.

"She would save most of her lunch for them. I grew concerned that she wasn't having enough to eat at school, so I asked her Nanny, Edna at the time, to pack an extra snack that she can use to feed the swans. Of course Edna always stuck to that ridged list Mr. Baldwin implements. Although Natalie's daily activities are decided by her Nanny, I was quite nervous when I stepped over my boundary and ask Mr. Baldwin myself."

"Was that like putting your career on the line, kind of chance?" Philip asked.

"Oh, quite possibly," she said with a wide eyed expression. "But of course, he approved it. Sometimes you never know, and then at times, he can appear very staunch and unapproachable," she said with a yawn. "Oh pardon me," she said.

Philip enjoy listening to Maureen, she has a way of painting a picture with words that you wouldn't have otherwise seen. William was right, he was enjoying her company, and she demanded it too.

"Mr. Lane sir you have arrived," she reminded him.

"Oh, that was quick," he said. "I would love to hear more of my fiancé's childhood, there's something special about the way you tell it."

"Without a doubt," she smiled. As Philip got out of the car...

"Would you require a lift back to the Manor, if so I can wait," Maureen said smiling warmly.

"Thank you Maureen, it's a wonderful suggestion, however, there's no need to wait. I will be driving the Jeep back to the Manor."

"Wonderful, then I'll see you when you return," she called.

"Absolutely," he calls and waved as she drove off.

After collecting their belongings, Philip went to the Hotel front desk to return the keys. Two smartly dressed young women, smiles as he approaches. They already knew who he was and were both very enthusiastic to assist him.

"Hello Mr. Lane, how are you today sir? This sure is fine weather we are having. Maybe you've brought some of that lovely California weather to London with you," Molly complemented.

"I should believe so," Philip replied. They then told him that all charges were being refunded to his credit card and that it would reflect in a few days.

"But how do you...?" before he'd finish his question.

"You are the American that's marrying the Royal Guard's daughter, aren't you?" Molly asked.

"But how in the world do you know that?"

"Well, your father-in-Law to be, had his accountant phoned this morning to have your hotel bills reversed," Amber replied.

"We know Richard very well, and we know that you had mentioned that you were here with your fiancé, so we put two and two together," Molly replied.

Philip shook his head in disbelief.

"Let's hope you're ready. And please say hello to the lovely Lady Baldwin for us," Molly said as he walks away.

"Thank you again ladies," he called. As he was about to exit the building he looked over his shoulders at the women..."You will not mention this to anyone."

Both ladies looked at each other and then back at him with guilty expressions on their faces.

"Have a lovely day, you're a very lucky man, Mr. Lane."

"Thank you again ladies," he called and took the elevator down to the parking structure. He wondered if everyone in London knew the Baldwin's.

Philip was in a hurry to get back to the Manor. As he drove toward Croydon, he noticed an open field of gorgeous wildflowers and he thought of Natalie. After pulling over to the side, he got out of the Jeep and began picking a variety of flowers. He wasn't sure what they were but they looked pretty, he thought. Philip didn't realize it but he had walked far into the field leaving a winding trail behind of all the places he had picked flowers. Suddenly, a large black bumble bee came out of nowhere and circled angrily around his head. Panicked, he ran out of the field, his unbuttoned shirt flying in the wind as he raced toward the vehicle. Finally, he reached for the door of the Jeep and dove head first inside. Tossing the flowers in the passenger seat, he sped away from his attacker. He was happy that he had managed to hold on to the flowers. That was a close call, he thought, and then realized that he had forgotten to carry his Epipen along. He felt lucky because he is deathly allergic to bees. He then laughed hysterically at the incident. When he'd finally stop laughing, he glanced over at the flowers.

"Bees or no bees, you are definitely worth it."

Before long he pulled into the Manor's entrance. It was the first time he realized that there was a security call box on the gate. There were instructions on the box; press zero for assistance it read. He pulled his Jeep up close to the box. After pressing zero, he waited but there was no response. Then he got out of the vehicle and peeked behind the box. There was a broken wire hanging loose. He wondered why no one had noticed before.

"This one doesn't work," Maureen called.

Philip looked up and saw her looking down from the upstairs balcony. She was holding a cocktail glass in her hand.

"I think I found the problem," he called.

"I can't believe it's still broken; it's been that way for three years. Richard snipped the wires because Natalie's boyfriend Bient was determined to get his permission to marry," she said with a chuckle.

"I think it's safe to fix it now, what do you think?"

"I'll be right back," she called but Philip's head was tucked behind the box and he didn't hear her. After repairing the wires, he drove through the now opened gate. He collected the flowers that were scattered on the floor of the vehicle and hurried to the kitchen to place them in water. As he walked out of the kitchen carrying the vase of flowers, he almost ran into William again.

"Back so soon, how was your trip into town?" he asked, staring at the flowers in his hands.

"Interesting," he replied

"How did you know; red poppies are her favorite. Should I get them to her?" he asked.

"Sorry Master Will, these flowers and I have formed a special bond, and we are not exactly ready to part," Philip said staunchly.

"Is that so?" the Butler said smiling.

"Let's just say, every beautiful thing comes at a price, and that I now admire every florist a great deal," he called.

"Well said, Master Lane. Don't forget these words, you will need them," he calls after him.

His fiancé was not in her room and he heard the shower running so he walked quietly across the carpeted floor and placed the vase on a corner shelf then hurried away. He was relaxing on the sofa in the guest room enjoying the sandwich and beer that William had brought him, when he heard a very happy squeal.

"Oh my goodness, I haven't seen poppies in forever," Natalie said joyfully. "These are just gorgeous," she continued.

"Is that what they are? I saw those on the way home and they reminded me of you," Philip said entering her room. At the sight of him she ran into his arms and began to kiss him viscously.

"Darling," he was about to suggest that she take it easy but he couldn't and began kissing her passionately.

"*I love you,*" he whispered. She shoved him gently against the wall, throwing her bathrobe across the floor. He made passionate love to her as when the sun drifts across the English countryside; bringing life and every flower to full bloom. The couple remained indoors for the remainder of the day to discuss their plans to marry.

"The majority of my family are here in Croydon; maybe we should get married here," she suggested in happy realization.

"Your mom and cousin Belle can fly in," he smiled.

"I should phone my cousin. I haven't spoken to her in an entire week," she said worried. "John seems nice but I'm still worried about her and those strange men she meets online," she said sounding more worried.

"I wouldn't worry. That's typical, and besides, she's a big girl, I'm sure she can take care of herself. Would you remind me to phone her in the morning?" she asked.

"You love her so much, sweetheart, almost makes me jealous," he laughs. "I've never met anyone like you before," he said, kissing her forehead. Philip gazed around her room. It was the room fitting for a Royal Princess. The more he got to know her, the more he realized that there was something extraordinary about her.

Chapter 10

It was hard to believe that he'd embarked on this journey. *What on earth was he doing?* he thought. His life had taken this very different, very unexpected turn and his excitement began to transform into fear. His fiancé had drifted off to sleep again and he wondered if that was normal. He got dressed and phoned the doctor's office. The assistant answered and forwarded him to Dr. Jeff.

"Hello Jeff, this is Philip, Natalie's fiancé."

"Oh yes, the American fiancé'," he said in his usual curious tone.

"Sir, I have some concerns."

"Is there a change in Natalie's progress?" Jeff asked.

"She's the same except she's sleeping a lot more during the day."

"I'm so sorry to hear that Philip. Yet, I have to assure you that this is expected. Fatigue after an adverse allergic reaction of the magnitude is quite normal. I can also attribute some of her fatigue to your time difference and possible jet lag."

"Oh, I see, yes that does make a lot of sense," Philip said, sounding relieved.

"Philip, I had prescribed some supplements for Natalie, have they arrived?" the doctor asked.

"I guess we forgot to fill it this morning," Philip replied.

"The prescription was sent electronically and is usually delivered by Royal Medical. Don't worry Phil, in time you will get used to being around her types," the doctor said with a chuckle.

"Do you have any more concerns at the moment sir?"

"Thank you Dr. Jeff, that will be all for now. I will phone you if anything changes."

"Philip, please don't hesitate," he responds warmly before hanging up.

Philip headed to the kitchen to chat with William. As he walks down the hallway, he notices a blue package from Royal Medical sitting on the dining table. He glanced at his watch. It was already after five in the evening. He remembered that Natalie's father had mentioned that he was stopping by later today. Just then, Maureen entered the living room.

"Do you have any further engagements in which I may be of any assistance sir?" she asked.

"No, ma'am, thank you for all your help today."

Just then the phone rang and the Butler answered.

"Baldwin's abode, how may I assist you?"

"Yes sir, I will pass on the message promptly," William replied.

"That was Natalie's father. He said that he will be staying at his other residence over in Purley, to afford you more privacy. He will stop by over the weekend to check in on his daughter, and to get more acquainted with you," William said.

"Thank you for that William. I didn't realize he lives in Purley."

"Yes, he does so from time to time sir," William replied.

"By the way Master Philip, it is also the end of my shift, can I trust you to take good care of Lady Baldwin?" he asked politely.

"Thank you for a most hospitable day Will and don't you worry, she's in excellent hands."

William nods in appreciation and leaves the room.

"I like this guy," Philip said with a curious expression.

"We all do, he's been with us almost eight years now," Maureen said entering the kitchen. Just then they both heard coughing sounds coming from upstairs.

"Alright then, I'll be in my room down the hall, if you or Lady Baldwin needs anything," she called.

"Oh, that's right, I almost forgot you live here?" Philip said, relieved.

"Yes on a full time basis; never heard of a lived-in Chauffeur?" Both laughed as Maureen excused herself and slipped into her bedroom at the end of the hallway. Philip thought it was nice having someone else around this huge mansion.

As he walked toward Natalie's room, she was standing at the doorway.

"Philip, where are you, darling?" she called.

"I'm right here sweetheart. I just got off the phone with dad, he suggests I get off my biscuits and grab some fresh air."

"Only, if you're up for it," Philip said worried.

"I'm not sure, but having slept almost all day, I won't be going to bed anytime soon. Besides, I'd like to show you one of my little secrets."

"Are you sure Hun, you really should take it easy my lady," he said taking her hands."

"I insist," she responded heading down the stairs.

"This way," she said pointing, leading the way through the kitchen and out into what looks like a garden.

"You have a beautiful home. It's your home now too," she smiled.

"Not at all, I'm just a humble American boy in love with a beautiful mysterious girl," he said brushing her hair with a kiss. She laughed.

"Honey, look around you," she called.

"This must be your garden; I recognize it from the photos upstairs," he said looking around in awe.

"It reminds me of something I would see on a postcard," he continues.

"This one over there is my cherry blossom in full bloom. I planted her when I was about seven. My goodness, look how much she has grown. Roses, Violets, Sunflowers, Zinnias, Lilies, everything's a bloom," she declared in awe. They strolled over to her garden bench and sat next to each other.

"And this over there must be your fountain and garden pond; it's truly a work of art."

"Thank you. Jake, our gardener is very gifted. Maureen believes that this garden was built with love. She always poked fun at me, and claimed that Jake was in love with me."

"Was he?" Philip asked, sounding playfully jealous.

"I hoped not, I was in my late teens, still a child when the pond and fountain was added to the garden and Jake was an adult in his late twenties. I would hope not."

"Late teens, and late twenties? Still possible." They both laughed.

"This has always been my little retreat and the place where I started thinking about falling in love. I was so upset with my father when I left England. I never imagined that I would see this place again."

"It couldn't have been that bad," he said looking over at her curiously. She became quiet for a while and Philip wondered why.

71

"His name is Bient Attaway. Long story, I'll tell you about it later," she said sounding exhausted.

"Alrighty then, let's get you inside. I'll prepare dinner. How's broth with vegetables?"

"That would be delightful," she said happily.

As they were about to leave the garden, Philip saw a reporter taking photographs of them. He said nothing because he didn't want to upset his fiancé. Excitement is the last thing she needs.

After dinner, Natalie took her supplements.

"These little red suckers haven't changed over the years," she said making a face.

"So you've seen these before?"

"Yes, I was anemic as a child and these were a big help."

"Don't worry about it babe, you will be feeling a lot stronger in no time," he said gazing at her lovingly.

"Let's relax in the entertainment room. Tomorrow, I will give you the grand tour; it will be one you'll never forget," she smiled proudly. He could tell that she was beginning to feel like herself again. He admires how strong she was. There was something very resilient about her. He knew that she would fit right into the American culture, if they ever so choose to make it their home.

"Let's turn on some lights. This place can get really dark," she said, opening her eyes wide to be scary.

"Trying to be scary, huh?" he teased.

"You started it. Remember the snakes, orange groves?" Philip laughed.

"I've never seen anyone more terrified of snakes."

She squeezed his arms and tugged his shirt collar playfully as they collapsed on a comfortable sofa facing a large HD television.

"Wow, you guys must own every movie there is. I love it," Philip said, reaching for the remote control.

"Ever heard of Netflix?"

"Yes, however, it's not the same as physically owning a movie. It's our preference," she said proudly.

"I don't believe I've seen them all, but it will certainly take me hours to find the ones I haven't."

"Let's watch Something's Gotta Give; it's an absolute favorite."
"Wait a minute, I cannot believe my eyes. I think I spot it. There it is straight ahead," she said excitedly, reaching for the case.

"Let's invite Maureen to join us," Philip suggested.

"Great idea; she would love too," Natalie said hurrying toward the stairs.

"Wait babe, I'll come with you," he called.

Before reaching the top of the stairs, Philip heard a thump and then laughter followed. He looks in time to see both women on the floor laughing hysterically.

"What's going on?" he asked looking puzzled. Maureen and Natalie continued laughing. Maureen got up from the floor and helped Natalie up.

"I was headed to the kitchen to grab a drink of water and somehow your fiancé ran right into me," she laughed.

"Well finally, this place sounds like someone lives here," he jokes.

"Would you like to join us for a film?"

"Oh I would love to, but I would not want to interrupt you two lovebirds," she smiled.

"Oh it's no interrupt," Natalie said, embracing and kissing her on her cheek. "Besides I haven't spent some quality time with you since I've been back," she said embracing Maureen tightly.

"Ok love, I'll join you two for a bit, but remember I work for you, so I can't stay up too late." Natalie continued embracing her Chauffeur tightly.

"In order for me to watch the film, you'll have to let me go now love."

They all laughed. Natalie releases Maureen and kisses her one more time on the cheek.

"I see you turned on the lights. Thank you."

"Don't you get the creeps doing this alone?" Natalie asked.

"It's your house, you'll have to get used to it," she teased.

"Would you ladies like a drink?" Philip asked, reaching for a wine opener.

"That's what I'm talking about," Maureen said in a partying tone. Philip reached for a bottle of Cabernet Sauvignon out of the cabinet next to the DVD's and popped it open with the wine opener.

"I had no idea you like red wine, Maureen." Natalie said surprised.

"There's a lot you don't know about me my dear."

"Is that so?" Natalie asked intrigued.

"I like her already," Philip laughed.

Natalie placed the movie into the DVD player and sat next to her fiancé. Maureen took the bottle of wine from Philip.

"Let me do the honors," she said boldly. After filling each glass with wine, she took a sip and said…

"So tell me, how did you two meet?"

Philip and Natalie looked at each other.

"Hmm, long story," she said.

"I'm up for it," said Maureen, making herself more comfortable on the sofa. Despite having their favorite movie on, Natalie's fiancé began telling the story. Maureen's eyes began to bulge.

"I still can't believe you went to America?" she said, shaking her head.

Natalie laughed.

"I didn't realize how upset I was. I literally went everywhere dad didn't want me to go."

"Glad I did," she said, touching Phil's hands.

"Shall I continue?" Philip asked, sounding like Scooby.

"Of course," she laughed. As Philip continues, Maureen's eyes widened and narrowed as he explored the details of how they met and their first date to the wineries. While some details had her in tears, she laughed out loud at others.

"So very romantic. Sounds like something out of a novel; truly remarkable," she concluded.

"I'm surprised that you too have yet to attract the London Press."

"There was someone…" Philip forgot and almost mentioned the person he saw earlier taking photos of them.

"Someone?" Maureen asked.

"Oh it's nothing, I was about to compliment the maker of this fine wine," Philip said, trying to sound convincing. Maureen refilled their glasses.

"Oh I saw him," Natalie said. "Someone spying on me and Phil in the Garden, nothing I'm not used to."

"I was hoping you didn't see him darling," Philip said.

"Don't worry darling, this will be good for our wedding. This will save us from having to send out all those invitations; it's a good start."

"The London press and your Grandma; you know that she's equivalent to the National Enquirer," they all laughed. Maureen had never really liked Anabelle.

"How's it going with Maddie?" Natalie asked.

"Oh, a Royal pain in the behind. Earlier this week, I drove her down to Trafalgar Square, it took hours, one would think that there's enough shoes and dresses…" Maureen paused and smiled.

"Nothing's changed, she's still Annabelle; the one we all thought would take the throne by now. Maybe I can hire her, her own personal chauffeur because now that we are in town we will need your assistance more often."

"That would be great love, I'm honestly at my wits ends with her," Maureen admitted.

"Who's Maddie?" Philip asked.

"My Grandma. Don't worry Hun, you'll meet her soon enough," Natalie chuckled.

"As soon as the morning," Maureen reminded her.

"Well my friends, I'd better call it a night. Thank you for the perfect end of a fine evening," she said standing. Natalie stood up and embraced her.

"I'll see you in the morning. Glad you could join us," Philip called.

"It was my pleasure. We should do this again sometime," she said with a smile and hurried up the stairs.

"She's great," Philip said.

"She's the best. Something's troubling her though; I can read her like a map. Maybe you can spend some time with her tomorrow," Philip said standing. He reached for his fiancé and kisses her. He lifted her up playfully and carried her up the stairs. They both giggled.

"Natalie." Having heard her name, she awoke and sat up in bed. She could swear someone had called her name, but who could it be, she thought? She looked at the roman clock on her wall. It was exactly four thirty in the morning. Natalie rubbed her eyes and tried returning to sleep. As she dozed off, it was like a dream. A soft yellow light filled her room and she could hear the cries of children. Then she heard someone call her name again, in a hushed tone.

"*Natalie.*" This time she got out of bed. Right there in front of her were babies in cribs and young children laying in small beds. There are women in white and grey uniforms tending to them. On the other side of her bedroom, she saw men, women and children sleeping on the street corners, covered in rags. As she observed, a sense of sadness came over her. Then she heard a female voice calling out her name again. This time she looked at the picture of Princess Annie on her bedroom wall. She's alive in the picture, but how? She thought.

"Natalie," she said pointing to the children.

"Please go to them. Please tend to the children and the less fortunate on the streets of England."

Then she was awakened by the sound of her fiancé's voice.

"Honey, are you okay?" She looked at him puzzled.

"You were having a dream," Philip said, wiping tiny drops of moisture from her forehead.

"It was so real," she said looking around.

"What were you dreaming about?" Philip asked.

"Don't worry darling, it was just a dream," she said embracing her pillow, returning to sleep. A Few hours later, Philip awoke to the sound of the phone. He was about to reach for it when his half asleep fiancé reached over and picked up the handset. She answered with a sleepy…

"Hello, who's calling so early?"

She sat up quickly. "Maddie?"

"Oh my goodness, it's Maddie and she's downstairs," she panicked.

"I'll be right down," she said rushing to the shower.

"Come here babe, let's hurry, Maddie is waiting."

"What's the rush?" Philip asked, stretching his arms.

"From what I've heard she's a pain in the behind," he laughed.

"We're supposed to be joining her for lunch."

"Please tell her I'm not hungry?" he joked.

Natalie laughed. "Trust me, you are."

Philip went into the guest bedroom to prepare for his visit with Annabelle. He wondered why his fiancé made it sound like the Queen of England was visiting. After a shower, he grabbed some cargo shorts and a pair of Polo T's. He then slipped on some Nike socks and his favorite Nike tennis shoes.

"Are you ready? Philip, what are you wearing?" she asked, looking frustrated.

"Come on, she's waiting," he said, teasing, and walk past her.

"I'm really not up for this," he admitted.

"Not dressed like this," she calls after him.

"Don't worry, she would love me. By the way, I'm glad you like the outfit," he said and disappeared down the stairs.

"Philip, wait!" she called.

Chapter 11

Phillip stared at his fiancé's grandmother from around the corner. She appeared much younger than a woman in her early seventies. She was dressed in Pink Capris, a white low cut blouse with matching pink and white polka dotted high heeled shoes. Next to her on the sofa was a white, wide brimmed hat and sunglasses. Philip entered the room and boldly sat on the sofa on the opposite side of the room.

"Well, well, well, you must be the American fiancé," Anabelle said glaring at Philip.

"And you must be Anabelle," Philip replied.

"Please, tell me how you manage to have met my granddaughter?" she asked, staring at Philip scornfully.

At that moment William entered the living room.

"Good morning Will, it's good to see you looking sharp as usual," Philip said in a pretentious British accent.

"I could say the same of you, Master Philip. What would you two like to drink this morning?" Will asked.

"I'll take the usual 'Cherie' Will," Anabelle said, keeping her eyes fixed on Philip.

"A cup of tea, make that two please. My fiancé is on her way," Philip replied.

"By all means, would you like breakfast or brunch, Master Philip?"

"Breakfast would be great, my good sir."

William nods and left the room. Philip returned his focus to Annabelle.

"Anabelle, maybe I can let Maureen enlighten you on how we met on one of your trips to London. She has a remarkable way with words," Philip said rudely.

All the while, Anabelle stared at him saying nothing. Philip ignores her rude demeanor. Suddenly he remembers.

"I wondered what happened to my Natalie."

"I'm right here darling," she said entering the room, carrying a vase of pink Roses in her hands.

"Hello grandmother, it's lovely to see you. I see that you've met Philip, my fiancé. These are for you, my garden did very well this year," she said placing the vase on the coffee table. She then kissed her Grandmother on the forehead.

Anabelle barely greeted Natalie. She simply smiled at her, all the while staring at Philip. Philip wondered if this was customary in England; and even if it was, he thought that it was quite rude.

"Hello darling, you look amazing," he said, shifting over to make room for her to sit next to him.

"Your father is on his way up, so is your aunt Jasmine and your cousin Katie," Anabelle said sounding entitled.

"That's great, but who invited them?" Natalie asked, slightly upset.

"I did," Anabelle replied.

"Geez Maddie, you should have asked me first. This is my home."

"And they're your family," she snapped.

Natalie wanted to walk out of the room at the moment, but didn't.

"Um, it was nice meeting you Annabelle, Natalie and I have had a previous engagement. Maybe we can catch up later," Philip said standing to leave.

"Maddie, I will phone Katie and others to make proper arrangements for them to meet Philip," she said.

She embraced her grandma before her and Philip left the room.

"Alright love, please don't forget to inform your uncle and others across town."

"Don't worry Grandmother; I'll take care of it," she called.

"What about your breakfast?" William called.

"Sorry William, we'll take our tea if it's ready and we'll have breakfast when we return in an hour's time," Philip called.

William thought it was quite strange. No one drinks tea while walking, it must be an American thing.

The couple walked away from the Manor, and when they were outside…

"Where are we going?" Philip asks.

"For a little stroll. I want to show you something," she said excitedly. As the couple walk toward a wooded trail behind the Manor, Maureen called from an upstairs window.

"Where are you two lovebirds off too? Would you be in need of my services this morning?"

Natalie laughed because although they could hear Maureen's voice, because of the dark window screen, they couldn't see her face.

"No thank you Maureen, you can take the day off, as a matter of fact you're off all week with full pay."

"I'm showing Philip around; we'll be back shortly."

"That's fantastic, the whole week off? Are you certain my lady?" As they continued to walk on the trail further away from the manor, they could hear Maureen still asking questions. They both laughed.

"She's so funny," Philip said. As they reached on top of a small hill, looking down at the Manor, they could still hear Maureen asking in disbelief.

"Are you sure, that I have all week off with full pay, my lady?"

"Yes Maureen, you're off, all week, full pay," Philip shouted from atop the hill.

"I love how devoted they are to you my love. She must have missed you a lot when you were away. Are you sure that you are ready to give them all up to be with me in America?" he asked sitting down on the grassy trail. She appears momentarily distant. This time she didn't have an answer.

"I'm really growing to like it here," he admitted. "Look at that spectacular view."

"This over there is Grandma's house, and over there is Aunt Jasmine's," she said pointing.

"Come along babe, there's lots more to see," she called.

"Where are we going?" he asked.

"Put on your sense of adventure, you are going to need it," she laughed running ahead.

Philip walked briskly trying to not lose sight of her.

"This way," she called pointing. As they turned a corner, in front of them appeared a green grassy opening, surrounded by a wooded forest.

"Wow," Philip remarked.

"I used to come here often to write poetry. It's very peaceful and brings out my wildest imagination.

"I see why," Philip said walking toward her.

"Who owns this place?"

"I think it belongs to Uncle Alfred, a horse herder who used to live across the way," she replied.

"A few months before my eighteenth birthday, while I sat writing, I saw the most beautiful horse running over there on the edge of the forest. I came here for months on end hoping to get another glimpse of her. It's almost as though I'd never really seen her." She said, sounding slightly mystified.

"Hmm, well maybe you'll see her one of these days," Philip said walking toward her. She turns to face him and he kisses her passionately.

"*I miss being alone with you,*" he said softly.

He held her close to him and she heard his heartbeat. His heart raced as though he was afraid of something.

"Are you alright?" she asked looking up at him. He assured her that he was fine but by the look in his eyes, she could tell that there was something on his mind.

"*Talk to me, sweetie,*" she whispered. He kisses her instead. She pulled away.

"No Philip, there's something on your mind?"

"I'm fine," he assured.

"No you're not," she said firmly.

"Okay fine, I'm afraid you wouldn't want to return to America with me. There you have it," he said, fearing what he said might be true. Natalie looked down at the grass.

"What makes you think that?" she asked, pretending to be surprised.

"Well, look at all that you have here; a beautiful home, family and friends who love you."

"You're right. I didn't realize how much I missed them. But there's still a lot of time to think about where we want to live. Don't you think? Please don't let this concern you," she said leaning her head against his chest.

"You're right," he said, kissing her softly on the forehead.

"Come this way," she said, walking toward the shade of a large tree.

As she got closer Philip notice a large tree stump with a tiny door.

"What's in there?"

"Come see," she called. She knelt and opened the tiny door and removed a clear plastic folder with a large zipper.

"I can't believe it's still here," she said excitedly.

"What is it?" Philip asked curiously.

"It's the blanket and my poetry journal."

"How long has it been here?" he asked.

"About four years," she replied.

"No kidding," he said surprised.

"I used to sit on this old blanket every morning in springtime to write and enjoy William's breakfasts," she said smiling.

"As I wrote, I used to wish that my true love would come out of the forest riding the blond mane horse, and take me away," she laughed.

"Really?" he asked.

"Maybe that dream did come true, of course in a different way."

"I think so," she said smiling. She opened the bag and pulled out a black journal and a green blanket laced in pink ribbons.

"Please have a seat, I'll read you some of my poetry" she said. She shook the blanket and the dust caused them to sneeze. After catching their breaths, they laughed. Philip listened as she read. He could hardly believe that she'd written such fine words. As she read, there was something in her voice that indicated her devotion to poetry, revealing her finest sentiments.

"That was remarkable love. You have an incredible talent for written art."

"I'm glad you enjoyed them. You are the first to have heard them," she said smiling proudly.

"I'm truly honored," he said standing.

"Let's head back, I'm starved," she admitted.

"I'm sure William's breakfast is cold by now," Philip said.

"Thank You for showing me your secret place, there's something very special about it," he said hugging her shoulders.

As they headed back on the trail Philip looked at the green open plain.

"So beautiful, are you always drawn to beautiful things?"

"Truth is darling, I don't even realize it, I'm simply drawn to certain things not even knowing why."

"It's truly magical here?" Philip admitted. "I think I would love to make this my home for a while."

Realizing what he'd said, she looked over at him surprised.

"Oh Philip, you don't have to decide now."

"My mind is made up; I'd like England to be my home, at least for now."

"Honestly, I was hoping that you would say that."

Overjoyed by his sudden decision, she embraced him tightly.

"Thank you for helping to make my dreams come true."

About an hour later, as they walked toward the manor, they heard commotion.

"I wonder what's going on," she said anxiously, walking more briskly. As they neared the manor, they saw a group of reporters holding microphones up to Richard's face.

He was yelling... "Get off my property! No comment!"

As Philip and Natalie approached, the reporters noticed and came hurrying toward them with questions.

"Natalie, is this your fiancé from America?"

"When did you get back?"

"Will Richard be able to keep his position at the Palace Manor?" They placed the microphone in Philip's face.

"Who are you, sir?" Philip avoided the question and as he and Natalie made their way inside, William stood at the front entrance.

"Would anyone care for a cold drink?"

Some of the reporters began to question William.

"Yes his name is Philip and he is Natalie's fiancé from the States. They plan to wed early June."

"Oh my goodness, William please don't!" Natalie called. The couple pushed past the growing crowd of reporters and neighbors gathering around and finally made their way inside.

When they were all inside Richard invited Natalie and Philip to join him on the balcony downstairs for a drink. When they were all seated, Richard filled their glasses with what looks like lemonade on ice.

"This here is the British version of hard lemonade, except this time I used a Caribbean rum called Clarkes Court and limes instead of lemons," he said to Philip.

"Sounds excellent," Philip said, sounding impressed.

"Did mum send you this bottle?" Natalie asked excitedly.

Richard smiled but didn't respond.

"So how are you enjoying your visit?" Richard asked.

"So far, I have no complaints. There's something about England that takes me away from the norm," he replied.

"Hmm, I didn't expect that. I thought by now you would be fed-up of how small everything was and left."

They all laughed. Then Richard's face became serious.

"Maureen took the pleasure of filling me in on how you met my daughter. As a boy my grandmother Sylvie used to say that there are no coincidences. I believe that it was for this purpose," he said pausing. The couple listened without interruption. Richard continued.

"I'm sure by now that Natalie must have filled you in on how I met her mother."

Philip nods.

"I was overjoyed learning that I was a father. The fact that I was new to the Royal Battalion, bringing Natalie to be with me in England has created many speculations regarding my moral standing.

"Is that still an issue sir?" Philip asked.

"Not at all. Of course Princess Annie, the only heir to the throne at the time met Natalie and fell in love with her at first sight. The fact that she shares the same birthday as her only son Prince Ethan placed her on top of the favorite's list to receive lots of incentives from the Royals. As a matter of fact, not only did she make headlines, she gained fame on her first trip to England; thus, becoming an anchor for my career.

Natalie laughed. "Dad?"

"It's true my dear," he said with a wink.

Natalie suddenly appeared withdrawn.

"What's the matter Hun?"

"Oh, I'm troubled by a dream I had this morning. I'm still wondering what it meant."

"Let's hear it?" Philip said.

"Yes, sweetheart, please enlighten us."

She told them how the Princess of Edinburg had appeared to her very clearly in a dream and it seems as though she is asking her to do something. She told them that although the request appeared urgent, it was unclear what it is, she was requesting.

"Maybe it's because you miss her darling."

"No dad, this was different," she assured.

"It was so real, that the picture of Annie on my wall came to life. It must mean something," she insisted.

"Don't worry honey, last night you were very tired. Maybe it will go away over time. As we all know Princess Annie, your beloved Princess has been gone over five years now," Philip said.

Natalie could tell that he didn't really care about her dream and it bothered her.

"Well, you two can say whatever you want but she was my friend and I believe she was trying to tell me something. But as usual, men will be men."

With that she stormed away.

"I believe you sweetheart," Richard called after her.

"Me too babe," Philip called.

"Yes and I'd like ice in my pudding!" she called. Both men laughed.

"Thank you for the fine drink, Richard. I have to say, that is some excellent rum."

"Thanks, I'm glad you like it. Natalie told me that you love Cabernet Sauvignon. Would you like to help me out at the Pub?"

"The Pub?"

"Didn't Natalie mention it? Oh that's right, she doesn't know about it. I purchased the Pub shortly after Natalie left for the Caribbean, from an old friend who's recently retired. I'm currently in need of a bartender, I'm thinking of letting go of Adam."

"It's a little unexpected, but I'd like to know more," Philip said.

"Alright, let's discuss it over the weekend."

Just then Natalie rejoined them.

"I've missed you darling, so have all your friends. How long do you plan on staying?"

The couple looked at each other.

"Let's talk about it over the weekend when we meet at the Pub," Richard said.

"The Pub?"

"Yes sweetheart, do you remember Uncle Alder?

"Yes, how is he?"

"He's gotten too tired to run the Pub and before moving to Wales he asked me to manage it for him. But of course, seeing that he was about to retire I paid him a good price for it."

"That was a fantastic opportunity dad, I'm glad you bought it from him."

"Yes, I think so too sweetheart. But it wasn't so easy at first. It was after months of arguing with him to take some money for it; he finally agreed to sell."

"That's wonderful, but a Pub and where in the world would you find the time to run this business?" Natalie asked concerned.

"Don't worry sweetheart, I have someone there now, but that's a different story," Richard said standing up to leave.

"Maybe you can fill her in Philip. Alright folks, I'll be in touch. If you need me, you can reach me over at the bungalow in Purley."

"Dad, please stay for a bit," Natalie urged.

"Come on sweetheart, I'm really happy you're back. I'll call you later." He embraced and kissed her on the forehead before heading out the door.

"It seems like there's other things on his mind. I'll be right back," Natalie said following her father out the door but he'd already driven off.

"Dad, wait!" she called. By the way he was driving she could tell that he was in a hurry.

Chapter 12

Phillip stood at the entrance of the door. "I'm sure he's alright."
"I know him too well, something's definitely bothering him. Come here babe, maybe you can talk to him about it later."

"Alright then, and besides, I have an idea," she said approaching Philip.

"What's that?" he asked curiously.

"It's time for the grand tour," she said with a girlish charm.

"Aww that's right," Philip said buttoning his collar and folding his arms to imitate a British gentleman. Natalie laughed.

"Let's start with the first floor," she said leading the way.

"This room here is the Entry Hall; the first room in the Manor that visitors would see upon entry."

"Wow, look at this furniture. Are all these antique?"

"Most of them," she replied.

"This room over here used to be a game room, but I turned it into the entertainment room."

"Oh yes, we were in here last night."

They continued down the hallway.

"That's a lot of books. Is this the library?" he asks whistling loudly.

"Yes, some of which dad got from his mum who inherited it from her mum and her mum before that."

"Wow, I don't imagine that you both have read this many books." he sighed.

"During my senior year of High School, I made a schedule that would have allowed me to read all the books on this side of the room in one year."

"How did that go?"

"I did it in nine months."

"No way!"

"Well, I do love to read," she said, removing a novel from a lower shelf.

"That's an understatement," he said.

"Want to test my knowledge. Start on the bottom shelf and I'll give you the back cover synopsis of every book from top to bottom."

"Excellent idea."

Philip lifted the first book and Natalie gave a clear description of what the book was about. When she'd given the description of about half the books on the shelf. Philip was convinced."

"Sorry, but I can't find the words. You're incredible."

"The power of an avid reader," she said in a scholarly tone.

"Alright then, shall we continue?"

"By all means," he replied. Philip gazed at her posture; the way she turns each corner and lifted her hands was almost poetic-and as graceful as she was, this huge place suited her well.

"This room over here is the Parlor; another guest room for entertaining close relatives and friends. And this here is our study."

"Very interesting, I like its location; away from any noise as though to prevent interruption."

"I quite agree," she said. "During my teenage years, this was my only playground. My father was very strict about my studies and because of this I was fortunate enough to have completed a University degree at the High school age of eighteen."

"That's incredible, how did you manage that?"

"One would wonder, but I did. More specifically, I attended a Catholic Prep school that has an accelerated option to complete High School as well as University at the same time. However, this option is only available to students who demonstrate superior performance in key courses," she said, this time appearing more serious.

"I think you're going to love this room," she said. "This over here is our Wine Cellar."

"Ahh," Philip said, this time leading the way into the Cellar.

"This brings back such fantastic memories," she said laughing out loud

"Mind sharing?"

"Oh you can have as much wine as you may, darling," she said with a giggle.

"I mean, the memories," Philip said, realizing what she presumes."

"Oh, that's right, silly me," she said, realizing. They both laugh.

No sooner she begins to recall the events; she would erupt in laughter.

Philip folded his arms.

"Well, we'd better sit down for this one," he said, taking a seat on the comfortable sofa. Natalie sat next to him.

"Before William, our current Butler, we had Frederick," she said holding back laughter. "On my seventh birthday, her majesty, Princess Annie very briefly attended my birthday party to personally deliver my presents. From my sixth birthday and upwards, I received many beautiful presents from the Royal family; due to the fact that I shared the same birthday with Princess Annie's son, Ethan. She paused after that statement. Frederick was a secret admirer of Annie and could barely contain himself around her. He became extremely drunk while entertaining our guests." With that, for a third time, Natalie broke out into uncontrollable laughter.

"Frederick sounds like my kind of guy, right on," Phil said waiting on his fiancé to continue.

"After spilling a tray of glasses filled with champagne, he went missing for hours during the party, and some of the guests had to pitch in to help serve the other guests."

"You're kidding," Philip laughed. "Where did he go?"

"Dad and some friends found him here in the wine cellar, passed out on the floor next to two empty bottles of Gin."

"Well, I have to say that Frederick is the only Brit at that party that knows how to have a good ole time," Philip laughed.

Natalie got off the sofa and dust off her behind. She laughed.

"I knew you'd like Fred."

"What happened to poor Fred after all this?"

"Well, it took dad and three other guests to carry him out of the cellar. They didn't do so without taking a few punches. Frederick was throwing punches and calling them the worst names ever, before they finally got him into the guest bedroom. I swore that it was the end of his job," Natalie laughed.

"Of course, the following day, dad wanted to fire him on the spot, but I talked him out of it. Poor Frederick, it was the first time he'd seen the Princess in person."

"Were you and Annie very close?"

"I admired her a great deal, but she was much closer to my father. Of all the Royal Guards, my father is a favorite of the Royal family. Some have even speculated that her Majesty had often complemented his good looks and gave him more privileges than the others."

"I have to admit that your dad has turned out to be a surprisingly decent bloke. I'm still wondering why he asked me to sleep in the guest bedroom the first night I spent here."

"Oh he was just upset. He assumed that Dr. Jeff was keeping something from him."

"And of course, he doesn't think anyone is good enough for his only daughter," Philip said with annoyance.

"Well are you?" she asked, poking his side.

"Hey, whose side are you on?"

"Mines," she teases.

"Come here young lady. This instant," he said pretentiously.

Just then Maureen interrupted their silence.

"Nat, are you down here? Someone's mobile phone rang and it woke me up."

"Thanks Maureen, we'll be right there," Natalie replied.

"I'll be right back," Philip called.

"Okay then, it's probably my mum or cousin Bella," she said.

"Or it could be my uncle, he has no idea I left the country," Philip called as he hurried down the hallway. As she sat waiting for Philip to return, she wonders about the vision she had of Princess Annie and the children. Thinking of this dream made her think of Lily, her previous nanny. Lily had a way of explaining dreams making them believable and easy to understand. She always had the most beautiful interpretations, some too beautiful to disregard. She always knew that Lily was simply too pretty to be a nanny. She knew that sooner or later that some handsome gentleman would notice her and sweep her off her feet. Of course it was the perfect timing. Two days before her eighteenth birthday, when Mark Anthony's Yorkie came running up toward them as they strolled through Tadworth Park. He was a cutie alright. He ran up to Lily and began licking her feet. Lily, having a natural love of animals picked him up and began patting his soft brown and white coat. Just then Mark called after his pet…

"Ginger you knotty boy, get over here this instant."

As Lily handed Ginger over to his owner, their eyes met. Natalie knew that this very moment would change everything for her favorite nanny. A few months after they met, the two moved to Australia and were married. Natalie and Lily stayed in touch but after Lily and Mark welcomed their first child, things got very busy for them both. It was then she realized that it was time to go visit with her mum and seek a new adventure.

As Natalie thought about Lily, she heard a rustling sound behind the cellar. She pulled back the curtain and peeked into the backyard. The trees back there had grown tremendously in the three years she's been away. She heard the rustling sound again but still couldn't see what was there.

"Who's there," she called. Then she heard cries which sounded like a baby animal of some sort. She tried the bolt on the Cellar door leading outside but it was rusted. She pulled against it with all her might but it didn't budge.

"Darn it!" she fretted. She heard cries again.

"Just a sec, I'll be right there," she called. She then noticed a heavy mallet hammer sitting in the corner. She reached for it and struck the bolt backwards and gently pushed the door open.

"Hello, where are you," she called.

As Natalie reached the end of the stairs, she missed her footing and fell into the brushes. As she tried to pull herself up, she heard cries and something running off. Just then Philip looked into the backyard.

"What are you doing back there my lady?" he asked with a silly smirk on his face.

"I thought I heard something," she called.

"You're bleeding," he said, hurrying towards her.

"Let's get you inside and take a look at that scratch on your knee."

"No, I heard something or someone crying, we must see what it is." Then she heard soft whining again. This time a little further away.

"Let's get you inside, and then I'll go have a look."

Although she insisted that she was fine, he carried her up the stairs and laid her on the sofa.

"William, would you be a champ and bring the first aid kit," Philip called.

91

"Please Philip hurry, something or someone back there might need our help."

"Alright babe, I'm on it," he called.

Philip searched through the thick brushes. He was uncertain what he was searching for but he kept looking. Then he saw something. As he got closer he couldn't believe his eyes. It was a puppy; with an all-white coat except for a cute brown spot on its right ear. The pup tried to run away but couldn't. She appears to be hurt.

"Hey there, don't worry, I won't hurt you," Philip said, lifting her up. Surprisingly, the pup didn't fuss. He held her close to his chest and carried her inside.

"How did you get back there?" Philip whispered.

The puppy licked him on the chin as though to thank him.

"You're welcome. Let's get you inside," he said.

As he entered the room carrying the adorable creature, Natalie was holding an icepack on her bruised knee and gasped in amazement at the sight of the pup.

"Oh my, look what we have here; she's adorable. Do you think she belongs to someone?"

"Well, she doesn't have a collar and it looks like the two of you would be off your legs for a while," Philip teased.

"Looks like you have double duty tonight Nurse," Natalie toyed. They both laughed. Natalie put her hands out to touch the pup but she grumbles at her.

"Wow, easy their girl," Philip said patting the pup's ear.

"Hmm, looks like she's been abused," Philip said trying to calm her.

"It's already late evening, let's look at her leg and we'll call the Vet in the morning," Natalie said, sounding exhausted.

"That's a great idea, Nat. But, where should we put her for now?" She pointed to a wooden box sitting near the entrance of the room.

"I think this will make a nice bed for her, for now," she said trying to sit up.

"No hunny, don't I have it."

"There are blankets in the hallway closet," she called. After making the pup more comfortable, Philip look at his fiancé's knee.

"Just a small bruise," he said.

He then opened the first aid kit and removed a small scissor, a band aid, cotton balls and an alcohol wipe. At the sight of the alcohol pad, Natalie shut her eyes tightly. Philip tore open the alcohol wipe and with one gentle but swift touch, cleansed and bandaged his beloved's knee.

"Thank you darling, that was excellent, I didn't feel a thing," she said, opening her eyes.

"Your other patient awaits," she said, patting Philip's head gently.

"You're most welcome," he said, kissing her bandaged knee.

"Natalie darling, are you down here?" Maureen called.

"We are all down here Mau," she answered. As Maureen entered the room, the puppy began to bark profusely. Surprised, Maureen froze at the sight of him.

"Easy their little girl," Philip called.

The pup calmed herself at the sound of Philip's voice.

"Well, who do we have here?" Maureen asked, sounding entitled.

"This would be, Cassie."

"Cassie?" Philip ask, surprised.

"She has a hurt limb, we found her in the shrub behind the cellar," Philip said.

"You poor thing," Maureen said, reaching out to pat her on the head.

"Careful Mau, she's a bit grumpy," Natalie warned.

"The pup grumbled but then allowed Maureen to pat her on the head.

"I'll be happy to have a look at her leg," Maureen said.

"Umm, it's alright Maureen, I'll take a look at her," Natalie said, sounding possessive.

"Someone's jealous," Philip teased.

Natalie shot him a stare.

"She looks starved. Maybe that's why she's grumpy," Maureen said.

"I don't think we have anything a puppy will eat," said Natalie.

"I'll make a quick run to the store," said Philip.

"There's a little store off Marden Road, just right around the corner," said Maureen.

"Alright then, I'll be right back ladies," Philip called.

Maureen sat next to Natalie.

"Perfect, now I have you all to myself."

"Something's on your mind, and by the way you look, something different?"

Maureen opened her mouth to speak but paused. She looks down at her hands.

"What wrong Mau?" Natalie asked, feeling anxious.

Maureen exhaled loudly.

"There's something I think you should know, about your dad."

"Dad, is he alright?"

"While you were in the Caribbean's, he met someone."

"You mean like a girlfriend?"

"I was hoping that he might have told you today, but by the way it looks I don't think he did."

"Did Richard mention anyone to you?"

"No, who is it?"

"She's a perfect nightmare; she treats everyone as her servant."

"You're joking?"

"I assure you not," she replied.

Maureen stood up and ran her fingers through her hair.

"There's more," she said, appearing nervous. By the look on Maureen's face, she knew it wasn't good news.

"She's pregnant!"

"She's what! Oh my goodness, that's impossible!" Natalie said staring at Maureen in horror.

"How far along is she?"

"She's about five months and due in October," Maureen said scornfully. Natalie couldn't believe what she was hearing. She sat in silence for a moment.

"What is she like?"

"You wouldn't care for her, she's extremely possessive. Twice divorce and treats everyone like Commoners."

"I thought dad was hiding something today, but this!"

"She acts like this home belongs to her. She's even hosted a few parties here for her horrible friends."

"And dad allowed all this?"

"I'm so glad you're home Nat. It's been impossible."

"I'm happy dad found someone, but from what I'm hearing, I don't think that he knows what he's doing."

"You know he's a saint. She treats him like an ATM Machine."

"Do you think he's with her now?"

"Without a doubt," Maureen admitted.

"Why didn't dad tell me about this? Does he plan on marrying her?"

"Oh goodness, I pray not," Maureen said expressing disgust.

"What's her name?"

"Marguerite," Maureen said rolling her eyes.

"I know him only too well, he would have proposed by now," Natalie said.

Please have a talk with him sweetie, and promise me that you won't let him know that you learned this from me," she pleaded. As Maureen left the room she said...

"You might want to have a look in the bedroom next to the guest room."

"What's in there?" Natalie called.

At that moment, Philip entered the room carrying a few bags. The pup wiggled his tail at the sight of him.

"I think she likes you Philip. So does all the ladies at the store," he laughed.

"You are handsome and you're an American."

They all know you very well over there," he said.

"Who's Bient," he asked with a curious stare.

Natalie looks away from him.

After feeding Cassie, Philip gave her a warm bath and bandaged her leg. Cassie appears no older than four months old and took a liking to Philip.

"Don't worry girl, you're safe here," he said, placing her back into the box.

"Why the sad face?"

"Do you remember when I mentioned that I thought something was going on with dad?"

"Yes, I just learned that he's seeing someone and that she's pregnant."

"You're kidding?"

"Not that there's anything wrong with dad being with someone, but by what I've learned, it doesn't sound very good."

Natalie filled Philip in on what she had learned from Maureen. Philip listened with great interest, now concerned about what this could mean for his fiancé.

"Pregnant, did your father ever mention wanting more children?"

"Never, and besides he's almost retired and always planned on retiring in the Caribbean. There's no doubt Marguerite has an ulterior motive. You're a God sent Philip. If it weren't for you; I wouldn't have been home to look after my father's interest."

Philip was silent for a while.

"Who's Bient Hun?" he asked a second time.

She looks directly at him but said nothing.

"Oh, I see," he said, getting up to leave.

"He's my ex-fiancé."

Philip stood with his back toward her and then turns slowly to face her.

"What?

"It's nothing to worry about, we were high school sweethearts."

"But you never mentioned him?" he said appearing slightly disappointed.

"I did mention him last night when we were in the garden. But I wanted to wait for a better time to discuss these unimportant matters. And besides, my father never liked him and was against us getting married. Two weeks before our wedding, I found out that he was having an affair with my cousin Katie," she said with tears appearing in her eyes.

"She was always so jealous of me."

Her tears didn't calm his need for answers. It only made him wonder if she still had feelings for her ex.

"Is he still around?" Philip asked, appearing a bit calmer.

"I haven't seen or spoken to him in several years. Believe me Phil, I'm over this jerk. I try to avoid the subject as much as possible."

"I'm sorry babe, don't worry about it," he said, returning to her side. He then kisses her gently, kissing the tears of her face.

Just then Cassie barked. They both laughed.

"I think someone's Jealous, maybe we should call her Katie?" Philip suggested.

This time Natalie laughed hysterically.

"I think that this is the first time in forever I've laughed when someone mention that name. My father has a saying; one should discuss the things that hurt the most to allow one to properly heal."

"Hmm, I think I would have to agree."

"Tell me more about your parents."

"Maybe after dinner," she said exhaustedly.

Just then William called them to dinner.

"Maureen mentioned that I should have a look at the bedroom next to ours."

"What's in there?"

"Not sure, we'll see," she said walking with a slight limp.

"Here babe, I got you."

"Phil my dear, that's a very long hallway, you won't be able to carry me this far. You're so strong, I love it," she said leaning her head on his shoulders.

"I love you."

"I love you too darling."

As they approached the kitchen, Philip suggested that they wait until tomorrow to find out what's going on in the room next door and Natalie Agreed.

"Something smells delightful," Natalie beamed.

"It's your favorite, Lasagna with a side of onion soup," William said proudly.

"May I interest you into a slice of homemade apple pie?"

"Absolutely, but only if you'd have a slice with us," Philip said. William laughed. As the three sat dining, William was suddenly quiet.

"I understand that you are only visiting for three weeks, does this mean you will be leaving next week?"

Natalie and Philip look at each other.

"There has been a change in our plans. Being home reminded me how much I missed everyone. And besides, I never intended to stay away this long."

"Does this mean you will both be staying?"

"I've given it some deep thought and I don't see why not," Philip said sipping on his lemonade.

"Of course I will have to return to America for a short while to tie up some loose ends with the business and other tid-bits."

"You'll do well listing your company for sale on the British Market," William said.

Philip's eyes widened.

"Hmm, great idea Will, I hadn't thought of it," he said in deep thought.

"Maybe you can hold on to it for a while. It could be a great vacation spot for when we do visit."

"An even better idea," Philip said.

"Don't worry William, we'll be around for a while," Natalie said ruffling his hair. They all laughed.

"It's been different around here without you Nat. Marguerite..." After that statement, William paused and tried to change the subject.

"Oh don't you worry Will, I already know about the mistress."

"You do?" William said, surprised.

"She's after your home, you should sit down with your father and talk some sense into him," William said, sounding straightforward.

"She already hosted several parties here. Her and her guests have been nothing but rude. She's requested my service which Richard approved for these so called parties. I've served her horrible guests for hours while being made sport of by these hooligans," William said, shaking his head.

"I cannot believe what I'm hearing, that's insane! This is quite unacceptable!"

"I'm sorry my lady, I didn't mean to upset you," William said, sounding worried.

"No one treats you this way and gets away with it. Not under this roof. I'm so sorry this happened to you Will and I'll see to it that you are properly compensated," she said leaving the table. And I promise you, Marguerite will not be allowed near this property again."

Philip patted William on the shoulder.

"Come here babe, you'll be seeing him tomorrow. You can discuss it with him then."

"I'm sorry my lady, I didn't mean to upset you," William said regretfully.

"No need to apologize William, it is I who need to apologize to you."

"William, may I ask, when was the last time you had a vacation?" Natalie said seating next to him.

"That was when we all flew to Lily's wedding in Australia," he replied.

"Will, that was over three years ago."

"It was a memorable one, and besides Butlers never takes a vacation."

"William, would you like to take a few weeks off?" Philip asked.

"I don't think I can and besides who will look after my Lady and the household?"

They both smiled at how devoted he was, even under the wrong circumstances.

"William, I insist. It's the least that I can do. Please take the rest of the summer off. As a matter of fact, we'll make flight arrangements for you, just give us the time and location. All expenses paid for two," Natalie said smiling.

William smiled at them both and removed his reading glasses.

"I don't suppose I have the option to refuse," he said.

"You've got that right," Philip said.

"Well, I've always wanted to visit Italy to see the Sixteenth Chapel."

"You've got it. We'll make all the arrangements for you tonight. As of now you're on holiday," Natalie said smiling.

"I can hardly believe it, thank you both very much," he said smiling proudly.

"You are most welcome, Master William. Please inform us who you would like to bring along with you and we'll take it from there."

"Well, I have to say that this is most unexpected," William said standing. "Thank you most kindly."

"You are most welcome Will," Natalie said, embracing him.

"I think I will invite Jane," he said, reaching for his Jacket in the kitchen closet. "I'll see you both tomorrow." He said happily.

"William, I didn't know you were seeing someone?"

"Well, my Lady, when I learned of your engagement, my heart was broken so I had to find someone else," he jokes. They all laughed.

"Oh my?" Natalie said, pretending to be crushed.

"Please enjoy your evening my Lady."

"You do the same Master William," they said simultaneously.

"Thank you for making the suggestion Natalie; I would have never thought of it."

"As would a noble Butler," Natalie replied.

William nodded once more and shut the door behind him.

Chapter 13

Marguerite let herself into Richard's townhome. Feeling exhausted, she relaxed on the recliner.

"Richard, are you home?" But there was no answer and she wondered if he was running late. Things between them are not on schedule as she had plan. She was hoping that he would have proposed by now. She enjoys Richard's company but the moment she's laid eyes on the Manor she was in love at first sight. She had to have it by any means necessary. Just then her mobile rang. It was her daughter.

"Danica, where have you been sweetheart?!" she asked, concerned.

"Oh I see. Certainly, you can have a party at the Manor this weekend. I'll speak with Richard and I'll get back to you, okay darling. I love you too sweetheart, cheers." As she put her mobile away, she heard the sound of keys at the front door. She rolled over and pretended to be asleep.

"Marguerite, are you here? Oh there you are, I thought that was your Compass parked out there," Richard said walking toward the sofa tickling Marguerite's feet.

"Richard, can't you see I'm asleep."

"Oh, come on? Can't a gentleman play with the mother of his child?"

She sat up and looked at him with a serious scowl.

"Richard, we need to have a talk," she said firmly.

"Yes sure what about?"

"What about? What do you mean?" she asked, surprised.

"Getting married, that's what."

Richard sat on the sofa beside Marguerite.

"Marguerite, the truth is that I never expected this to happen. I already have a child and she's a grown woman."

"What are you saying?"

"I'm saying that this is very much unexpected and I'm not sure where to begin."

Marguerite pretended to be hurt by Richard's words.

"I'm not saying that I don't care for you. I'm simply not ready to be married, not like this."

"Richard, is there someone else?"

"No there's not. You've asked me this before," he said, sounding slightly annoyed.

Marguerite got up and began walking toward the door. Richard hated to see her upset.

"You don't have to leave," he said. He was only trying to calm her emotions but she turned around and began kissing him viciously. Unable to resist her, he returned her affection. Realizing, he pulled her away gently. Before he said another word, she began kissing him again.

"Richard, I love you, please say you'll marry me," she pleaded. Caught up in the moment Richard shook his head as if saying yes to marguerite's invitation to propose and she quickly accepted it as his proposal. Not realizing what she thought Richard look into her eyes.

"Marguerite, I do care for you."

"That's all I needed Richard," she said gazing at him in a pretentious way.

The following morning Natalie woke up earlier than usual by the sound of Cassie whining. She tiptoed quietly over to her. Cassie was making sounds but she was fast asleep. She must be having a dream, she thought heading back to bed. A few hours later, she was awakened by the sound of a cup resting on a saucer. It was her fiancé bringing her a cup of her favorite tea.

"Good morning darling," he said, kissing her gently. She looks lovely as usual in her sleepwear.

"Oh Philip it's a bit too early for tea, I'm still sleepy," she said sitting up in bed. He took the tea and placed it close to her soft pink lips. She sipped a tiny bit.

"Yum, that's peppermint," she said, her sleepy face appears inviting.

"Please close your eyes for me darling," Philip said. Before her eyelids touched, Philip's lips met hers kissing her intimately. The smell of peppermint filled the room bringing out their deepest desires.

A few hours later, they were awakened by a soft knock on the door. It was Maureen, she pointed to the bedroom across the hall. Natalie threw on her robe and hurried to the door.

"My lady, you might want to have a look in here," Maureen said pointing.

"*Now*?" Natalie asked, rubbing her eyes. Maureen nods...

"Yes my lady." She led the way and waited as Natalie entered the room. She couldn't believe her eyes.

"Who are you, and how did you get in here?"

"Hello, I'm Danica. I got in through the front door. Don't you knock!" she asks rudely.

. "What do you mean through the front door?"

Danica took a set of keys out of her handbag and shook them in Natalie's face.

"You've got keys to this house? And you're still not telling me who you are."

"Are you deaf, I said my name is Danica!" she yelled.

"Maureen, please call Bobby's, tell them there's an intruder in my home."

"Right away my Lady," Maureen called.

"Please, don't call the Police, I'm Marguerite's daughter."

"Maureen, it's okay, I think we've got her attention," Natalie called.

"Who are you?" Danica asked.

"I'm Natalie, Richard's daughter, and this is my home. How did you manage to get keys?" Natalie said, sounding a little bit calmer.

"I'm off college for the summer and my mum said that it was okay for me to stay here," she said, sounding uncertain. Natalie could not believe her ears.

"Does my father know that you are here?" She didn't respond.

Having heard conversations, Philip peeked out the door.

"What's going on?" he asks, joining them.

"This young lady has keys to my home. She says that her mum gave her the okay."

"You're kidding," Philip chuckled.

"How long have you been living here?"

"I've lived here every summer the past two years," she said nervously.

"Is that so? Who else has keys?" Philip asked.

"Umm, my boyfriend," she stuttered. They could hardly believe what they were hearing. Natalie turns her back toward Danica. She didn't want to insult her any further but she knew that she couldn't have someone she hardly knows living in her home. Natalie paused for a moment in deep thought, then looked directly at Danica.

"Young lady, I understand your predicament, but it is my permission that you need to be here. You can stay tonight. However, in the morning, you will render your keys. I do not wish to discuss this any further," Natalie said before walking away.

"My lady, would you join me for a moment," called Maureen. Philip motioned that it was okay.

"I'm not leaving!" Danica yelled and slammed the door shut behind her. Natalie ignored her outburst and followed Maureen to her room.

"Oh I love what you did with your room," Natalie said looking around. Maureen smiled but the smile quickly disappeared. Natalie recognized that look; something was very wrong or very urgent.

"What's the matter Maureen?" She asked, sitting next to her.

"At first, I thought I might have misplaced it, but then another piece went missing last week," she cried.

"What's missing?" Natalie asked, rubbing her back.

"My Great Grandmother's Broach," she sobbed.

"You've got to be joking," Natalie said.

Maureen nods no.

"I'm not pointing any blame, but since Danica and her boyfriend have been coming around, things have begun to go missing. I've searched everywhere, I've been searching for my grandma's broach for weeks and it was when I couldn't find my mother's necklace I realized that it was stolen," she said, drying her eyes.

"Don't worry Maureen. We both have a sneaking suspicion who it might be. I'll ask my fiancé to assist in the search; I pray we find your keepsakes," Natalie said embracing her.

"Thank you, sweetie," Maureen said gratefully.

"We'll find it, I promise," Natalie said, shutting the door behind her.

Richard's mobile rang. "Hi Sweetheart, I'm headed over to the Manor to see you, I want to discuss business," he said, sounding happy.

"That's perfect; I'll see you when you get here. Love you, dad."

"Love you too sweetheart."

Even if she had brought back a fiancé, Richard was happy that his daughter was home. He was unsure of how he would handle telling her all that had happened in her absence. He was considering putting it off until after her wedding. His phone rang again and this time it was Marguerite.

"Richard, Danica is not here at the Town house. Her keys to the Manor are also missing," she said sounding concerned.

"Marguerite, she's only allowed at the Manor on weekends during the summer," he said annoyed.

"I told her that it was alright to stay there until we find a new home," Marguerite said.

"You know that my daughter is home now, you should have discussed this with me first," he said pulling over to the side.

"Richard, I thought your daughter was at the Palace Hotel?" she said, sounding entitled.

"Marguerite, did you expect my daughter to stay in a hotel, while your daughter lived in her home?" She was silent.

"Richard, please don't be upset. I've also created a nursery at the Manor for the baby," she said. Richard remained silent for a moment.

"Marguerite, we'll discuss this when I return."

"I love you," she called. But he had already hung up and didn't hear her. Richard didn't appear upset about the nursery, and Marguerite took it as an indication that he was okay with her unplanned arrangements. In her thoughts her plan was slowly coming together.

As Richard drove through the busy London streets, he wondered what he was going to say to his daughter. They never kept secrets from each other and he wondered what this was going to do to their relationship. He only hoped that she would not become upset and return to America. He was certain that she would never get over how he came between her and her first fiancé. At least, she realized that he was right about him. He remembered when he'd first met Marguerite. For the first year things were perfect and he even contemplated marrying her. Then he thought of the baby, and smiled. Although he was thinking about retirement, he thought that perhaps this would be a good change for him. Maybe he could retire and be an even better father than he was to Natalie.

As Richard pulled up in the driveway of the Manor, he dials his daughter's mobile. He couldn't keep this a secret any longer. He had to tell her before she found out on her own. Natalie's phone rang but there was no answer so he dialed the landline.

"Hello, Baldwin's residence, how may I help you?" Danica said.

"Danica, what are you doing? Does my daughter know that you are here?"

"Umm, yes she does." His fears were confirmed.

"Would you ask Natalie to take the phone please," he said firmly. Without saying a word, she knocks on Natalie's door.

"Natalie, your father is on the phone, he wishes to speak with you!" she called rudely. By the time Natalie open the door to confirm what Danica was saying, she was gone. Having overheard, Maureen told Natalie that her father was on the phone.

"Thanks Maureen. Hi dad, are you headed over?" she asked.

"I'm already here, sweetheart," he replied.

"Please come downstairs darling, I need to speak with you alone."

"Okay dad, I'll be right down." She already knew what he wanted to discuss. However, by the sound of his voice, she feared that there was something more.

As she approaches, he motions for them to sit out by her garden.

"Dad, please, let's sit in the shade by the pool." Her garden was her place to make good memories and she didn't want anything negative to influence her memories.

"Sure sweetheart," he called. Before sitting down Natalie reached out and embraced her father.

"I love you, dad. I don't like seeing you so worried," she said. When they were seated, he told her everything that Maureen had already told her.

"There's one more thing," he said. Natalie became nervous. "I wasn't sure that you were going to return to England so I had placed this house on the market and I've already received a few generous offers," he said looking stern yet concerned. Natalie was prepared to hear about his girlfriend and the baby, even Marguerite's disrespectful daughter, but her home, the home she's built most of her childhood memories in and where she hopes to raise her own children...

"You did what!"

"Well you were so upset with me, then I was so upset with you, I couldn't tell who was more upset with the other," he said smiling.

"That's not very funny, it was your fault. You introduced Bient to Katie knowing that I was engaged to him!" she yelled walking away from him.

"You know Bient made it sound much worse than it actually was. He wanted you to blame me and that's exactly what you did," he said, slightly more upset, this time.

"Dad, it doesn't matter how you put it, it's still very upsetting," she said returning to her seat.

"They belong together. Bient has no ambition. He was unemployed and ready to start a family. He was after your family's money and you know it. Honey, I'm sorry let's change the subject," he said.

"You're right dad, and besides I have Philip now." They both smiled.

"Dad, about the house...would you please take it off the market? I'm not sure what my plans are yet but I know I'm not quite ready to give up the Manor. And besides, you will never get its worth in this Market," she said.

"Alright. I'll make arrangements, but there's going to be some very disappointed prospective buyers," he said.

"Dad, one more thing, you promised that when I was eighteen, that you would make me the beneficiary of this home, I'm almost twenty-two now."

Richard looked at his wrist watch.

"Maybe we can talk about this another time," he said.

"Now is the time dad, you're having a baby and this could create a lot of confusion." She was right and Richard knew it. His girlfriend already had her sights on this place.

"We'll go see my Attorney on Monday, please remind me," he said standing up to leave.

"Dad, wait."

"Yes sweetheart?"

"What are you going to do about Danica, she's been very disrespectful to me."

"Don't worry, she's only around for the summer," he said.

"No dad, she's been living here with her boyfriend and now some of Maureen's Jewelry is missing."

106

"Is she certain?"

"Dad, she's sobbing her eyes out over them, I've never seen her this upset before." Richard returned to his seat.

"Honey, I'm sorry, I'll have a talk with her," he said. Natalie expected Richard to be more upset.

"I've already asked her to leave."

"The truth is sweetheart; she has no place to stay at the moment. Her mother just went through a terrible divorce and lost everything to her husband."

"That's unfortunate, but it's not our problem."

"What about her father?"

"Marguerite and her first husband were quite young and divorced shortly after learning of her first pregnancy. This was her second husband, Danica's stepfather."

"Oh, I see. But dad, you still have to be careful, she can't stay here for too long. She'll have to find a job and try to get out on her own. She's an adult."

"I didn't want to mention this, but darling, she has a long record of delinquent behaviors. This might prevent her from employment for a while," Richard said.

Natalie became a bit jealous because her father seems to care for this girl.

"That's her tough luck, she needs to learn responsibility! By the way dad, where did you meet Marguerite?"

"I met her at our Pub," he smiled.

"The pub? Dad for goodness sakes!" They both laughed. Then Richard's face became serious.

"What's the matter?"

"Oh, it's nothing to worry about," he said pretending to be okay. But she knew him only too well.

"Dad, please let it out?"

"Marguerite is thinking about marriage," he said.

"What do you think?" he asked.

"Well, when am I going to meet her? I think this will have to happen first," Natalie said.

"Let me know when you're ready and we'll arrange it," he said.

"About marriage, I think you should wait, in time it will sort itself out," she said.

"It's good that you're home sweetheart, I've missed your wisdom. Here's the address to the Pub, please give this to Philip and ask him to meet me there later. I have a business proposition for him." They both stood up and embraced each other.

"Okay sweetheart, I'm happy we got a chance to talk."

"Sure dad, me too."

He kissed her on the forehead and waved one more time before slipping into his car. She loves her father very much. Other than her nannies, it has always been just the two of them. Like two peas in a pod. They had promised that they would always take care of each other no matter what. The thought of Marguerite made her worry about him. Did she get pregnant on purpose? They had only been together for a short while; this doesn't sound like her father at all. If these people were going to be a part of her life, she must find out who they are, and soon.

Just then her phone rang.

"Hi babe, where are you? I saw your dad left quite a few minutes ago," he said possessively.

"Hello darling, I'm out back, by the pool, I'll be right up," she called.

"The pool? How big is this place? I didn't know you had a pool."

"Want to join me for a swim?" she asked seductively.

"Would love to," he called.

"Can I join in?" Maureen asked.

"Sure, the more the merrier," Philip said tossing a towel over his shoulders. Just then her phone rang. It was William; he has new information in regards to his plans for vacation.

"Absolutely William, Phil and I would make the arrangements tonight and you and your friend would be on your way to Italy in no time. You are very welcome, take care now. Bye, cheers."

"What a splendid view," Philip said with a loud whistle. Maureen follows behind him carrying a basket with a few glasses and two bottles of champagne from Rockwell creek's winery.

"Good call Maureen," Philip said.

"I was wondering when you two was going to enjoy these fine bottles of California champagne," she said, removing her sunglasses. The couple laughed.

"What's the occasion?" Natalie asked.

"Well, how about you being home and us having the Manor all to ourselves," Maureen laughed. Although Natalie knew that Danica would be around for a little while, she dared not ruin the moment.

"Absolutely," Philip cheered. He then dove head first into the pool and did a couple of laps.

"Very impressive, and he is in such excellent shape. *Look at those abs, yum*," Maureen said.

Natalie chuckles.

"Just keep your pretty panties on my friend," Natalie teased.

"I'll try," Maureen laughs.

Natalie opened the umbrellas over the lounge chairs for shade.

"Boring," Philip called and tossed water at them. Maureen and Natalie screamed.

"Now that's not the way a gentleman should treat a lady," Maureen called. Natalie simply laughed while slipping into her swimwear.

"Who said anything about being a gentleman? Open up that bloody champagne and get in here ladies!"

"Oh you are so going to get it," Maureen scolded and tossed some ice from the container at Philip, barely missing his head. Philip dove under water to avoid being hit and both women jump into the pool. Philip surfaced and wondered where they went.

"Hey ladies?" he called. They seemed to have disappeared. Unnoticed, Maureen came up from the water and then Natalie followed. Natalie motioned for Maureen to be silent. She dove quietly under the water and grabbed Philip's legs, pulling him under. After a few seconds, she releases him. Startled, he resurfaces and screams like a lady.

"Yikes, what the heck was that?!" he said pretentiously and jumps out of the pool. Maureen couldn't believe how petrified he was and laughed hysterically.

"We got you," Natalie said splashing.

"I couldn't take any chances, after all this is an eighteenth century remodeled Mansion. It could have easily been a corpse selling noodles."

They all laughed. Philip opened the champagne and poured them each a glass.

"I have to say, it's very early for such a fine drink," Philip said.

"It's five o' clock somewhere," Maureen said.

"Cheers to that," Natalie said.

The party of three sat enjoying their morning while discussing wedding plans and other fun things to do around Croydon. It was now May and their wedding date was previously scheduled for June second.

"That's only four weeks away," Maureen said.

"Maybe we should hire a wedding planner. I just want a small wedding, however, it has to be perfect," Natalie said. Just then Philip looked up and saw someone with a camera taking photographs of them.

"Hey, you there!" he yelled. This time he was very annoyed.

"Don't worry love, you'll get used to it," Natalie said.

"Think he heard our conversation? He was really close. I'm sure he heard," Philip said throwing a small rock in the cameraman's direction. After her fourth glass of champagne, Maureen appeared drowsy. She got up and attempted to stand and almost tumbled into the pool.

"Well, I think that's it for our buddy, what do you say?" asked Philip.

"Poor baby," Natalie said.   Philip hugs one of Maureen's shoulders and Natalie hugs the other and they helped her to her room. Afterwards, they return to the pool.

"I'm going to miss William; at least he would have ensured we had breakfast instead of champagne this morning," Philip said.

This time Philip watches as Natalie dove into the pool; a perfect needle. When she surfaces, her long wavy hair hugs her shoulders and her fair slim body shined in the glistening pool. Unable to resist her angelic appearance, Philip dove into the water. The moment he surfaced he took her into his arms. Before she had a chance to mumble a word, Philip covered her lips kissing her madly. She wraps her legs around him and he kisses her like never before.

A few hours later as they prepare for the day...

"Want to head over to the pub? Dad asked us to drop by. I think he has a proposition for you."

"Alright then, but maybe we should wait for Maureen to wake," he suggested.

"Of course," she replied. Suddenly she appears distant and Philip wondered what was on her mind. She's had a lot of reality thrown at her the past few days and he could tell that there was something new on her mind. As he slipped on his sunglasses, he thought of his Parents. He wishes they were alive to meet the woman he loves. Besides his aunt, uncle and cousin, he was alone in the world.

Suddenly they heard Cassie bark.

"Hmm, she sounds upset," Philip said.

"I'll go check on her," Natalie said hurrying off.

"Cassie was looking out of the bedroom window into the backyard. She wagged her tail at the sight of Natalie but then continues barking.

"What's the matter girl?" Natalie looks out of the window in time to see the blond mane horse disappear into the brushes. Philip followed after her.

"What's   going   on?"

       "It's her; it's the horse that I've seen running on the edge of the forest, I can't believe it," she said excitedly.

Philip watched as his fiancé prance about excitedly. At times she seems no older than a sixteen-year-old, but much more mature when she spoke.

"I'm going to go after her," Natalie said, slipping on her Jeans and water boots.

"We can't, I have an appointment with your dad."

"There's time, I'll be right back," she called.

"Let's go babe," she called.

"Wait a minute, where are we going?" Before he had a chance to follow she was gone. She was determined to capture this horse. Even more determined now that it has found its way to her. She disappeared in the thick brushes and Philip heard her whistle. She must be close he thought and picks up a light pace.

"Natalie, wait up Hun, this could be dangerous!" he shouted.

Natalie ran down hill for a little while and stopped at a small pond nestled in the middle of a wooded area. She didn't remember a pond being here and wondered how much it must have rained the last few years. Everything was taller and much greener than she remembered. She turns around in time to see Philip.

"She's gone," she said.

"Alas, she's proved that she's much too beautiful to be captured, making me more jealous and more determined than ever. Oh well," she cried.

"Chasing after her would only make her wild, maybe if you let her alone she would find her way to you," Philip said, walking toward her. Suddenly they heard someone call. It was Maureen. Someone was on the phone for Natalie.

"Who is it?" she asked.

"It's Marguerite," Maureen called. Natalie was quiet for a moment.

"Please inform her that I'm not available at the moment and that I'll return her call shortly."

"Okay love," Maureen replied.

As they head out of the wooded area, the couple heard a loud crackle. They turn around in time to see the horse walking toward the pond and began to drink.

"No way," Philip said.

"She's magnificent, and sneaky too," Natalie said.

As they gaze at the gorgeous creature, she looks up and stared at them. The horse began to approach, but then hesitated. She was looking at Natalie. She then lifted up her right hoof and whined loudly. They couldn't believe their eyes. Philip began to slowly back away.

"What are you doing?" she asks.

"I think she wants' you, I'm a distraction," he said.

As Philip backed further away, the horse began to approach Natalie. She came close enough where she was able to reach out and touch her.

"Careful," Philip called. As Natalie lifted her hands to touch her, she whined softly.

"It's alright girl," she said fiddling the horse's mane.

"Okay babe, we should go now," Philip called. At the sound of Philip's voice, the horse turned and ran off. Natalie was thrilled.

"Yes!" she shouted. "Why do you think she came up to me like that?"

"The same reason I came up to you that fine evening at the Mall," he said. They held hands and headed back to the Manor.

"That was amazing," Philip finally admitted.

"She seems to know you. Not sure, this is the first time she's ever come this close," Natalie said.

"I think you're jealous," she teased.

Philip giggles. Maybe so, but I'm the one that get to take you home," he boasts.

"Maybe so for now," she smiled.

As they strolled back to the manor, they noticed a car in the driveway with the Royal seal on the license plate.

"Looks like you have company," Philip said.

"Looks like the Palace Chauffeur. Probably looking for dad," Natalie said. As they entered the door, they heard a male voice.

"Hello madam, you must be Natalie, I'm Nathaniel York," he said removing his hat and slightly bending his knees. The respect given to the first daughters of Royal Guards.

"Ma'am, I... I... was sent here with a message from the Baroness," he stuttered.

"Oh," Natalie said surprised.

"Yes, she heard that you were home and would like to see you as soon as possible," he said standing upright, with both hands at his side.

"Do you know why she's requested my presence?"

"No madam, I was only asked to deliver the message to you," he replied. Natalie was only a child when she was last invited to the Palace Manor and it was to have tea with Princess Annie. She was the first and only child of a Royal Guard ever invited to visit the Palace.

"Nathaniel, Palace messengers are only sent to request the presence of someone when it is of high importance. Kindly inform the Baroness that I have accepted her invitation and will visit her at fourteen hundred hours, on the first day of next week."

The chauffeur nodded gently. Philip saw him to the door and watch as he got into his vehicle and drove out of the courtyard. After the messenger had left, Natalie was slightly concerned and wondered the reason for the sudden invitation to the Palace Manor. Philip enters the guest room.

"Wow, what did he want?" he asked, surprised.

"Phil, that was Nate, the Palace's Public Chauffeur and messenger. I was invited to the palace."

"Hmmm, I see that he regarded you very highly."

"Oh Philip, don't be silly. That's how Palace employees greet Guard families. It doesn't appear that the Baroness knows about you or I'm certain she would have invited us both."

"Maybe we can talk about it later. Let's head over to the pub," Philip reminded her.

"Oh you're nothing short of a Yank," she teased.

"A Yank, oh you are so in for it," he said, pulling her closely. Natalie sunk into his arms hoping to be kissed; instead she was swept off her feet and placed on a large Piano in the Parlor. Philip reached in his pocket for his drawing pad and pencil.

"There's something about this place that makes me want to sketch beautiful things."

"Ah, sounds interesting, but there's no time," she reminds him.

"That's all the time I need," he said. Before she became too uncomfortable he had sketch a beautiful image of her sitting uncomfortably on the oversized instrument.

"That's it?" she called.

"Yep," he said walking away.

"No way, get back here handsome," she called.

"That's what you get for calling me a Yank," he played.

An hour later as they drove to her father's pub, Philip suddenly became silent. He began to wonder if they were ready to be married. The things he'd learned about his fiancé, her popularity with the Royal family and the London Press made him a bit anxious about his promise. Was he ready for this excitement? It's the least he expected when he ran into this dazzling. Little did he know that he had laid eyes on the most popular girl from the heart of London. As Maureen drove the couple through the streets of Croydon, every now and then she would glance at them through the rear view mirror. She had grown quite fond of them as a couple but somehow she has always believed that Natalie's life was meant for greater things. From the time she was a child, she had stolen the hearts of everyone who set eyes on her. She couldn't picture her living a simple sheltered married life. There had to be something much greater to be accomplished.

Maureen pulled the Limousine to a stop in front of a busy pub named 'A lady's Abode.'

"Here you are my lovelies," Maureen said stepping out of the vehicle to open the door for her guests. Natalie had fallen asleep on the way and awoke to the sound of the Bobby's' siren as it blared through the busy London streets. Before Philip had the chance, Maureen reached for the door and took Natalie's hands, helping her out of the Limo. Some recognized the Baldwin's Limousine and took photos while others whispered. Although it was only Thursday afternoon, the Pub was already quite busy.

"That's what I'm talking about," Philip said as they entered the building. Of the many Pubs in London, A Lady's Abode has a well-organized bar, a restaurant, a game room, and a place for relaxation. Adam the bartender saw them entered.

"Natalie, is it really you?" he called, walking briskly toward them and embracing her.

"Your dad is on his way and should be here shortly. May I fix you a drink?" Adam pretended to not notice Philip as they sat at the bar.

"Adam, I want you to meet my fiancé, Philip Lane; Philip is an American."

"A Yank, pleasure to meet you," he said pretentiously.

"Careful, the last person that called him a Yank, had the pleasure of eating a bunch of dirt," Maureen warned.

"Is that so," Adam said, folding his arms.

Philip laughed.

"Adam, one Incredible Hulk, straight up!" Maureen called, banging her hands on the counter. Most of the guests at the Pub engulf in laughter.

"Atta girl!" someone cheered.

Just then a young African girl who appears to be in her late teens appeared behind the bar. She mixed a few drinks and served a glass containing a green drink to Maureen.

"Ah wonderful," Maureen said, lifting the glass to her lips.

"This is my girlfriend Makayla. She is out of College for the summer and is helping me out at the Pub. She's got quite the singing voice and has attracted a nice crowd here last weekend," Adam said proudly.

"That's good to know Adam, but you know that you're not responsible for hiring around here," Maureen reminded him. "Does Richard know about this?" she asked.

"I was planning on discussing it with him today and besides it's none of your business!" he scolded. Natalie watched as two other young ladies went behind the bar and began serving drinks to customers. She was pleased that they were helping out, however they appeared much too young to be at the Pub.

Just then Adam took Natalie by the hand.

"Let's show you around my Lady," he said, leading her toward the restaurant.

"Ladies and Gentlemen, employees of A Lady's Abode; meet Natalie Elizabeth Baldwin; the beautiful daughter of Sir, Richard Baldwin, whom we all know as the highest ranking Royal Guard to his Majesty, the Prince," he boasted.

"Adam that's not necessary," Natalie said. Most of the employees came forward and introduced themselves while visitors applauded and took photos. A short while later Richard walked in with Philip and Maureen by his side.

"Richard?" Adam said surprised.

"Adam, you're just the man I want to see. Natalie, Philip, Maureen, please join us, if you may," Richard said leading the way.

When they were all seated, without hesitation, Richard turned to Adam.

"Adam, for the last three years, you've done a great job managing A Lady's Abode for which I am very grateful."

Adam smiled proudly.

"Sir as you know, this Pub is my home away from home, I treat it the way I would treat my very own property."

Richard smiled but just as quickly, his face became serious.

"Adam, is it true that you've hired three unlicensed, under aged young ladies to assist at the bar? Is it also true that you've also been serving free drinks every Saturday for the past year to High School students?" Adam looks at Natalie and then at Richard nervously. He tried to find the words to address Richard's accusation, however, he had no response. Richard glanced over at Natalie.

"I've received mail from the Business Administration threatening to shut down my operation for serving drinks to minors. I've been very busy the past year... Adam, how could you've done a thing like this?"

"But who reported it?" Adam asked, upset.

"Is that all you have to say for yourself Adam? Did you even ask them to present identification?" asked Maureen. Adam said nothing.

"Two parents of High School students are currently filing lawsuits to shut me down," Richard scolded.

Philip looks over at Adam.

"What are you looking at," Adam said scornfully.

"You're fired," Philip said toying with him.

"You can't fire me!"

"He sure can," Maureen said.

"As of this moment Adam, you are being relieved of your duties. You will receive a full explanation within a week," Richard said.

"And please take the young women with you," Maureen said.

"This is absurd; what's this place without me?"

"You're right about that, it will be much better without you," Maureen called.

Adam stormed out of the room. After he left, Richard revealed that Adam was also suspected of embezzling monies to fund his mother-in- law's new club-the one over on Trafalgar Square that's almost completed. The group of four made new arrangements for hiring a Bartender. In the meantime, Philip, who has previous experience offered to take Adams place until Richard found a replacement.

Maureen glanced at Philip... "There are only two conditions."

"And what's that my friend?" Phil asked.

"Please don't drink all the booze, and if you plan on it, promise you'd invite me," she warned. All laughed.

Natalie spoke to her father about the young African girl that Adam hired. She asked him to consider hiring her to sing at the Pub on weekends. Richard agrees to hire her only if she was at least eighteen. Natalie excused herself and went to find Makayla. As she searched for the girl, she noticed Adam arguing with her outside the Pub. Then she saw him grab her wrist angrily.

"Adam, stop it!" Natalie called.

"Stay out of this Natalie, this is none of your business," he yelled.

"As a matter of fact, it is now my business because you are harassing a prospective employee of my father's!" Adam looks at her furiously.

"So, are you going to give my girlfriend my job?"

"Not sure, but we are seriously considering it," Natalie said, staring at him disappointedly.

Makayla pulled her arm out of Adam's grasp and ran into the lady's room.

"Adam, it's best you leave the premises," Natalie scolded. He got into his car and sped away from the pub. Natalie followed Makayla into the lady's room. As she entered, the young girl was splashing water on her face.

"Pardon me, my name is Natalie. I don't think that we were properly introduced."

"We weren't, but I know who you are," she said, drying her hands with a paper towel. She appears upset and Natalie wonders if it was a good time to discuss the opportunity with her.

"May I ask, how old are you?" Natalie asked. She didn't respond and appears slightly annoyed. Natalie turns to leave.

"Twenty-two, why?" she responded. Although her attitude was less than appealing, Natalie discussed the opportunity with her. After their conversation, she learned that Makayla was only a visitor, and was in England temporarily visiting family, therefore she could not have accepted the opportunity. Natalie offered her an opportunity to obtain an employment visa but she told her that she'd missed her family in Johannesburg, and was looking forward to returning home. Makayla thanked Natalie for considering her.

A moment later, Maureen entered the restroom. As Natalie turned to leave...

"I'll think about it," Makayla called.

"That would be lovely," Natalie said smiling at her.

"Maureen, have you been drinking? How in the world are we going to get home?" she asked.

"A lot has change in three years sweetheart," she said, cupping Natalie's face.

"I can fire you for this you know," Natalie joked.

"Well, why don't you, you know that you're nothing without me," she said mockingly.

"Now you are starting to sound like Adam." They both laughed.

As they headed toward the bar, Philip seems to have everything under control. Maureen thought he looked handsome with his white sleeves rolled up as he rearranged the bar to his liking.

"No more for you," Natalie warned.

"Just getting started sweetheart," Maureen said with a wink. As they sat at the Bar, Anthony the chef entered.

"Madam, your lunch has been served. Richard wishes you all to join him."

Before leaving, the Chef bent his right knee toward Natalie and headed back to the restaurant.

"What manners, I like this bloke," Maureen said. As they sat dining, Natalie shared the news of her invitation to the Palace Manor with her father. He didn't appear surprise and she wondered how much he knew. She pried him for information but got nowhere. After lunch, since it was his first day, Richard gave Philip the okay to close the pub early. Philip admitted that he was not nearly prepared to take on a full day's work.

He glanced at his fiancé. He was ready for some alone time with her and wondered if that was possible with all the new events that was on her schedule. He never thought that their vacation would take so many interesting turns.

"Darling, are you alright?" she asked. She noticed how reserved he's been lately and it worried her. After all this was supposed to be their time. Maybe this is turning out to be too much for him in such a short time.

"I'm okay Hun, just a bit exhausted," he said. But she knew that look. He was jealous in a cute kind of way; the too much too soon kind of elusive American look. She knew that they had to get away soon.

A few hours later when Maureen was sober enough to drive, the three headed back to the Manor. When they arrived, Maureen received a call from her sister Claire and a short while later, without a word, she hurried out the door. From the way she left, Natalie knew that something was urgent; she was concerned but thankful for the time alone with Philip. As they headed up the stairs they heard Cassie bark and Natalie's heart sank.

"Oh no, Philip we forgot to feed Cassie," she panicked.

"Don't worry, I took care of her before we left," he assured. As they entered the room, Cassie leaped out of her bed and ran to Philip. They were finally happy to be alone together when they heard someone scream.

"Did you hear that?"

"Sounds like it's coming from the bedroom across the hall," Philip said. They both ran out into the hallway but Philip asked Natalie to wait while he investigated.

As he opened the door, he saw a teenage boy shoved Danica against the wall.

"Where is it?" he yelled.

"Hey you, get away from her," Philip yelled.

At the sight of Philip, the boy released Danica.

"Who the hell are you, punk!"

"This is none of your business," she yelled.

"It is my business, when it happens in my fiancé's home," Philip yelled.

Natalie entered the room.

"Danica, what's going on, and who's this?"

"Get out of my room, both of you," she yelled angrily.

"That's it, I'm calling the authorities," Natalie said dialing. At the sound of that, the boy grabbed his belongings and ran toward the door.

"Larson, wait," Danica called following him.

"So much for a quiet evening," Philip said annoyed.

"That's it, she's out of here in the morning, I have no idea who these people are in my home. I still don't understand why she lives here," Natalie said storming away in frustration.

"I was trying to do this for my dad, but I'm not sure if it's going to work. This girl needs some kind of help before it's too late for her," she said.

"Let's go sweetheart, don't worry about it," Philip said, taking her hands; we'll discuss it with your father later. As they head back to their room, he tickles her tummy playfully. She giggles. He didn't want her to worry about anything. He wants to be her Rock; and most of all the love of her life. He felt slightly jealous that she was once engaged. His plan is to erase all memory of her previous romance with this high class jerk, she was engaged too, and the pain he has caused her.

"It's not fair, you know I don't like the tickles," she laughs. She grabbed a pillow and tossed at him. As he reached for the pillow, she hid behind her hutch. He looked up and noticed her shadow reflecting against the wall. Very cute, he thought and pretended to not notice her hiding place.

"I'm set on fire for you darling, and if I don't find you in the next half of a second, I may die with passion." Then he remembered their first date at the Winery, among the orange groves. He recalled what he'd done to get her to come out of hiding. He transforms his face as the Wolfman and made that eerie howling sound. He heard a muffled giggle and began walking away from the hutch. She peeked and saw him stopped in his tracks, then just as swiftly he pointed in her direction…

"There you are," he said pointing and making the veins in his neck protruded as he gaped his teeth. Natalie screamed and jumped onto her bed pulling the linen over her head.

"Ah, there you are," he said returning to his human form.

As she waited for him to get into bed, he sneaked off into the shower. Where is he? she thought and just then she heard the shower running.

"No way," she said disapprovingly and followed after him. As she opened the curtain, Philip pulled her into the shower kissing her passionately. She smoothed her hands over his chest. Unable to withstand her overwhelming beauty, he lifted her up in one swift move as she nestled into his arms embraced in showers of passion.

The couple spent the rest of their evening indoors. They had plans with Richard and Marguerite but what was broadcast as a light shower has transformed into a thunderstorm, cancelling all plans into the perfect evening of love's unfolding rose. Philip got out of bed and sat on her sofa watching her sleep. Natalie rolled over to face him but discovered emptiness. Realizing that he wasn't in bed she awoke.

"Philip?" she said sitting up in bed. He didn't respond, he wanted her to return to sleep. As he sat watching this beautiful princess, he fell asleep and had a dream. As though he was back in the States in his Condominium and Natalie was not with him. He called her name several times but she didn't respond. He awoke to his fiancé soft touch.

"You were dreaming," she said wiping moisture from his forehead.

"What were you dreaming about?" she asks concerned. He pulled her close to him and kissed her.

"Let's elope," he said.

Her eyes widened. He looked worried and it scared her.

"Um…" before she said another word, he kisses her again.

"What's the matter babe?" she said, pulling away from him.

He walks toward the sink and splash water on his face.

"Let's go back to the States, there's still time to catch our flight." He said, wiping his face. She appears as though she'd seen a ghost.

"What's going on babe, is everything okay?" she asked, slipping into her nightwear. Philip appears overwhelmed and she knew that everything was happening much too quickly for him.

"Maybe you can accompany me to the Palace to meet Baroness Esther?" she said.

"What do you think it's about?" he asked.

"Not sure but I have a feeling that it's something to do with Princess Anne," she said smiling.

"If that's the case, you may not have any time for me," he said.

"Is this why you want to return to the States?"

He didn't respond and it surprised her.

They sat quietly and she knew that she had to figure out her priorities before she lost focus on the most important thing in her life.

"Please babe, don't worry," she pleaded.

He remained silent. He wanted her to agree into marrying right away.

"Please Phil, please say something, you know that I don't like the silent treatment."

Still, he said nothing. She sat on her sofa and hugged a pillow tightly.

"Alright then Mr. Lane the game is on, silent it is," she fussed.

Just then Cassie barked and they both erupt in laughter.

"Alright girl, I promise there would be no more silence in this house," Philip said patting her head.

The couple spent the next few days indoors. It was the first time in a while since they were alone on the weekend and they loved it. This gave her time to think about Phil's proposal and to prepare for the coming week. As she sat on the upstairs balcony overlooking the driveway, someone in a grey BMW pulled up and began approaching the gate. At the same time, Philip joined her on the balcony.

"Gorgeous view out here," he said sitting next to her. She motioned for his silence and pointed to the woman approaching.

"I don't recognize her, she seems upset," Natalie said.

"I'll go out front to see what she needs," Philip said hurrying off.

Natalie watched from upstairs as Philip approached the gate. At the sight of Philip, the woman cried in a panicking voice and pointed to the nearby woods.

"Help, my daughter fell in a large ditch over there and she is not responding."

Did you call Paramedics?" Philip asked.

"No I had no way of calling. My daughter had my phone when she fell in. Come quickly, there's no time," she urged.

Philip reached into his pocket, removed his phone and dialed emergency. Overhearing their conversation, Natalie went to get Cassie and hurried outside.

"Hello, I'm Natalie; please take us to your daughter's location. We'll follow you there," she said getting into their Jeep. The woman led the way and they followed in close pursuit. They drove about a mile off the main road and then the woman made a sharp right turn onto a rugged unpaved trail.

"Looks like she's headed to Alfred's property. As they turned off the main road, not too far off, the woman's car came to a stop.

"Please come quickly, please help my little girl," she cried running ahead. Natalie took Cassie and Philip grabbed a rope and some equipment and followed after the strange woman. When they arrived at the scene, Philip got on his knees and peered into what looked like an abandoned Well. Luckily there were tree roots growing horizontally across the Well, which prevented the young girl from plummeting to the bottom. Philip observed her for a moment. There were minor bruises on her face and knees, but she showed signs of life.

"What's her name?" Philip asked looking up at the woman.

"Allie, Allie Rockefeller and I'm Jenny," the woman cried.

Philip call the girl's name and she move her toes once. Cassie barked and struggled to get away from Natalie.

"She's alive, but we need to hurry," he said.

"Phil, would you be able to help her?" Natalie asked nervously.

"Where are the frigging Medics, they are never on time!" the woman said anxiously.

"Don't worry ma'am," Natalie said, placing a hand on her shoulders. We'll do everything we can to help." Philip quickly tied the rope around his waist in a climbers knot and tied the other end to a nearby tree. With one swift move he climbed into the narrow well.

"Please hurry sir," Jenny cried.

"The Medics are here," Natalie called.

Cassie began barking at the sound of the sirens blaring.

"I have the girl, please tell the crew that I will need them to pull us up, there isn't much time," he shouted.

Philip looked up to see four faces looking down at him.

"We have the rope sir; on the count of three we will pull you up." Natalie and Jenny joined in the effort to pull Philip and Allie out of the Well. As they neared the top, the rope made a crackling sound.

"Hurry!" Jenny cried.

As Philip reached the surface, Medics took the girl carefully off of his arms. Just then the sound of more sirens could be heard, but this time it was the cops. Curious neighbors and onlookers began to crowd the scene.

"Isn't this the woman I saw on the evening news?" someone said pointing at Jenny. As Jenny was about to get into the Ambulance, she was apprehended and placed into a police car. An angry Caucasian male jumped out of a black SUV and began shouting at Jenny.

"You really thought that you were going to get away with this! She's my daughter, and you can't take her away from me."

"You monster!" Jenny yelled from inside the police vehicle.

As the ambulance sped off, an officer approach Natalie and Philip and began asking questions about the events surrounding the incident.

"What's going on?" Philip asked.

"The young girl you assisted was being kidnapped by her mother. She's now facing charges of kidnapping and child endangerment," the officer said. They couldn't believe what they were hearing. The officer thanked them for their time and headed back to the car where Jenny was being held. Although Jenny was a complete stranger, Natalie knew by the looks on her face that there was more to this story. She borrowed a piece of paper and a pen from someone in the crowd and jotted down her name and phone number. She then ran up to the officer and asked him to give the note to Jenny. She watched as he handed her the note. As the squad cars drove off, Jenny looked at the couple and thanked them.

"I hope the girl will be okay?" Philip said.

As they headed back to their vehicle, Philip looked over his shoulders in time to see reporters from KTV News channel from downtown London running toward them.

"Darn it, I've had enough excitement for one evening," Philip said. He took Natalie's hand, got into their Jeep and sped off as they drove back to the Manor....

"We'd better close the gates to the entrance and the one behind the manor because reporters will be swarming around here all weekend," Natalie said.

"I'm sick of making headlines!" Philip yelled.

"But you saved a little girl's life, you should be proud," Natalie reminded him. He didn't respond. He was upset and hardly felt like a hero. Seeing how upset he was, Natalie embraced him.

"I'm sorry babe, let's get away this weekend," she said excitedly. He glances at her but didn't respond. When they arrived at the Manor, Philip wasted no time securing the gates.

"I'll go activate the security cameras," she said, hurrying.

"We have no idea who these people are; did you see how upset the girl's father was?"

"Don't worry, we'll discuss it later," Phil said reassuring her.

"This could have been much worse," he said.

"You're right, this was careless on our part," he said.

"But it was your idea to reach out to the woman when she came up to the gate. You could have ignored her, you know," she said.

"You seem to have forgotten that this isn't the States where you answer the door when some salesman come knocking," she said with a chuckle. Philip was silent for a moment. She expected him to be upset or at least annoyed by her prejudice, except he laughed till his tummy ached. When he had stop laughing, he looks at her squarely.

"Is that what you Brits think?"

"I'm sorry babe, I didn't mean it," she said feeling embarrassed. He wasn't upset anymore. She looked adorable sitting on the stairs in her brown guard boots and white beret in the middle of spring. He sat closer to her.

"Is this the typical British stereotype of Americans?" He asked now, smiling.

"Please tell me some more popular stereotypes you folks have managed to conjure up of us adorable Americans," he said, tucking her hair behind her ears.

She blotted out... "Gullible Yankees," they both laughed hysterically.

"I think it's hilarious," he said, pulling her closely.

"I'm glad you were able to help that little girl," she said smiling.

"I'm happy I was able to help. But Nat, you can't save the world you know.

"But I can certainly try," she said. Unable to resist her charm he took her in his arms and submitted to another tender moment.

That night Natalie had another vision. This time she was running on the beach. Although she has a fear of heights and was high above the surf, she was unafraid. As she neared the edge of the cliff, she came to a stop. The wind stirred and the rough waves of the awakened sea splashed upon the rocks, sprinkling her with wet kisses. At that moment, someone said her name...

"*Natalie!*" To her right on a patch of grass is the Princess of Edinburg. She is arrayed in glowing white and a warm yellow light shone around her.

"My lady!" she said bowing gracefully. "What can I do for you?"

"Natalie I have chosen you to complete my unfinished work in England. You will be given instructions in another vision."

"But why me, I'm not of Royal blood," Natalie said nervously.

"There's none among them worthy of this calling. Yet, it is not a matter of ancestry, but a matter of the heart." Before Natalie could say another word the Princess was gone.

Chapter 14

Marguerite stepped on the patio of Richard's Townhouse. It was almost summer and a gentle wind rustled the apple branches nearby. As she sat thinking about the baby, she felt a sudden sharp pain in her lower abdomen. She's had a few of these and Richard's doctor told her that they would pass, but this felt different.

"Oh my, oh no," she cried; feeling yet another sharp pain in her back. She knew something was wrong and she phoned Richard.

"I'm on my way, only a few miles away," he said frantically. By then she was in even more pain; something was very wrong. Barely able to walk, she pats her tummy, and as she staggers inside she felt warm liquid running down her legs. Dreading, she glanced at her feet and broke into tears at the sight of blood.

"Richard!" she screams collapsing on the floor. Just then Richard came rushing through the front door. At the sight of Marguerite, his heart sunk.

"Marguerite, Hunny, what's happening?" he cried.

"Please save our baby Richard," she cried. Without hesitation, he lifted her up and carried her to his car. Luckily, they lived only a short drive from the West Middlesex Hospital.

"Please hurry Richard," she cried.

"You should have called the Royal Medics," she complained.

"Please try to relax and besides it would have taken them much longer to arrive."

Richard pulled his car into the crowded parking lot. He took Marguerite in his arms once more and rushed into the busy emergency room.

"Please, hurry, we need help. She's only six months pregnant and there's blood everywhere. Please hurry," he urged. The nurses immediately recognized him and rushed to their side. Richard was furious; he couldn't believe they wanted him to sit in the waiting room. As he sat waiting he reached for his phone and dialed Natalie.

"Sweetheart, it's dad, I'm at the hospital."

"Dad, are you okay?"

"I'm fine, it's Marguerite."

"I'm on my way," she replied.

"Natalie no, you don't......" She hung up before he'd finished speaking. He didn't want her to meet Marguerite this way. He then phoned Danica. She said that she was on her way, and would be there in twenty minutes. A few minutes later, Richard saw the Head Nurse walking briskly toward him, before she said a word, Richard hurry toward her.

"Where's Marguerite? How's the baby?"

"She's in room 212." Before she said another word Richard ran down the hallway and entered the room. Marguerite appears pale and lifeless. There were five nurses doing everything they could to revive her. He rushes to her side.

"Marguerite, Marguerite, please darling wake up," he cried. He couldn't believe it.

"Mr. Baldwin, you are going to have to wait outside, " the Head-Nurse pleaded. Natalie came just in time to help escort her father out of the room.

"Please dad, come with me. I'm sure they're doing everything they can to help her," Natalie said embracing him.

"She looked so pale," he cried. As they sat in the waiting room, Richard told Natalie how panicked he was when he came home and saw Marguerite collapsed on the floor.

"Dad, I think you might be in love with her," Natalie admitted.

He was quiet for a moment.

"I didn't expect to be a father again," he said.

"Dad if you don't mind, how old is Marguerite?"

"She's almost forty-eight," he replied.

"I see."

Richard glanced at the time and realized it's been over twenty minutes and Danica still hadn't arrived.

"Where's Marguerite's Daughter?" Natalie asked.

"I was just thinking the same thing," he replied.

"How's she?" Philip said joining them in the hallway.

"Hello Philip, no word yet," Richard said sorrowfully.

"I'm sure she'll be fine," Philip assured.

"Thank you, Philip," he replied.

"Richard, Margaret's awake!" the nurse called. Natalie, Richard and Philip rushed into the exam room.

"Marguerite has lost quite a bit of blood, but they are both going to be okay," Dr. Jefferies said. Just then Marguerite screamed. Philip looks at her Monitor.

"Looks like she's in labor," he said.

"How do you know?" the nurse asked.

"I spent almost three years in Med School," he replied." Natalie and Richard both looked at each other surprised. Marguerite screamed again, this time Richard and Natalie rushed to her side.

"It's alright honey, I'm here," he said kissing her forehead.

"Who are you?" she asked, staring at Natalie.

"Marguerite, I want you to meet my daughter, Natalie, and her fiancé Philip" he said.

"Oh my goodness you are…" before finishing her statement, she was interrupted by another contraction. The nurse prepared a syringe and as she was about to administer the shot…

"What's this," Richard asked.

"It's Tubulin, it helps to stop Marguerite's contractions."

"How many doses have she already had?" Philip asked.

"This is her fourth dosage," the nurse replied.

"The first or second dosage should have stopped her contractions," Philip said. Marguerite cried again and the monitor showed a very large contraction.

"She's in preterm labor; I don't think she needs anymore Tubulin," Philip said to Richard.

"I think my water broke," Marguerite cried. The nurse rushed out of the room to get Dr. Jefferies.

"Richard, I think the baby's coming," she cried.

Dr. Jefferies entered the room.

"Amanda, please check Marguerite's dilation." he said to the Nurse.

"We'll wait outside," Natalie said kissing her dad on the cheek.

As they sat in the waiting room, the nurse reception told them that it was okay to wait in the family room. She showed them to a large suite designed for Royal Guard families. There was a king size bed, a large pull-out couch and a small kitchen with a fully stocked refrigerator.

"Ah, not bad," Philip said opening the small pantry reaching for a bottle of wine.

"You never told me that you went to Med school," she said staring at him curiously.

"What else do I need to know about the man I'm going to marry?" she asked, flopping down on the couch.

Philip reached for a glass.

"Only that it's the craziest few weeks I'd ever spend while vacationing?" he said pouring her a drink.

She laughs while reaching for the half-filled glass out of his hands.

"It's awful what's happening to Marguerite. I feel sorry for her and dad. Needless to say, I'm still mystified by the whole idea of dad, Marguerite and Danica; I smell a fish, if you know what I mean."

"What are you saying?" Philip asked.

Just then, there was a knock on their door. It was Richard, he looks exhausted.

"You have a baby sister," he said smiling. She weighed a little over four pounds; she's beautiful."

"How's Marguerite?" asked Philip.

"She's doing great and is now in recovery."

There was another knock. Richard opened the door and it was Danica.

"Where's my mum?" she asked slightly berated. She stared in Natalie and Philip's direction.

"What are they doing here?" she asked.

"It's best that you go check on your mum and leave quietly please. We've all had a very long day and no one has time for this," Richard said firmly.

"Where's my mum?!" she asked this time almost yelling.

"Danica, the baby came, and your mom is in recovery," Richard said.

"She had the baby and you are all in here while she's all by herself!"

"No one's allowed in recovery for the first hour. You should be able to see her in another ten minutes," Richard said glancing at his watch.

There was another knock on the door. This time it was Dr. Jefferies.

"Come on in Jeff," Richard said.

Dr. Jefferies took Richard aside.

"Richard there's a problem. We couldn't use the blood transfusion that you gave for the baby.

"What! What do you mean?"

"According to your blood type, you're not the father."

"That's absurd, there's got to be some kind of mistake!"

"We thought so, so we ran the test a third time."

"What's going on? Is the baby okay?" Danica asked nervously.

"I'll give you a minute with your family," Dr. Jefferies said leaving. But we need to find a solution quickly; the baby needs a transfusion right away," he said before leaving the room.

"Danica, your sister is in need of a blood transfusion."

"I don't think that I can. I've had a few drinks," she said, now in tears.

"I'm sorry Richard," she cried, and hurried out of the room.

"Danica, wait…" Richard called.

"What's going on dad?"

It's been a long evening and Richard didn't want to share what he had learned. Trying to hide his disappointment, he thanked Natalie and Philip for being there for him and Marguerite. He then told them that it was okay for them to go home.

"Okay dad, I'll stop by tomorrow to meet my baby sister. Oh by the way, what names do you have in mind for her?"

"We haven't really thought of any yet; maybe you can think of something for us?"

"You bet," she replied. Natalie embraced her dad and Philip shook his hand, to congratulate him. Exhausted and a little bewildered, the couple left the hospital.

As they drove through the busy streets of London Natalie gazed at the familiar places where she'd spent endless evenings with Bient. She hadn't seen him since she's been back and although he was still married to her cousin Kate, she couldn't help but wonder what it would have been like if things had worked out between them. So many things have changed since she's returned to London. Her dad had moved on and now has a new baby. She knew with the new baby, that things would never be the same between her and her father. Suddenly, she felt lost, being faced with many decisions. As much as she loves Philip, she wonders if she was ready to marry the fiery American that has bought fireworks into her life. She also wondered if she was ready for the sudden changes that marriage would bring. As she reflects on her nightly visions, she knew that somehow that they would affect her many decisions.

As Philip pulled into the Manor's courtyard, Natalie broke into tears.

Confused, he tries to comfort her.

"Honey, what's wrong?" She didn't respond but continues to cry. Puzzled, Philip opened her door and helped her inside. At the sight of them, Cassie barked and wiggled her tail. After helping her into bed, Philip sat staring at her lovingly; a million thoughts race through his mind. He loves her, more than he loves himself. Maybe now that she's seen this many changes, she would agree to elope and marry.

The following morning Philip awoke to the smell of coffee. He went to the kitchen and was surprised to see William.

"William, back soon?" he asked, surprised.

"I couldn't do it Phil; I couldn't be away from Lady Baldwin for this many weeks."

"What happened, what about your friend?"

"Oh don't worry," he said looking embarrassed.

"Will I'm so sorry, don't worry, you don't have to talk about it," he said.

"Please join me for coffee," Philip said. When they were seated, he shared with Philip how much he cares about Natalie and how much he thought of her while he was in Italy. He told Philip that his girlfriend became jealous and got the wrong impression about why he was so devoted to her. He told Philip that he felt that his purpose in life is to be her Butler and nothing more. Even Philip became a little jealous listening to William as he discussed the woman he loves. He then filled him in on the events that occurred while he was away. William couldn't believe his ears. As surprised as he was about the new baby, William was just as suspicious of Marguerite and her daughter Danica. As Philip stood to leave…

"Philip, please don't forget that her appointment with the Baroness is today," William reminded him.

"That's right!" Philip said, remembering. "It's good to have you back Will; it was a little strange around here without you." They both laughed.

Nathaniel York arrived promptly at 12:30pm to take Natalie to the Palace Manor in Edinburg for her 2:00 pm appointment with Baroness Ester Edmund-Cromwell. Maureen opened the gate and the Royal Chauffeur pulled up into the Manor's courtyard. At the sight of him Maureen clears her throat.

"Hello there, who might you be?"

"I beg your pardon?" he asked scornfully.

"I'm Nathaniel York of course, the Prince's public Chauffeur."

"Oh, that's right; today's Natalie's appointment with Baroness Cromwell," Maureen smiled proudly. Nathaniel rolls his eyes.

"What's with the attitude? You and I aren't so different you know. I too I'm her chauffeur," Maureen boasted.

"Nathaniel, I see that you've met Maureen. I'm happy that you came but I'd prefer it if she took me to the Palace."

"Madam I have strict orders to get you to Edinburgh Palace to meet the Baroness at fourteen hundred hours sharp," he replied respectfully, yet with an edge. Philip and Maureen watches as Natalie argue with Nathaniel, finally allowing him to help her into the limousine. She was now in the care of the Royal family and as important as Philip and Maureen was to her, there was nothing she could do to get them involved. Natalie was silent the entire way and although the Chauffeur was curious, he didn't mind because he didn't want to release any information regarding the Baroness's invitation. After what seemed like hours, Nathaniel drove through a gate made of solid gold, covered in white roses. Natalie finally broke her silence.

"This looks like the back entrance."

"That's correct Ma 'dam. This meeting was kept as private as possible to prevent any information from being leaked to the media," he replied.

As they pulled into the entrance, she recognized some of the Royal Guards who are friends of her father. Recognizing the limousine, the guards gave the order to open the gate. Natalie hadn't seen this entrance since she was about ten years old and was in awe of the variety of flowers that grew there. Even more astounding are the magnificent tabletop fountains that watered them.

"Welcome to the Palace Manor Madam, you are right on schedule," he said. As Nathaniel led her through endless hallways, she became nervous. It's been over a decade since her last visit and she didn't know what to expect. Nathaniel gazed at Richard's daughter. He couldn't help but notice her beautiful attire and what a lovely young lady she has become. Although he'd brought many people into the Manor, he knew that this meeting was more important than any other he'd help organize. They have entered through many doorways and as they were about to enter into Prince Ethan's chambers, Nathaniel paused…

"Madam, you've arrive. Please remember the courtesies due to the Baroness." Reaching for Natalie's hand he escorted her into what used to be Princess Annie's Royal chamber. At the sight of the Baroness, both Natalie and Nathaniel bent their right knee and bowed gently.

"Your grace, Lady Baldwin has arrived."

After this Nathaniel kissed Natalie's right hand and departed promptly.

Natalie looks up slowly at Ester; she wonders why she was seated in the place of her friend; if anything this should be Prince Ethan's place.

"Lady Baldwin, it is lovely to see you. Thank you for coming at my request."

"The honor is mine, your grace," she replied. After this, Ester stood up and asked Natalie to join her for tea in her private guest room. A little surprised, Natalie was then escorted by one of the palace servants into a small room. As they were about to be seated, the Baroness's grandson, Prince Ethan entered the room. As he was about to speak to his grandmother, he paused at the sight of Natalie.

"Pardon me grandmother, I didn't realize you had company," he said and was about to leave.

"Ethan, surely you must have remembered Lady Baldwin, Richard's daughter," she called. He turns around slowly to face her. Remembering, he looked at Natalie and smiling, he said in a hushed voice.

"*Hello, it's good to see you again*," then hurried off before she responded.

"Pardon my grandson, he's been very distant since the loss of his Parents," she said apologetically.

"Surely, I understand, your grace," Natalie replied.

She was growing anxious, as she wonders why she was invited to the Palace and before long, the Baroness lifted up her right hand and one of her servant's brought her a tiny golden box which she opened with a small key. Natalie looked on as Ester open the box and removed a sealed envelope which she handed to her servant who presented it to Lady Baldwin. Her name was written on the envelope. Surprised, she unfolded the letter and immediately recognized the handwriting as her deceased friend, Princess Annie.

"Natalie, my dear friend, I pray this letter finds you safely. If you are reading this letter, know that my heart is overjoyed because as I've learned, you are the only person I can trust in this entire world, with such matters. As much as I wanted to be here to say this to you in person, I could not have shared this with you, while I lived." As Natalie read through her friend's words, she knew that her life would never be the same. She looks up from the letter to meet the now narrowed eyes of Baroness Ester.

"What does it say?" she demanded. Surprised by her change in attitude, Natalie simply smiled.

"Your grace, Princess Anne has requested my assistance in delivering a message to specific charities that she's sponsored here in the United Kingdom and around the world. She's also left me a small inheritance; her wardrobe and private capital that I am to use to assist the less fortunate. After this, Ester's appearance appeared a bit softer. She glared at Natalie as though fearing a possible hidden agenda.

"Lady Baldwin I have to admit, you've grown into quite a lovely young lady," she said, now smiling. "Your father must be very proud."

"Thank you, for your kind words, majesty," Natalie replied. She was hardly flattered by the Baroness's new attitude and wondered why she was so nervous about the content of the letter.

"Your grace, may I ask, when was this letter discovered?"

"My grandson discovered it while he was going through his mother's things. We were preparing for an auction to raise monies for the orphanages and charities in remembrance of how much they'd meant to Annie."

"I see," Natalie replied.

"This letter was discovered in the perfect timing."

"You are absolutely right, my dear. Annie had a lot of unfinished business. I am surprised that she didn't entrust such a task to someone of her more immediate family," Ester replied with jealousy.

"Lady Baldwin, I was hoping that since we were already in the process of handling the donations for the charities, if you would be pleased to allow me to manage the final proceedings entrusted to you?" she asked looking curiously at Natalie.

"As much as I would like too, my Lady, I owe it to my friend who's entrusted me with these tasks; allowing me to honor her final wishes," Lady Baldwin replied smiling, yet firm.

"Although I hope that you will reconsider, I will respect your decision," Ester said pretentiously. Natalie wondered if she would have been given the chance to read this letter hadn't Prince Ethan discovered it.

As they were speaking, Ester's servants brought in teacups and saucers and served tea. Natalie glanced at the servant pouring her tea.

"Thank you," she said.

"You're most welcome, Lady Baldwin," the servant responded warmly. Why did it seem that she was liked by the palace staff? Natalie peeked to her right in time to see a group of Servants and Butlers staring at her from around the corner. As Natalie and the Baroness continued to converse. On the other side of the room, the Palace staff was whispering among themselves.

"We can't let her leave, we need to come up with a plan, and quickly," Jasmine urged.

"What do you have in mind," asked Oscar, the Lead Butler.

"Well, we can't strike her over the head with a pan, so what do you suggest?" Rusty demanded.

"Well, why does everyone expect me to have all the answers," Oscar fretted.

"Well we won't get anywhere just standing here bickering. Look they are preparing to wrap things up, quickly, we must do something," Jasmine said hurrying toward the kitchen.

Jasmine spun around the kitchen looking for anything; anything that would help to stop a beautiful lady in her tracks. Unable to find anything, Jasmine hurried to the exit where she knew Lady Baldwin would be sure to pass. Suddenly she heard voices and hid herself neatly behind a door. She watched as Nathaniel and Natalie entered the fore area and found the perfect opportunity when Nathaniel excused himself to the guest bathroom. Without wasting another moment, Jasmine hurried toward Lady Baldwin. Startled by Jasmine's sudden entry into the room, Natalie slipped, falling backwards barely missing the grasp of the Prince, hitting her head against the marbled floor. Shocked, Nathaniel and Ethan reached for her, but she was unconscious.

"Lady Baldwin!" Nathaniel panicked.

"How did this happen?!" Prince Ethan demanded. The sound of commotion came to the attention of two Royal Guards who entered the room. At the sight of Lady Baldwin on the floor, they ran to her side and felt for her pulse.

"Her pulse is strong," one of the guards assured.

"Well someone should phone the Royal Medics," Jasmine said entering the room, pretending to have just arrived. The men eyed her suspiciously.

"We already did," the guards replied. Just then Natalie began to stir.

"Ouch, my head," she cried. Prince Ethan and Nathaniel ran to her side.

"Madam, are you all right?" Ethan asked.

"What happened?" she asked, looking puzzled.

"It seems that you have taken a fall," Nathaniel replied.

"I think you should rest in the guest bedroom until you are properly evaluated," the Prince suggested.

"Thank you, your highness, but I'm alright," she replied.

"Lady Baldwin, it's common courtesy and I insist," he said nodding to the servant to help her into the guestroom. A few seconds later, Royal Palace Medics arrived and was directed into the guestroom. After properly evaluating Lady Baldwin, they said that she had sustained a small concoction and should remain overnight and be monitored by the Palace Nurse.

Jasmine hurried to find her friends.

"I'm not sure, but I think we did it," She said.

"How, what did you do?" Rusty asked suspiciously.

"Apparently, Lady Baldwin wasn't very taken by my haggard appearance and she fainted at the sight of me."

Oscar and Rusty laughed hysterically.

"What?" Rusty asked.

"Well, all you did was send her to the hospital," Oscar continued.

"Come, follow me," she said leading the way. Puzzled, the two men followed Jasmine down the hallway and into the guestroom.

"Hello Lady Baldwin." Natalie looks up.

"I'm Jasmine and I will be your help while you're here.

"This is Oscar the Baroness's Butler and Jasper, Prince Ethan's Butler. We are truly sorry about your incident this evening and hope that you feel better soon."

Natalie had taken some meds for her headache and was feeling sleepy.

"Thank you," she said softly. Jasmine handed Natalie a small remote control that she can use to communicate with her. Then they left the guest room quietly.

"She's so beautiful," Jasper said.

"Truly Prince Ethan must have noticed her," he continued.

"Jasmine!" called Oscar. "You are dreadfully wicked," he said and they all laughed.

"Yes, who knew I was the Phantom," she replied.

"I did," Jasper said, placing a gentle kiss on her cheek.

"You'll be mine someday," he said, staring at her seductively.

"In your dreams," Jasmine said scornfully. They all laughed.

Chapter 15

Maureen and Philip sat on the Balcony overlooking the courtyard. They were enjoying one of Philip's cocktails when they saw Nathaniel's Limousine pulled into the gate. Excited that his fiancé was home, they both hurried outside to meet them. At the sight of Maureen and Philip, Nathaniel came out of the vehicle and walked slowly toward them.

"Good evening messenger, where's my fiancé?" Philip asked.

"I'm afraid that there has been a little incident at the Palace and Lady Baldwin would be spending the night for observation."

"What? What in the world happened?!" Philip yelled.

"We don't need the French Nathaniel, you are not at the Palace Manor, just speak plain English please," Philip scolded.

"Sir, I'm very sorry, your fiancé has taken a fall inside the Palace and suffered a small concoction," he replied nervously.

"How did this happen?" he demanded. Before Nathaniel replied, the landline rang and Philip ran inside to answer it.

"She was in your care; this is your fault. Do you know how much she means to us? I don't suppose you do," Maureen said walking away.

"I'm truly sorry, but wait I'm not finished," he called.

"We are finished here Mr. York, and thank you for coming," Maureen said walking away. As Maureen entered the living room, she saw Philip on the telephone.

"Who is it, is it my Lady?" Maureen asked and Philip nodded yes. A little relieved she sat waiting for her chance to speak. A few moments later Philip replaced the handset.

"I still don't understand why they couldn't bring her home," Philip said, sitting next to Maureen.

"That's routine; any minor incident that occurs on Royal property is monitored for at least twenty-four hours. No one, not even family has precedence over this rule other than the Baroness or of course his Majesty," Maureen said.

"How is she doing otherwise?"

"The medics said that it's nothing serious."

The phone rang again and this time it was Richard. He wanted Maureen, Philip and Natalie to meet him at the guest house in the morning. Apparently he wasn't aware of the incident with his daughter and the fact that he was occupied with Marguerite and the baby, they didn't feel the need to inform him. Feeling annoyed that he was spending the evening without his fiancé, Philip spent the rest of the evening with Maureen and William who was kicked out of his flat by his jealous girlfriend.

"But William, this is your home, why is she kicking you out?"

"I didn't want to bother fighting her."

"You are a true gentleman," Maureen replied embracing him. She's very fortunate. Too bad for her that she can't see that," Maureen said.

Back at the Palace, Prince Ethan brought the news to his grandmother of the incident. She was pleased that Lady Baldwin was not seriously hurt and applauded her grandson for offering up one of the guest rooms to her.

"How did this happen?"

"I'm not sure grandmother, but I do remember the floor being sleeker than usual."

"Strange?" she said.

"Oh by the way, I'll be visiting with the Prime Minister today to discuss a new proposal. Do you have any messages for him?" Ethan asked.

"Not at the moment, but please send him my regards."

"I certainly will, grandmother," he said. The Baroness called Jasmine to her. "Please see that Richard's daughter has everything that she needs to make her stay as comfortable as possible."

"Absolutely my Lady," she replied. As she was leaving…

"Jasmine," the Baroness called. This time, slightly more nervous, Jasmine turned around slowly.

"Yes, your grace." Ester was suspicious that Jasmine might know something about the incident regarding Lady Baldwin, but she changed her mind.

"Oh, never mind, please be excused," she said smiling warmly.

"Thank you, your grace," she said, then hurried off.

Natalie awoke very early the following morning to the clanging sound of a teacup being placed on a saucer.

"Good morning madam, I pray you slept well," Jasmine said, placing tea on the nightstand. Startled, Natalie sat up quickly.

"Are you alright Madam?" asked Jasmine.

"Who are you?"

"I'm so sorry madam; would you like to rest a while?" asked Jasmine. Natalie reached for her tea, took a sip and returned it to the night stand.

"My favorite, but how did you know and you didn't tell me who you are? Where am I?" Natalie asked, looking around puzzled, getting out of bed.

"Don't you remember? You are at the Palace Manor, you were invited here yesterday by the Baroness," Jasmine said growing concerned.

"The Palace Manor?" she said hurrying out of the room.

"Oh boy!" Jasmine said, running her fingers through her hair.

"But wait, Lady Baldwin, wait!" Jasmine called hurrying after her. The small disturbance came to the attention of Prince Ethan who came hurrying.

"What's going on Jasmine?" he asked, slightly annoyed.

"It's...it's...nothing sir." She stuttered.

"Come on Jasmine, you are a terrible liar," he laughs. Although Jasmine had worked at the Palace the past year, she had never spoken to the Prince for more than a few seconds at a time. Slightly embarrassed she looked at the floor.

"It's Lady Baldwin sir, she seems to be having trouble remembering things."

"Is that so?" he asked.

"Where is she now? Have you mentioned this to anyone?" he asked.

"No majesty," she replied.

"Good, tell no one about this till we locate her," he warned. Jasmine nodded and led the way.

Back at the Manor, Philip barely slept that night and woke up earlier than usual, to welcome his fiancé home. They had never spent the night apart since they'd met and he felt a strange sense of fear creeping upon him. Something has happened, he could feel it and it terrified him. He paced back and forth across the guest room and

141

was interrupted by a soft knock. It was Maureen; she wanted to remind him of their meeting with Richard.

"Thanks Maureen, I'll be ready in a couple of hours," he called. He was about to reach for the phone on the wall when it rang. It was Lisa. She hadn't heard from her daughter in months and was concerned.

"Hello, I'm Lisa Natalie's mom, who am I speaking with?"

"Hi Lisa, I'm Philip, um, Natalie's fiancé."

"You're engaged to my daughter? Are you American?"

"Yes ma'am," he replied.

"That's wonderful, but how, where and when did all this occur?" After Philip told her how they met, Lisa told Philip that she was on her way to England and requested that he kept it a surprise. After he got off the Phone, he was deep in thought.

"I think I might have passed the preliminary review," he said and winked at his handsome reflection in the mirror. A few hours later Maureen and Philip arrive at Richard's home in Purley. They were surprised how overwhelmed he seemed.

"Hey guys come on in, I hope you're hungry; I made us lunch." When they were all seated…

"Is everything alright?" Maureen asked.

"I'm afraid not," Richard said, turning away from them. Philip placed his hamburger back onto the plate and approached him. He placed his hands on his shoulders.

"Want to talk about it?" Richard turns to face them, his eyes filled with tears.

"She's gone," he said breaking down.

"Who, who's gone?" Maureen asked puzzled.

"Marguerite, she's gone. She passed away while in recovery." Maureen's face went from curious to complete horror.

"Richard, I'm so sorry?" Philip said. "How did this happen?"

"She wasn't supposed to have any more children," Richard said crying uncontrollably.

Philip and Maureen stood in utter shock at what they had just learned.

"I'm so sorry," they said repeatedly.

"But why didn't you phone us sooner and what about the baby. Where is she now?" Philip flooded him with questions.

"I spent the last few days at the hospital, and after several tests that I insisted on, it is confirmed that I'm not the baby's father. Danica admitted to me that Marguerite had quite a few relations with Adam shortly before we started dating."

"I can't believe what I'm hearing? Richard, this is horrible," Maureen said sitting next to him.

"Is there anything we can do," Philip asked.

"There's one thing, I need your advice."

"Sure, anything," Maureen said.

"I'm not sure what I should do about the baby…" he said.

"I'm not sure what you mean," Maureen said. "There's only one thing to do; we find that bastard and have him tested. If he's the father, have him take responsibility for her.

"This Adam guy is a real jerk," Philip said standing.

"I agree with Maureen."

"That's the thing, you see I've bonded with Abigail and it would be difficult to simply hand her over to, like you said Philip, the jerk." Philip almost laughed but didn't.

"He doesn't deserve her. A few days ago, I went to the NICU to visit with her. I placed my index finger in her tiny little palms, and boy she has the perfect grip," he said a smile returning to his face.

"Where's Danica, how's she handling all of this?" Philip asked.

"She is heartbroken, but one thing's certain; she doesn't seem to care about Abigail. She hardly visits her. It's been a week since her birth and she's only been to see her once," Richard said.

"I see your concern Richard," Philip said

"What about Marguerite? Does she have any family around to handle her funeral arrangements?"

Richard shot a glance at Maureen and excused himself from his guests.

"Geez Maureen, he's just lost his girlfriend, maybe he doesn't want to discuss this right now," Philip said while staring at Maureen in disbelief. She rolled her eyes.

"Other than the baby losing her mummy, I think that this is the best thing that could happen to him."

"You're horrible, why would you say that?" Philip said; throwing a cushion at her. She giggles.

"Trust me Phil, you don't know her like William and I do, she was horrible. She was after Richard's money and nothing more. Possibly her and Adam both," she said, taking a bite into her hamburger.

Chapter 16

As they sat adjusting to the news, Richard's landline rang. "Maybe you should get that, the area code looks like the Palace Manor," Maureen said.

"Palace Manor?" Philip said quickly, reaching for the handset.

"Baldwin's residence, Philip speaking, how may I help you?" There was a silence on the other end of the phone.

"Is anyone there?" Philip asked.

"Is Richard home, please tell him it's his daughter and I need him to come to the Palace Manor to get me out of here, as soon as possible." Recognizing his fiancé...

"Darling, is it you? It's me Philip."

"I'm sorry, who's Philip? Are you a friend of my dad's?"

"Nice one Hun, very funny," he laughed.

"We are over at your dad's place; he needs you sweetheart. I'm sorry, but I still don't remember...who's Philip is... Do we know each other?" Before he responds, there was silence on the other end of the phone.

"Natalie, honey, are you there?"

Maureen stares at him...

"You look like you've been smacked. Is everything alright?"

Prince Ethan and Jasmine searched everywhere.

"Where could she have gone? She seemed to have disappeared in thin air?" Ethan fretted. As they neared the entrance of the Palace, they heard commotion.

"There she is," Jasmine pointed. Natalie was in the Palace gallery arguing with one of the guards.

"Oh no," Ethan said, hurrying toward her.

"It's okay Jasmine; I've got it from here; please phone Richard and tell him that he is needed here immediately."

Despite Natalie's aggressiveness towards the guard, he didn't respond, but continuously stood in his required position. As Prince Ethan approached, the guard immediately relaxed and stood, at ease.

"What happened?" Prince Ethan asked.

"I, I, apologize, your Majesty, but Lady Baldwin seems, seems, to be trying to locate her father who is currently on leave," he stutters.

"She seems a bit…out of it," Ethan said, finishing the guard's statement.

"Natalie, do you know where you are?"

"No you tell me!" she yelled.

"Lady Baldwin, please calm down."

"Please do not tell me to calm down, some bloke name Philip was calling me sweetheart and no one is telling me what I'm doing here at the Palace Manor!" The Guards, Lester and Jim glanced at each other.

"Do, do you need my assistance, Majesty?" Lester stuttered.

"Thank you Lester, you can return to your duty, I'll manage," he said, sounding confident.

"Natalie your father should be on his way, would you please follow me inside, and I'll see that you are properly taken care of," he assured her, approaching her cautiously…

"May I?" he asked, taking her hands.

"By the way, who are you?" she asked in a more relaxed tone.

"I'm Prince Ethan, you were invited here yesterday."

As they walked through the palace, Ethan gazed at her. She was more beautiful than he remembered.

"Where have you been all these years?" he asked.

"Last I remembered I was in Grenada with my mum."

"You went to the Caribbean's?"

"Yes, that's where I was born, my mum's still there. I wonder how she would feel when she's learned that I ran out on her on such short notice," she cried.

"It's all right your dad will be here shortly, he'll explain everything," Prince Ethan said.

As they sat in the Parlor waiting, Natalie shared with Ethan everything that she remembers. He had only spent a few moments with her but was already beginning to develop an attraction toward her. Her demeanor, the way she spoke was that of a woman he could love. Ethan was bold and never hesitated to reach for what he wanted. As she sat opposite him, sharing her experiences, he leaned over and kissed her affectionately. He could no longer resist her fiery display with the guards on the balcony and the innocent expression

146

in her eyes. He was drawn to her vulnerability. To him it was now or never. Surprised, Natalie tries to pull away but could not resist his charm. He took her in his arms...

"Ethan, what are you doing?"

"Please say my name again," he replied. Before she said his name a second time, he reached for her lips like new wine, kissing her tenderly. He was on fire for her when someone suddenly knocks on the door.

"Who is it?!" he said annoyed.

"It's Jasmine, Natalie's family's here," she called.

"Darn it. Alright, thank you, he replied, trying to sound formal.

"Does Lady Baldwin need my assistance?" Jasmine asked.

"I don't think so," he replied.

"Yes, I need her. If you don't mind please leave," she said scolding the Prince.

"Are you upset?" he asked.

"Natalie, I've loved you since we were kids, I just never got the chance to tell you," he confessed.

"Don't you remember when we played together out on the Palace grounds? You promised that we would marry when we are old enough. Don't you remember?"

She broke into tears.

"I'm sorry, I don't remember anything," she cried. Growing concerned over what was taking so long and overhearing their conversation...

"Is everything okay?" Jasmine asked again. Surprised that she was still at the door...

"Go away, Jasmine!" Ethan yelled.

Shocked, Jasmine hurries away. She was embarrassed and hid her emotions as she approaches Natalie's family.

"Where's my fiancé," Philip asked, growing anxious.

"She will be out shortly," Jasmine replied trying to sound formal.

"Welcome to the Palace Manor, may I interest you in some tea while you wait?"

"Thank you kindly Jasmine, but we're more interested in what happened here last night?" Richard replied.

"I can ask the same question," Ester said entering the room. At the sight of the Baroness, they all stood up, folding their hands behind them.

"Richard, what a privilege, please be seated," she said kindly.

"Can anyone explain to me what's going on in my home?" her smile fading quickly. As Jasmine was about to speak, Natalie and Prince Ethan entered the room. At the sight of his fiancé, Philip hurried to her.

"Honey are you alright?"

Puzzled, Natalie looked over at her father.

"Father, I don't remember anything," she sobbed.

"Lady Baldwin, madam, you took a fall last night and I'm afraid it might have affected your memory," Jasmine said fearfully.

"What! How did this happen?" Richard scolded.

"I, I, I don't know," Jasmine said nervously.

"I remembered the floor being more slick than usual," Ethan said a second time.

"Richard, since this happened here at the Palace, it is customary that the Royal family takes full responsibility of all Medical care preceding this incident," the Baroness argued.

"I agree," Ethan replied.

"Ester, your generosity is much appreciated, but I believe that Natalie will be better served with her own family, surrounded by those who care for her the most."

"If you insist Richard, however, please allow me to refer her to the best Physician that would see to her care," the Baroness insisted. Jasmine, you would also accompany Lady Baldwin to her home and assist her in any way that she needs," she ordered.

"Yes my Lady," Jasmine replied, appearing relieved.

"But grandmother, this is not the usual route of handling such matters, it's customary that she remains here to be looked after," the Prince argued. Philip realized that there were other things on Prince Ethan's mind than his fiancé's care and he stared at him suspiciously.

"Ethan, you have my permission to visit the Manor weekly to ensure that my daughter is being properly looked after." Philip couldn't believe what was happening. Suddenly, he felt like he had no say in a matter.

"I'll see that she is properly taken care of, she's my fiancée," Philip said, finally speaking up.

"This is not the place or time, Philip," Richard said, sounding surprisingly harsh. Even Maureen was surprised and looked over at Richard.

"I had no idea she was engaged," Ester said.

"She's engaged, how is it that we are just learning of this?" Ethan said.

"That's enough Prince Ethan, this is none of your business. It's alarming enough that you've kept the Baldwin's waiting," his grandmother scolded.

"Alright then, if it's settled, I will have a specialist at your home shortly," Ester said. At the same time Nathaniel entered the room.

"Nathaniel, you are just in time," she said.

"Ester, your kindness is much appreciated."

"As always, it's a pleasure, Richard," she said with a smile. Please take as much time as you need with your daughter," she assured. Then she looks over at Natalie who appears as puzzled as she was and said...

"Rest assured that you are in good hands," she said before excusing herself from her audience.

"Natalie, I'll see you one week from today," Prince Ethan called. He nods at Richard before leaving the room.

As they entered the Palace Manor's courtyard; Richard and Natalie got into the Royal Chauffeur and Philip rode with Maureen.

"Are you sure you didn't want to ride with your fiancé?" Maureen asked.

"It seems I have a lot to think about?" Philip said looking at his watch.

"What's to think about? You can't give up on her when she needs you most," she said.

"What's the use, she's forgotten all about us," Philip said feeling hurt and frustrated.

"I'm sure this is temporary; she will come around. I'm very suspicious as to how all of this happened in such a short time. I don't mean to jump to conclusions but I believe it could have been a setup," Maureen said.

"These Royals could never be trusted," she warned.

"Do you think that this was the plan all along? What do you think they would want with my fiancé?" he asked.

"Well, she was a very close friend to Princess Annie; Prince Ethan's mum. They were all very close, until Annie and Ethan's father who was also named Philip, suddenly disappeared on one of their yearly yachting trips to the British Isles."

"You're kidding," Philip said.

"I assure you not. Some claimed that they took an unplanned route and encountered rough waters off the coast of Scotland. No one except the Captain survived the trip. The Yacht was found shattered, and they were not able to recover any evidence from it," she continued. Philip listened in disbelief.

"The captain is currently serving a twenty-year sentence for reckless endangerment."

"That's difficult to believe," Philip said.

"Many people have speculated that the Baroness had something to do with their disappearance, but I doubt that she would want to hurt her own son," Maureen Continues.

"You mean Philip was her son?"

"He sure was," she replied.

"It's possible that her son was supposed to live through this, maybe she was targeting Annie," Maureen assured.

"I wished you'd told me this before Maureen, I wouldn't have let my fiancé anywhere near this place," Philip said angrily.

"During his trial, the captain swore that the engine was in perfect condition and he believed that there was sufficient petrol to survive the trip. However, somehow the engine gave out during the rough waters, just when he needed it to get them to safety."

"All very suspicious," Philip said.

"There was word that the Captain, after hearing his sentence began yelling that the Baroness paid him to fault the engine, but no one believed him," said Maureen.

"Who is this Baroness, I mean really?" Philip asked as they pulled into the driveway.

"She's earned her title from her Marriage to Baron Earl De La Ray; a knight honored by Princess Annie's Mother. They bore one son, Philip- Ethan's father."

"Then if Philip was merely the son of a Baroness, then how is Ethan a Prince?" asked Philip.

"Philip marries Annie the daughter of the late Queen Ann."

"Hmm I see," Philip said. As he sat processing everything he'd just learned, they became distracted by a loud commotion coming from the Manor.

Maureen glanced at him...

"She needs you Philip; you should go to her."

"Maureen, I need your help," he said hurrying toward the Manor.

At the sight of Philip, Natalie ran toward him and embraced him.

"Oh Philip, what happened?"

Puzzled, Philip looked over at Richard.

"What's going on?" he asked.

"Philip I wouldn't rely on it; she remembers for a little while then completely forgets. He needs rest," Richard said, leaving the room.

"Honey, are you okay? What do you remember?" he asks holding her at arm's length.

"What do you mean?" she asks, feeling frustrated.

"Why is everyone acting this way?!" she yelled and hurried to her room.

"Natalie, wait!" he calls, hurrying after her. Natalie enters her room and locked the door behind her. Philip could hear Cassie whining playfully.

"*Hun, open the door, we need to talk.*" Philip called.

"What do you mean!" she yelled.

"First, you would have to open the door," he called.

"I know what you're going to say. I know that you want to call off our engagement," she cried.

"Wow," Philip laughed.

"Wait a minute, that's great you remembered our engagement?"

"Well why on earth would I forget something like this," she said even more upset.

"Why is everyone acting so strange?" she called.

"Go away, Philip, there's nothing wrong with me and I'm not letting you in so you can end our engagement!"

"That's not the plan at all sweetheart, if you let me in, I'll explain," Philip said in an even gentler tone.

"Explain what?" she said opening the door to a creek. At the sight of her, tears in her eyes, Philip drew her to him in a ravaged thrust, kissing her madly.

"Where's everyone," asked Maureen, peeking into the kitchen.

"Oh hi Maureen," Richard said who was seated at the dinner table enjoying a glass of wine.

"Please join me," he said, pouring her a glass of wine that William had brought back from Italy.

"Long day?" she asked, taking a seat next to him.

"I never thought that my life would be this complicated at fifty-three," he laughs.

"You have my permission to not think about any of it right now," she teased, patting his shoulders.

"Well thank you," he said smiling at her. Maureen ran her fingers through Richard's hair. She wondered how difficult everything must have been for him. Before he said another word, she leans forward and kisses him. Surprised by her sudden move, Richard looked into her eyes. Unable to resist her, he leaned forward and kissed her softly. Then realizing, he pulled away.

"Oh Maureen, I'm sorry," he said standing.

"Please Richard don't be sorry, it was me," she apologized. He turns to face her.

"Maureen, you are very attractive, but you're my employee," he admitted.

"It's all right Richard, we've all been through a lot," she said approaching him.

"I find you very handsome Richard, I think you can use a friend," she said, placing both her hands on his shoulders.

"Maureen, please," he chuckled. Being aware that he might have had too much to drink, she removed his tie and kisses him again. She was right about one thing, he needed a friend, and without saying another word, she took him by the hand and led him to her room down the hall. As they passed next to Natalie's room, she placed a finger over her lips to signal his silence. The moment they were inside, Maureen pushed Richard onto her bed and plunged into his arms. She has imagined this moment for a long time. Barely conscious, he whispered softly. *"Oh Lisa,"* he called.

Chapter 17

The following day, Natalie awoke to the sounds of soft scratches on her door. Still sleepy, she walks across the room and opened the door slowly. It was Cassie; she wagged her tail at the sight of her.

"Hey sweetie, how did you get out here?"

As she reached down to lift Cassie up, she noticed Maureen's door slightly opened. As she thought of peeking inside Maureen's room, she heard whispers. She took Cassie by the collar and led her into the room. As she watched from her barely opened door, she saw Maureen embracing her father asking him to stay. As Richard was about to leave, she leans forward and kisses him.

"Alright Maureen, I have to go before someone notices," he said and walks away briskly. Shocked by what she'd just seen, Natalie embraced Cassie.

"How could they?" Overcome by emotion, and close to tears, Natalie stormed out of her room to confront Maureen. She knocks repeatedly on the door. Assuming that it was Richard, Maureen opened the door with a broad smile which quickly disappeared.

"How could you?!" Natalie yelled. An embarrassed Maureen was about to apologize but instead became infuriated with Natalie.

"This is none of your business!" she replied.

"It's not up to you to decide who your father sees! Why don't you just marry already and move on!" Natalie couldn't believe what she was hearing. It's obvious that Maureen had ulterior motives.

"Maureen, I've known you since I was a child, you've become like family to me. You are the closest friend I have ever had. How do you expect me to look at you after sleeping with my father?" Natalie sobs.

"I love Richard, I've always loved him, but he never notices me," she yelled.

"He was always too busy worrying about you, you spoiled brat!" Shocked by Maureen's confession, feeling puzzled and betrayed,

Natalie ran from the Manor, got into the Limousine and sped out of the driveway.

Philip, having heard the entire conversation between Natalie and Maureen, came into the hallway where Maureen was still standing.

"You, you stay right there, not another word from you!" he yelled and hurries after Natalie.

"Natalie! Where are you," he called searching everywhere. He looks over the balcony into the courtyard and noticed that the limousine was gone.

"Maureen, darn it, she's gone! She should not be driving like this," he yelled.

Philip hurries into the Jeep and sped off after his fiancé. As he approaches the intersection of Mistlethorpe and Marden road, he made a sharp left turn without stopping for a bold yellow YIELD sign and collided with an incoming car, toppling the small Jeep. The stranger in the grey Mercedes Benz came out of his badly dented vehicle and hurries toward Philip. After phoning paramedics…the stranger approached Philip.

"Sir, sir?" he called. Philip didn't respond. He appears lifeless and his shirt was covered in blood. At the sight of Philip's lifeless body, the stranger began to shout for help. Not too far off, was Natalie's Limousine. She was not too far off when she heard the collision. Other drivers began to rush to the scene. Recognizing the overturned Jeep, as in slow motion Natalie rushed to the scene. Seeing Philip trapped inside, she kicked open the passenger window, climbed through the window and tried removing Philip from the vehicle, but he was jammed by the seat belt, still intact.

"Philip! Philip, Sweetheart," wake up she sobs.

"Ma'am, please, let us help," called an older gentleman.

"No, that's my fiancé!" she said sobbing uncontrollably. She dug through the glove compartment and located a pocket knife. She quickly flicked open the knife and cut through the seatbelt. She tried moving Philip but he was much too heavy for her.

"Please ma'am, we'd like to help!"

Then Philip mumbled.

"He's alive!" she cried. She inched her way out of the capsized vehicle and two men pried open the driver's side of the Jeep. They pulled Philip out and placed him on the gurney. As they placed him into the ambulance, Natalie climbed into the back of the vehicle.

There were two ambulances on the scene and Paramedics placed the other passenger who had passed out at the sight of Philip, into the Ambulance and then sped off.

Natalie could not believe everything that was happening. Suddenly her whole world seemed to be coming to an end. As they rushed Philip through the Emergency ward, Natalie followed close behind.

"I need Dr. Jefferies to be in charge of this operation," she called.

"Ms. Baldwin, you'll have to wait here. I'm sorry," called one of the paramedics who recognized her.

"No!" she yelled angrily. Richard, who was at the hospital making arrangements with an adoptive family for Abigail, overheard his daughter.

"Sweetheart, is that you?" he called' hurrying over to her. At the sight of her father, all anger toward him subsided.

"Dad, I'm so happy to see you. It's Philip, he's been in an accident and it doesn't look very good," she sobbed.

"What, what happened?!" She didn't want to tell him that Philip must have gone looking for her because she would have to tell him why and he would discover that she knows what happened between him and Maureen.

"I'm not sure," she cried. Richard hated to see his daughter like this. As he embraced her, Dr. Jefferies walked into the waiting room. Seeing him from the corner of her eyes, she feared the worst.

"Natalie, it's alright," Dr. Jefferies assured.

"According to the assigned surgeon, Philip suffered a minor impact to his frontal lobe, and a broken leg and arm. He's also lost quite a bit of blood. However, he's stable and is expected to make a full recovery. You can see him now," he said smiling. Natalie embraced Dr. Jefferies and then ran out of the waiting room. As she entered Philip's room, she was overcome by emotion. She could hardly believe what had happened. She took his hand in hers.

"Philip," she called. At the sound of her voice his eyelids blinked rapidly. A short time later Richard walked in. Tears began to well up in her eyes.

"Phil, you cannot leave me now, please say something to me," she cried.

"I am so sorry sweetheart," Richard said, wiping tears from his eyes.

"I know you love him, or else you wouldn't have brought him all this way to get my approval." By then Natalie was sobbing out of control.

"He will get through this honey, don't worry," he said, embracing her. A few hours later Natalie and Richard reluctantly phoned Philip's relatives in the States to inform them of his accident. At first Becky thought that the two were greatly mistaken, because they didn't believe that their Nephew was abroad nor engaged. But after Natalie explained to them what seemed like a short scene from a movie, they went from excitement to complete horror. The couple said that they would catch the next flight and would be in London as soon as possible. It was the first time that Natalie ever had to deliver such frightening news and it broke her heart. She prayed that she would soon have better news for the Lane family.

Back at the Manor, a Specialist in Amnesia, sent by Baroness Ester had arrived to evaluate Lady Baldwin. William and Maureen sat in the Parlor and spoke with him about Natalie's improvement. A short while later he left. Before his departure, he told them that he would return the following morning to examine Lady Baldwin.

Back at the Hospital, Richard made arrangements with the adoptive family and a Judge who agreed to meet with the family at the hospital to finalize and approve the adoption process for baby Abigail. Danica was present to show her support. Before signing the paperwork, Richard asked Danica for the fourth time if she was certain that this was what she wanted for her sister. With tears in her eyes, she admitted that she was in no position to care for a newborn. She has been traumatized both by her parents' divorce and the sudden loss of her mother. Even though it was an open adoption, Richard was still heartbroken to give Abbie up. It's already been three months since Abigail's birth, and she has been approved by the Intensive Care Unit Physician for release. The family adopting Abigail knew Richard very well and they understood his situation. They agreed to an open adoption since his decision was made during an emotional period. With a heavy heart, Richard kissed baby Abbie, and hurried out of the ICU.

As he got off the elevator, Danica approached him. She appeared as though she'd been crying. Richard thought immediately that it was because of her mother.

"Danica? I thought you had already left. Are you all right?" She told him that she wanted to move out of the Manor but she didn't have anywhere to go.

"I thought you were moving in with your boyfriend," he said. She told him that she had broken up with him. He offered to pay for a hotel room for the night and in the morning he would help her to lease an apartment. She became momentarily happy and embraced Richard. He had promised her mother that he would be there for her and he meant it. As they pulled into the parking lot of Staybridge Suites in Surrey, Danica told Richard that she has the Urn with her mom's ashes in the trunk of her car and asked him if he would like to hold onto it for a while.

"Absolutely," he replied. Richard walked to the hotel parking lot with Danica. She took the Urn out of the car and brought it to Richard. After handing it to him, she said...

"Mum had one final wish. She wants us to have a small service for her. Then she wants her ashes to be sprinkled over the Thames River." Her eyes were filled with tears as she handed the Urn over to Richard.

"How can I thank you Richard?"

After embracing him once more, she got into her coupe and drove off. Richard was worried about her but he knew that she was going to be okay. He was meeting her in the morning to assist with an apartment. He has her contact information and was going to keep his promise to Marguerite to be there for her.

As Richard headed back to the hospital, his mind weighed a thousand pounds. For the first time in forever he knew it was the saddest day in his entire life. After checking in with his daughter, she told him that she was spending the night at the hospital. He told her that he would go to the Manor to get her a change of clothing and return shortly. She told him that he could rest and return in the morning...

"It's alright sweetheart, I don't want you to be alone tonight and besides everyone that I love is here," he said smiling.

After Richard left, Natalie fell into a deep sleep. She dreamt that she was running towards Big Ben and no matter how fast she ran, the further away it seemed. Then the River Thames made waves like the ocean, which washed over the tower of London. It seemed as though the waves were about to sweep her away. She looked in time to see

Prince Ethan speeding toward her on the blond mane horse. He swept her off the ground onto the horse, saving her from a seemingly horrible demise. Then she awoke to Philip's monitor beeping rapidly.

"Philip," she called. This time his eyelids blinked rapidly.

"Phil, it's me" she calls, touching his hands affectionately. He murmured and his eyes blinked to an open, then he fell back asleep. She hurries into the hallway and calls for the nurse. Four nurses came hurrying toward Philip's room.

"He said something," Natalie said excitedly.

"Hmm, not possible," one of the nurses said.

"He's suffered deep trauma," said another.

"No I heard him speak," she said emotionally.

"I'm sorry Ms. Baldwin, maybe it's possible you imagined it," Lydia said.

She sensed that this nurse was against her relationship with Philip and her close relations with the Royal Family. She then requested that this nurse not be allowed to assist with her fiancé. The other nurses offered her some comfort after the others left.

"We believe you Ms. Baldwin, just keep having faith, his numbers look really good," they assured her.

Dr. Jefferies entered Philip's room and confirmed his brain activity. The nurses smiled at her and left.

When Richard arrived at the Manor, he was happy to see that William didn't leave yet for the day. William could tell that by Richard's annoyed appearance that something was very wrong. He walked to the entrance to greet him.

"Mr. Baldwin, it's good to see you, sir."

"Hello William, I have some news, you might want to fix us a stiff one, will ya?"

William prepared their favorite hard Lime laced with Clarkes Court Rum and served it on the rocks. When they were seated Richard told him about Philip's accident. The horrified Butler sat wide eyed.

"How and when did this happen? He's going to be alright. We've informed his relatives in the States and they wanted him home immediately. However, he's engaged to my daughter, there's more to it than just sending him home."

"I quite agree," Will said.

"In any case they will be flying into Heathrow within the next few days."

"Of course," William replied, still in disbelief.

"Will, I want to discuss something else with you," Richard said, placing his glass on the campaign table.

"A lot has changed over the past few months, and I don't believe it will be the same from here onward," he said looking at Will regretfully.

"Yes sir?"

"Will, how would you like to conduct some house hunting starting today?"

"In search of a new home Sir?" asked an even more confused Will. Richard smiled.

"I'll tell you what, search for a home around the Thornton Heath area and as soon as you locate one you know for sure that I will absolutely love, you let me know," Richard said standing.

"Absolutely sir," Will said with a curious smile. After shaking hands with William, Richard headed upstairs and packed two days' worth of clothing for his daughter and headed back to Middlesex Memorial.

On the way to the hospital Richard's phone rang.

"Maureen, I was hoping to see you at the Manor. Oh I didn't realize that you're visiting with your mum? I'm sorry, no one told me that your mum was ill," he replied.

"Alright then, please come by in the morning, I need to see you. Please give my love to your mum," he said then hung up. A few moments later his phone rang again.

"Mother, where have you been? It's been months? You're what? This is nuts; when did you get married? Mom, I've been trying to reach you, Natalie's fiancé has been in an accident. Yes, a lot has happened since your last visit; we need you here. Okay Mother I'll see you in a few hours." As Richard pulled out of Marden road, he noticed a taxi cab headed in the direction of the Manor. He wondered who it might be. Of course, if it was anyone he knew they would have recognized his Black Royce, he thought. As he drove to the hospital, he began contemplating retirement. Despite everything, he'd missed Marguerite terribly, but somehow he couldn't have imagined spending the rest of his life with her. He's been in love with one woman his entire life and has never really given it much thought until now. It would have been futile to pursue this with such a demanding career. As he thought of Lisa he felt a warm sensation all over and he knew it was time.

Chapter 18

L isa's cab pulled up to the gate, but there was no one at the Manor to let her in. She asked the cab driver to take her back into London to the Palace Hotel where she has a reservation.

"Absolutely Ma'am," the cab driver responded. He stared at her from the rear view mirror and found her very attractive. As a Cab driver, he has a great reputation in London and didn't want to make it obvious that he was interested in her.

"What time did your flight get in?" he asked.

"About two hours ago," she replied.

"Then you must be exhausted," he replied.

"Do you have something in mind?" she asked.

"I'm about to retire for the evening, I was wondering if you might like to grab a bite to eat," he replied. Lisa was silent for a moment, then she replied...

"I'm sorry, but I hardly know you and besides, I've had a very long day and would like to catch up on some sleep; maybe next time?"

"That's alright, ma'am, I used to have a Caribbean girlfriend and I never got over her when she left," he admitted.

"Sorry to hear, how about tomorrow evening?" she asked.

"Sounds like a date," he replied smugly.

Lisa smiled at his reaction. As they approached the hotel entrance, the doorman hurried toward them and took Lisa's luggage from the taxi cab driver.

"Lisa, will I see you tomorrow around noon?" She only smiled. She was about to pay for her lift, however, the cab driver kindly refused.

"Maybe next time," he said, getting the rest of her things from the trunk. After a relaxing shower, Lisa was beyond overwhelmed and fell into a deep sleep.

Maureen was filled with regret as she thought of the night before, yet she could not deny the affection she felt for Richard. She thought of quitting her job, but she also thought of how this would look on top of everything. She was beyond frustrated. Unknown to everyone at the Manor, she's been in love with Richard from the moment they met. But was it worth losing the lifetime of respect and friendship that she has earned from the only people who, other than her mother, has been like family to her? As tears ran down her face, her mum called for her.

"Maureen, where's my beautiful daughter?"

"I'm here mum, I'll be right there," she said, drying her eyes with a napkin. As Maureen entered her mother's room, she noticed that she'd been crying.

"Talk to me sweetheart, what's bothering my angel?" As she was about to deny her mother's suspicion, she was reduced to tears.

"I love him mum."

"Whom?" her mother asked.

"Richard."

"Oh my dear child, I'm so sorry," she said half asleep.

Puzzled by her mother's reaction, Maureen stared at her.

"What do you mean mum?"

"Not now honey, maybe I'll talk to you later," Mrs. Taylor said rolling over to sleep.

"Mum, what is it?" Maureen pried.

"Mau, I said not today," Mrs. Taylor replied and drifted off to sleep.

After tucking her mother into bed, Maureen sat thinking about Richard. It was beginning to bother her that she was over thirty, unmarried and without children. She knew that elsewhere, that this was no major issue, however here in her neighborhood, after age thirty, folks begin to talk. What do they know about love anyway? Richard had a way with words and would often say, that 'neither place or time decides the matters of the heart. "This I agree with," she said falling asleep. Exhausted, uncertain and overwhelmed Maureen fell asleep and didn't awake until morning. She awoke to the sound of birds and as she slowly opens her eyes, the clock on the wall said that it was almost 7:30 in the morning. She found it strange that her mum didn't call on her an hour earlier. As she enters her mother's bedroom, she notices her mom sleeping in an awkward position.

"Mother?" she called. She walked closer to her mother's canopy bed and took her hands in hers: they were as cold as ice. Imagining the worst, she called at the top of her lungs…

"Mother!" she screamed but still no response. She placed her fingers on her mother's upper neck and felt no pulse. Fearing, she buried her head into a pillow and sobbed. Then she felt someone touch her shoulders. Panicked, she looks up staring into her mother's warm smiling face.

"Sweetheart, what are you so upset about?" Maureen looks at her.

"Mum! I thought you were gone," she cried.

"Gone where?" her mother laughed.

"Come on honey, how old do you think I am?" laughed a seventy-seven-year-old Mrs. Taylor.

An overjoyed Maureen embraced her mother tightly.

"Mum, you rascal," she laughs, wiping tears from her face.

"Maybe now you'd realize who loves you more than anyone in this world, my child," she reminded her as they embraced each other.

Having heard about Natalie's fiancé's accident over the news, Jasmine searched everywhere to find Prince Ethan. Then she saw him relaxing by the family pool. He looks like a tourist in swim trunks and sunglasses.

"Pardon me Prince Ethan, would you please come quickly," she called. After throwing on his bathrobe he came hurrying toward his mother's favorite servant.

"What's going on Jasmine?" He asked, running his finger through his wet hair.

"It's Lady Baldwin."

At the sound of her name the Prince became more alert.

"What happened, is she okay?"

"Yes it's her fiancé, he's been in an accident," she said nervously.

"My God, is he alright?"

"Yes, he's at Middlesex Memorial."

"How did you learn of this?" he asked.

"Sir, it's all over the news."

"Thank you for informing me of this important matter, I'll go visit them at once," he replied.

"You are most welcome," she replied. As she turned to leave…

"Jasmine, see that no one knows of my whereabouts. I do not want the press to hinder me."

"Understood sir," she said and left the room.

About an hour later, Prince Ethan arrived at Middlesex Memorial. Unknown to him, his Bodyguard Jim had followed him there. As the Prince pulled into the hospital parking lot, he saw a young man in his late teens wearing a black Motocross hoodie T-shirt and offered him some money for them. Recognizing the Prince, the teen was thrilled.

"Prince Ethan, no need to pay me sir!!" he said bowing, while removing his shirt. After handing the shirt to the Prince...

"Here, take this for your shirt and your silence," the Prince urged.

"Gee, thanks," said the tattooed Mohawked teen who got on his bike and disappeared. Looking at him from a distance, the Prince's Bodyguard smiled while shaking his head at the Prince's new appearance. He was completely undetected in his second hand hoodie. The Prince took the Elevator to the 4th floor of the hospital. The Nurse at the front desk refused to give him information on the Baldwin's unless he was family. The Nurse looked at him suspiciously as he walks away in a hurry. As he was about to get onto the elevator, he saw Richard.

"Richard, wait up."

Recognizing his voice, Richard stared at him in disbelief.

"Prince Ethan, I hardly recognized you in this clown's outfit," he laughed. "What are you up too kid?" he asked.

"I heard about the accident," he said.

"How's Philip?"

"Philip is making rapid progress, he's lucky to be alive," Richard said relieved.

"How's Natalie?"

"She's barely hanging in there, but strong like her mother. Come I'll take you up to her," Richard said pressing the elevator button. As the elevator took them to the seventh floor, they discussed Natalie's Amnesia, which has been more temporary than they'd expected. As they entered Philip's unit, Natalie had dozed off and awoke to the sound of the door shutting.

"Hi Sweetie, look who's here."

Prince Ethan removed his hoodie and at the sight of him Natalie's heart leaped.

"Prince Ethan, what are you doing here?" she said surprised.

"I heard what happened and I came to offer my support," he said embracing her. Then Ethan glanced over at Philip still unconscious.

164

"His numbers look very good," he replied.

"I'm so sorry but may I ask, how did this happen?" As Natalie reflected back on the events leading up to Philip's accident, she realized that she hasn't told her father what she had learn about him and Maureen-the same reason she fled the Manor which led to her fiancé's accident. She fought back tears.

"Father, there's something I need to tell you."

"Should I wait outside?" ask Ethan.

"No it's alright" Richard said. Natalie hesitated...

"Dad, I know about you and Maureen," she said. Richard looks at her curiously.

"You do? But what does this have to do with the accident?" he asked.

"I heard Cassie scratching the door. She must have gotten out somehow. As I was letting her back in, I overheard you and Maureen talking, because her door was partially opened. After you left I confronted Maureen and she didn't take it very well. I've known her for such a long time and I've never seen her so upset. She said some things to me that I simply couldn't handle and I fled the manor. Philip came to find me…" Her voice faded and she was reduced to tears one more. Richard stood in horror. He couldn't believe that he was partially responsible for this. Both men couldn't believe what they'd just learn. Richard's emotion turned into anger. Unable to look at his daughter, he left. He went into the guestroom and poured himself the strongest drink he could find. He couldn't be responsible for this, he thought. Within an hour he had emptied a bottle of Johnny Walker Whisky and fell into a deep sleep.

Ethan and Natalie had hope that Richard would have returned by now.

"Maybe I should go find him," she said standing.

"I know he's going to be okay and besides, I wanted to apologize to you," he said looking at her with deep care.

"What about?" she asked. It's obvious that she'd forgotten about his attempt to disrespect her that day at the Palace, however, he still felt obligated to apologize to her.

"I was overcome by how much you have change since I last saw you and I had behaved improper toward you," he said looking away.

"You did? Hmmm, I don't mean to be rude but maybe you should leave," she said opening the door.

Just then, Philip mumbled and Natalie ran to his side.

"Phil, Philip did you say something?" she calls desperately. Then he began to slowly open his eyes.

"Oh my goodness, Philip darling," she beamed with excitement. Forgetting her anger toward Prince Ethan she embraced him excitedly and then she ran into the hallway to get the nurse.

"Wait, there's something else I needed to tell you," Ethan called. Natalie returned to Philip's side.

"Honey, it's me." Then Philip said her name.

"Oh thank God, you're going to be okay honey. I wish dad was here," she beamed.

"Hey Nat," he called, his eyes half opened.

Sobbing… "I thought I'd lost you," she said wiping tears from her eyes. As she was about to kiss him, the Nurse enters the room.

"I'm sorry Ms. Baldwin, but I would have to ask you both to wait outside while we examine Mr. Lane."

"What!" she fussed.

"That's absurd!"

"It's okay Nurse, no problem we'll wait outside," Prince Ethan said. The Nurse looks at him suspiciously. He took Natalie by the hand and led her out of Philip's room. As they sat in one of the guest rooms, she looks at him and giggle.

"I just noticed, what are you wearing?" she laughed.

"Long story," he said smiling. The Prince glanced at the door and saw someone look away. He quickly got to his feet.

"What is it?" Natalie asked.

"I'm sure I just saw my Bodyguard peeking at me through the glass," he panicked.

"I see, did you sneak out of your sheltered life at the Palace," she teased.

"But really, what are you doing here?" she asked, looking at him suspiciously. The Prince stared at her longingly.

"Do you remember when we were shooting arrows in the garden?"

"Was it at my house?" she asked.

"No, it was at the Palace Manor. Mom had invited you over." Natalie was deep in thought as she races through the hidden memories in her mind.

"Oh yes, it was my tenth birthday!"

"Yes," he said excitedly.

Then she remembered something. On that same day, she had her first kiss, and they had made a promise to each other. Remembering, she looks at him.

"Ethan, we were only children," she whispered.

"But, I've kept that promise to this day, and I intend to live up to it," he said, taking her hands.

"But Ethan, that's impossible, I'm engaged," she said softly. Then there was a knock on the door. It was the nurse, she told them that it was okay to see Philip now. As she left the room Prince Ethan follows after her.

"I think it would be wise if you wait here, your Majesty," she said. Before he said another word she shut the door behind her.

When she arrived, Philip was wide awake and his face lit up at the sight of her.

"Oh Philip," she cried. The nurses look at each other and smile. They knew that they were looking at something that most women would wait a lifetime for.

"How do you feel honey?" she asked.

"I'm just a little bit puzzled why I'm here in this hospital bed," he said looking at the cast on his right leg arm.

"Haven't they told you?" she said looking over at the nurses.

"We leave this up to the family of the patient," Molly said, the youngest nurse. The nurses then called Natalie to a far side of the room.

"It is best that you tell him as little details of the accident as possible. This will help us to determine how much he's remembered. Also, the Doctor is on his way. Dr. Jefferies went home earlier so it would be Dr. Michaels," Molly said. She then thanked the nurses for all they've done for Philip. After everyone left, she leans forward and kisses him gently.

"I missed you." Then she remembered.

"Philip, I should go find dad," she said and hurries out of the room. Then she remembered Ethan. She searched the guest rooms and found her dad passed out on a leather sofa.

"Dad, come on get up, Philip's awake." Then she noticed the empty Whisky bottle on the floor. Richard opened his eyes briefly and Natalie was able to help him onto the sofa. After removing his shoes and socks, she covered him with a blanket and left. She opens the door to the guest room where she had left Prince Ethan to find him gone. He'd left her a note.

"Natalie, I'm so sorry but my Bodyguard came and I had to leave. I would like to see you again. Here's my phone details, please contact me as soon as you can, so we can arrange a more appropriate time-Xx Prince Ethan." As she headed back to Philip's room, she thought about Ethan. It's been almost twelve years since their visit in the garden. How could he have taken this silly promise they'd made to each other so seriously? Even now it's impossible because she couldn't image her life without Philip.

Natalie spoke to Philip for a few hours until he drifted off to sleep. Since it was already after four in the morning, she took the bag that her dad had brought her earlier into one of the guestrooms and after a long shower, she fell fast asleep. That night she had another vision. This time it was about her mother. They were all having dinner at the Manor and everyone was there, including all three of her nannies; Sofia, Edna and Lily. As everyone sat dining joyfully, Maureen entered the room and began yelling at her mother. "Who invited her into my home? Get out, get her out of my home!" she yelled. A moment later, Maureen was escorted out of the room by two Royal Guards. Troubled by the dream, Natalie stayed awake for a while and slept until noon the following day. Realizing the time, she got dressed and hurries to Philip's room. When she arrived, her father was already there.

"Darling, we have great news," her father said smiling proudly.

"I bet I already know what it is," she said happily.

"Wow, dad, you look great. How did you manage to shake off that whiskey so quickly?" she laughed.

"What?" he asked, looking puzzled. She smiled and winked at him.

"Where's Philip?" She asked, her smile fading.

"Oh you knew?" her dad replied.

"Yes I was there when he woke up last light," she said looking around the room.

"Dad, where's Philip?"

"He's undergoing a few exams darling. Dr. Jeff said that it will take a few hours. Maybe we should head back to the Manor to check in," he suggested.

"Um, okay, let me tell him I'm leaving for a little bit and that I'll be back. Which room is he in?"

"Ms. Baldwin, maybe I can take a note to him for you," the nurse suggested.

"Actually, I think it's better if he thinks that I didn't leave," she realizes.

"I think you're right sweetheart," her dad replied. The nurse agreed.

As they headed to the Manor, Richard discussed his plans for retirement with his daughter. She was hardly surprise and agreed that it was a brilliant idea. Richard's been eligible for retirement for over ten years now but never really had a good reason to put in the request. As they pulled up to the gat, William, noticing them from the kitchen, entered the code and the gate swung open. Exhausted from the day's events, Richard parked his Rolls Royce onto the red brick courtyard.

Chapter 19

Lisa had just return from her dinner date with the cab driver whose name she learned was Dominick Bates. He was very sweet and the perfect gentleman, however she was certain that she would not do dinner with him again. He constantly complimented her which was beyond flattering but she had only come to London for one reason; to see her daughter whom she had not seen in what seems like decades and was not interested in romance at the moment. Dominick was returning to her hotel in an hour to take her back to the manor, so she got ready. She couldn't wait to see everyone, especially her daughter's new fiancé.

Just as promised, an hour later Dominick arrived on schedule to drive her to the Manor. He told her more about his Caribbean girlfriend whom he claims was from Barbados. However, Lisa was the least bit interested in the conversation and finally dozed off. He smiled as he gazed at her through the mirror. Not paying attention to the road, he barely missed another taxi avoiding a head on collision. Lisa was awakened by the sharp swerve.

"What was that?"

"Everything's alright madam," he replied, and blamed the other driver. Lisa looks at her wrist watch.

"Are we almost there?"

"Please don't worry Lisa, we took a shorter route," he said in a caring voice. She was upset that he didn't tell her before taking another route. She reached for her mobile and dialed her daughter's number. Recognizing the London area code, Natalie thought it might be the hospital.

"Hello," she answered in a panic.

"Mother, is it really you?"

"What! You're here in London, where about? Oh that's right around the corner. Okay, we'll meet you at the gate, please don't worry."

"Dad, it's mum, she's here in London."

"She is?"

"Yes, the taxi has taken the other route and she's almost here."

"You're not kidding?" he replied, somewhat excited, yet nervous. "She took a taxi?"

"I wish she would have informed us of her plans," he admitted. Lisa couldn't wait to get out of the cab. She was irritated with Dominick and was never using his service again. As the cab pulled into the courtyard, Natalie hurries to get the door. Overjoyed at the sight of her mother, tears sprang into her eyes.

"I can't believe you're here mum," she said embracing her.

"Oh honey, I've missed you so much," Lisa said kissing her beautiful daughter all over her face.

William looked down from the balcony at Natalie and her mother in the courtyard.

"What a beautiful sight. They are almost identical," he whispered.

Richard joins William on the balcony and smiled at the sight of Lisa and Natalie. She looks exactly the same from the first time he'd seen her. She couldn't have arrived at a better time, he thought.

"Lisa, what a pleasant surprise," Richard said. As she looks up to meet his eyes, a million memories raced across her mind.

"Richard, my goodness, how have you been, you look terrible," she teased as he embraced her.

"Well, I wish I could say the same. You look lovely."

As William observes from the balcony, he felt a wind of change rustle through the nearby trees.

"Your lunch is ready," he called.

"Come on my lads before Cassie has her way at the table. She's been licking her chops and I don't believe she can resist the sight of that omelet any longer," he joked. All three laughed at Will's timely sense of humor.

"Hello William, we finally meet again," Lisa said, reaching out to shake his hand.

"That will never do," William said embracing her warmly.

"Will you be joining your daughter and her father at the table?"

"Smells wonderful, but I've already had lunch earlier," she replied.

"Well there's always room for desert," William insisted. Showing all three to the magnificent dining room where a feast awaited.

171

After lunch, the party of three sat in the Parlor. Richard and Natalie filled Lisa in on all that had happened over the past few months. Lisa's eyes widened in horror.

"I can't begin to imagine what it's been like for you both. I can't believe that Philip's been in an accident. Why didn't you call me sweetheart?"

"Everything happened so quickly, there was no time mum. But look, you're here now, how did you know?"

"A mother always knows sweetheart," she said. As they sat conversing, Richard couldn't take his eyes off Lisa. Then the Landline rang. It was the hospital. Philip was out of surgery and was asking for Natalie. Richard stared at his watch.

"It seems we've lost track of the hour."

"I'll accompany you, after all we're the only family that Philip has in London at the moment," Lisa said.

When they arrived, Philip appears relaxed and was wide awake.

"Hello Philip," Lisa said.

"Hi, I recognized your voice from the phone, you must be Lisa," Philip said, his eyes racing wildly.

"If it weren't for those bandages around your head, I'd say you look well enough to walk out of here," Richard said jokingly.

"I have to agree," Natalie said.

"Well, they said I could go home today, only if I agree to take the pain pills they prescribed, but I hate pills," he grumbled.

"But you will need them after General Anesthesia fades out."

"Oh that's right, you're a Nurse," Philip said smiling broadly.

"Yes, she is," Richard said.

"But she's on vacation, so you're out of business," Natalie said playfully.

"A Nurse is never on vacation," her mother reminded her.

"See there, I'm in good hands," Philip grinned. All four chuckled.

"Okay kids, Lisa and I will be down the hall," Richard said taking her hand.

"Thank you both," Philip called.

When they were alone, the couple discussed their plans to marry.

"After what happened, I think we should marry right away. We shouldn't wait any longer," she said concerned.

"Honey, have one good look at me, other than this pretty blue robe, I look like a cartoon character," he joked.

"That's not very funny," she giggled.

"Well, not as funny as marrying you with my head wrapped like a sandwich. Honey, let's discuss our wedding later. Maybe in a couple of days after I get out of this place," he sighed, gazing at her sorrowfully. He saw something in her eyes he never saw before and it concerned him. Why the sudden rush? The main focus right now should be my recovery, he thought.

"Hun, are you okay?"

She shook her head and smiled.

"I thought I had lost you babe, I swear."

"Come here," he said and he reached out his available arm to pull her closer to him.

"And besides, you don't want to look back at your wedding photos and be reminded of this accident, would you?" he laughed.

"You're right, that would be horrible," she admitted. She opened his robe to examine him. There were a few small bandages and a larger one just under his left torso. She placed small kisses on each bandage.

"I think you should come home tomorrow; I'll take care of you. We have our very own Nurse at the Manor now," she said smiling. When Richard and Lisa returned, Philip told them that he was thinking of leaving the hospital the next day. Lisa was concerned about his hurry to come home. But after explaining how much he'd miss the sounds of nature and the wind rustling the trees in the morning, they all agreed.

"Besides, nature is the best healer," Richard put in.

Back at the manor William rustled through the piles of listings that he had found of beautiful homes that he believed would be of Mr. Baldwin's liking. Most of which were newer built Mansions and Manors. Then he halted when he saw this specific home. It was almost American style with an automatic garage, a large modern kitchen with a middle aisle, marble countertops and an open pantry large enough to accommodate a family size of at least twelve. Then he looks at the number of bedrooms and gasped at the almost nine bedrooms which it boasted. This wasn't a manor, nor was it a Mansion; it was a humble abode. One that he believes would be the kind of change the Baldwin's would embrace.

As he looks through the other listings, he heard someone enter through the front door.

"William, are you here?" It was Maureen.

"I'm out on the balcony. Would you care to join me?"

"Sure, but only for a minute, I'm here to get my things," she replied.

"What's all this?"

"Not a thing, just shuffling through old papers for Richard."

"Hmm, I wonder what he is up to?" she said looking around.

"Where have you been Mau? It's been a few days."

"Was looking after my mum, you know."

"Oh yes, I heard that she's in remission?"

"She was until yesterday when we found out that the leukemia has returned," she said, her eyes welling up with tears.

"William has never seen her like this; she appears pale and there was a painful sadness in her eyes.

"Is there anything I can do to help?" She was going to lie to him but couldn't.

"I'm losing my mum Will. I won't have anyone left. My sister Claire is married and hardly has time for me anymore," she said reduced to tears. Puzzled and a little unsure of what to do, William approached her and took her in his arms.

"I never knew you felt this way? You've always been such a happy person," he said reaching for his handkerchief in his shirt pocket, gently wiping the tears off her face.

"Would you like some tea?"

"I'd love some."

"Don't forget, you've got Master William, who's always here for you with the finest cup of tea in Great Britain," he cheered.

"You always find a way to make me feel better. You know that, don't you?" Will laughed.

"It's because I know you so well," he replied.

Two days later Richard helped Philip out of the Rolls Royce into the guest room where he stayed when they first arrived.

"In case you're wondering, the king bed in this room is the most comfortable. Lisa loves this bed. She's slept in here a few times on her previous visits."

"And you're letting me have it?"

"Sure," Richard said with that familiar look in his eyes.

Hmmm, what are you up to Richard... Philip thought, staring at him suspiciously. As Richard walks out of Philip's room into the hallway, he heard a door shut down the hall. As he attempted to investigate, he saw Maureen carrying a large suitcase. He cleared his throat to get her attention.

"Richard, pardon me, I didn't see you there," she said looking slightly embarrassed.

"What's going on?" he asked.

"I'm going home for a little while to help look after my mum," she replied.

"And you weren't going to discuss it with me?"

"I'm sorry Richard, I've had a very rough week. It's best we discuss this later," she said firmly.

"I'm sorry Maureen; I never meant to hurt you," he said walking towards her. "I'm also very sorry about your mum's condition. We all thought that she was improving."

"She was, but you know."

He nods. I can hire a moving company to help you with the move; seems like a lot," he said looking around.

"No it's alright Richard, I have everything under control," she said trying to be strong.

As Richard was about to leave, she called out to him.

"Richard, wait," she said leaning up against him.

"I love you," she cried. Richard stroked her hair, and then gently held her at arm's length.

"I'm sorry, but this is not the time Maureen. Lisa is here and so is Philip and Natalie. Did you hear what happened with Philip?"

She nods yes.

"William told me yesterday," she said, drying her eyes.

"You are still very young Maureen, I'm sure there's someone out there just waiting to meet someone as wonderful as you," he said.

"Please Richard, hold me one more time," she said embracing him. His heart raced as he held her closely. She looks into his eyes and unable to resist, he kisses her then forcefully pulled himself away.

"I'm sorry Maureen, let's discuss this at a better time," he said and walks away.

"Should I phone someone to help you with the move?" he asked. She nodded yes and returned to her room to finish packing. As she packed the last of her things, she thought of what it would be like to be with Richard. What she would give to have him in her life. She refused to believe that it was over. As the movers packed the last of her belongings, a spark of hope filled her heart when Richard appeared on the balcony and wave to her. Natalie and Lisa joined him to see Maureen off.

"I can't believe she's moved out. Is this temporary?" Natalie asked.

"I'm not certain. She's leaving to help look after her mother," Richard said, trying to sound formal.

"She's been so wonderful to us mum. Dad, maybe there's something we can do for her."

"Is she the Chauffeur that's been with you since you were five?" Lisa asked.

"She is mum," Natalie said leaving the balcony.

"Maybe there's something we can do for her Richard," Lisa agreed.

"What do you have in mind?" he asked.

"How about a surprise going away party?"

"Hmmm, I like that idea a lot," he said smiling.

"I'll be right back Richard," Lisa called and slipped inside to grab them a drink.

He still couldn't believe that she was here. It's been over seven years since her last visit and he wondered what else other than their daughter's engagement had brought her to England. Despite being raised by a single father, their daughter is now a young adult considering marriage, and has grown up to be a wonderful young lady. Lisa is still one of the finest people he's ever known and is proud to have shared a daughter with her. As Richard contemplates life after retirement; still shaken from the sudden loss of his girlfriend Marguerite, the thought of Lisa and Maureen created new fears. Something he may not be prepared to embrace.

"Richard," Lisa called rejoining him on the balcony.

"Lisa, what's that you're holding?"

"It's a little surprise from Grenada," she said, handing him a tall champagne glass.

"I see," he said, taking a sip.

"Delicious, what is it?"

"It's lemonade," she replied.

"You're kidding," he laughed.

"I kid you not," she winked.

"What else have you bought from Grenada?"

"My lovely self," she replied walking toward the other side of the balcony. Richard placed his glass down, and followed her. As she turns around to face him, his eyes met hers. Before she said another word, unable to postpone his more than twenty years of feelings he kissed her savagely. She tries to pull away from him several times but he only kisses her more passionately.

"Richard," she said her voice muffled. He releases her temporarily and she slipped away from him. He pursues her, and as she tries to open the door to the Levorotatory, he stops her.

"Stop it Richard," she replied, slapping him gently.

"You shouldn't have done that," he said with a knotty expression on his face. He took her by the hands and led her back toward the balcony.

"*Why are you here?*" he whispered. Removing her white scarf from around her neck. He then took her in his arms and kisses her once more. This time she didn't resist.

After what seems like a lifetime of kissing, she pulls away.

"Richard, please stop it," she scolded and slipped away from him. This time he didn't pursue her. Lisa entered the guest room and splashed water on her face. What's gotten into him? she thought, a smile forming on her face. As she looks at her reflection in the mirror, it took her back to when she first met Richard. It was her day off and she was spending it at the beach. It wasn't the weekend so she didn't expect to see any tourists at the beach. She was only twenty-five and had the perfect figure. Most people would agree that she would make the perfect runway model, but of course it was no desire of hers. Although she was highly desirable; she had just ended a five-year relationship and had no intentions of meeting anyone new. Richard was bold. The minute he noticed her, he came right up and sat next to her.

"My, my, are you beautiful. What's your name?" Of course she was snobbish and ignored him. That did not get rid of him. He was determined to speak with her and was not leaving until she responded. Whether he likes it or not, she completely ignored him. She couldn't forget how handsome he was with perfectly sculpted abs and face like an angel. She chuckled as she remembered him following her from the beach...

"What are you doing?" she asked finally.

"Ah, now there you are, you spoke," he said staring at her intensely. "For a moment there I thought you were mute."

"And if I were," she replied hastily.

"Then I would have my way with you resting assured that you wouldn't be able to tell a soul," he laughed. She couldn't believe his boldness; but she liked it. She lived on a little hill not too far from the beach so he followed her for a while. Then he asked her if she would be at the beach tomorrow.

"No, I have to work," she replied sharply.

"What about after work?"

"Maybe," she replied and slipped inside before he said another word.

The following day, late evening around dusk, she went to the beach to see if he was really there. As sure as his boldness, there he was laying on a towel with his surfboard beside him. She choked back laughter at the sight of him. Overhearing her giggle, he looked up.

"You came," he said excitedly.

"It's late I cannot stay very long," she replied.

"Look at that sunset, isn't it beautiful. It looks like fire across the sky," he said approaching her.

"It's what I've seen since childhood and it never gets old," she admitted.

"What's your name?" he asked. She looks down at the sand and almost in a whisper she said *"Lisa."*

"It suits you well," he said looking at her intensely.

"Come sit with me, tell me all about Grenada."

As she reflected on the day she met Richard, someone knocked on the bathroom door.

"Mum, are you in here?"

"Yes sweetheart, I'll be right out," she called.

"What's the matter darling?" she asked, surprised to see her daughter upset.

"It's Philip mum, he has a very high fever."

"Is he taking his prescribed medication?"

"I'm not sure mum," Natalie said worried. Lisa followed her daughter to Philip's room...

"Hi Philip, how are you doing handsome?" Lisa said, playfully.

"Not so good," he replied, sounding exhausted.

178

"Did you take your meds?"

"No ma'am, I hate pills."

"Well sweetie I'm afraid you're going to have to take them or else you will keep feeling like garbage," she said in a serious yet sarcastic tone.

"See these tiny red ones; they are iron pills which helps to rebuild your red blood cells and are crucial since you've lost so much blood," she warned.

"These large white ones here are your antibiotics which helps prevent infections. So you see they are important," she said patting him on the head.

"Sweetheart, please bring him some clean sheets, these are soaking wet."

"I don't get why I have the shakes and why am I sweating so bloody much? I really don't like my fiancé seeing me like this," Philip frets.

"It's because of your low red blood cell count. Thus the reason you should take your meds," she smiled. Without hesitation, Lisa removed two pills from the pack and reach for the glass of milk that William had brought. Lisa sat next to him...

"Come here sweetie," she said in a motherly tone.

Philip laughed.

"Alright," he said, taking the milk and the two tiny red pills out of her hands.

"I will leave you two alone now. If you or Natalie needs me I'll be in the kitchen helping William prepare dinner," she said and shuts the door behind her. A short while later, Natalie and William return with linen for Philip's bed.

"Hey guys, what's up?" Philip greets them trying to sound like his old self.

"Hey there buddy, any plans for a party later?" William joked.

"Sure Master Will, what's the occasion and where's my dress?" asked Philip, in a sarcastic tone.

"Cut it out you two," Natalie laughed.

"Come here Will, do you mind helping me to place my fiancé on the recliner, so I can put some Linen on his bed?"

"Not at all, my Lady."

Philip thanked William, then chased everyone out of his room.

"Sorry guys, I'm exhausted. Thank you Master William, come back later with that dress and we'll discuss the party some more," he said yawning loudly.

"You are most welcome, I'll bring your dinner up shortly," Will said, shutting the door behind him.

"But honey, I wanted to discuss something with you," Natalie said folding a blanket over him.

"Maybe later," he replied, dozing off. It was a bit chilly in the guest room. Before leaving she turns on the fireplace and shuts the door partially.

After dinner with her parents, Philip was still fast asleep so Natalie spent the evening indoors with Cassie; thinking about Philip and Prince Ethan.

"Come here girl," she calls Cassie.

"My have you grown; what has William been feeding to you?" Cassie licked her face in response.

"Yuck, what did you eat?" she asked, hurrying to the bathroom to wash her face.

Cassie drops her head appearing embarrassed.

"You can't be," Natalie laughed.

"I'm sorry sweetheart, we'll have to get you some doggie toothpaste, and yes like that pink one we saw on Television."

Her ears flicked right up. Natalie couldn't believe how intelligent she was, and patted her gently.

"I have to admit, I could use some entertainment in this room. It's rather outdated. What do you think girl?"

This time Cassie just wagged her tail. As her thoughts returned to Prince Ethan and Philip, her phone rang. She didn't want to answer it but did.

"Hello. Oh hi Jasmine, yes I'm available tomorrow evening, you can come by then. Yes, I would love to see you. I can use the company for that matter. Ok Jasmine, I'll see you tomorrow evening, cheers." Natalie wonders what she meant when she asked if she remembered her but she soon shrugged it off. She hasn't spent an evening alone in a long time and for the first time she was bored.

As she dug through her old book shelf to find something to read, she saw the letter that Princess Annie had written to her.

"My goodness, I almost forgot about you," she whispered, removing the envelope from behind a large Webster's dictionary.

"Well this gives me something to do," she said. After reading the letter a second time, Natalie realized that Princess Annie had written a coded message in the last paragraph. "Please tell my son Pri(n)ce Eth(o)n that he is (t)he la(s)t ch(a)nce for England and is loved and highly (f)avor(e)d. The coded words spelt (not safe). Her final words left Natalie in utter shock. It is and has always been my hope that you would wed my son. With you as his wife, only then he would be the rightful heir to the throne. Overcome by a combination of fear and joy, she knew what all this would mean. But she was engaged to another man. How would she release this news to Philip? It would break his heart. Then she thought that no one needed to know and maybe she could keep this information to herself. But then she remembered the warning: Ethan was in danger. All thoughts of ignoring her friend's letter had left her. But how, she thought...

What can the daughter of a Royal Guard do to protect the only surviving Prince of Edinburgh? Then suddenly, she thought of Jasmine's visit.

"I can't trust anyone," she said. Without hesitation, she reached for the phone and cancelled her plans with Jasmine. Slightly stressed by the sudden responsibility that was bestowed upon her, she wished that Maureen was here. She always found ways in which to help her figure things out. Maybe it wasn't so bad after all. Her fiancé had been very fortunate and was recovering quickly. And maybe, just maybe Maureen truly loved Richard. But everyone who knows Richard knows that he's in love with my mother. Maureen was simply setting herself up to be hurt. Hopefully, she accepts their invitation and allows them to throw her a party. A little while later, she checked in on her fiancé and was surprised to find that he was still asleep. She glanced at his dinner tray sitting on the lamp stand and was relieved to see that he had eaten. He appears almost angelic and much younger than thirty-five. But of course someone this tall and ruggedly handsome was no boy at all. It's been three weeks since his accident and she's missed him. It almost feels like she'd lost him. But God knows, she now had a lot more than her engagement and Philip's injuries to be concerned about. Overwhelmed, bittersweet, yet honored by Princess Annie's final wish; she climbs into bed next to Philip and fell into a deep sleep. Her mind filled with unmade decisions, as the pages of her life unfolds.

The next morning Philip awoke to the sound of paper rustling beneath his feet. The smell of Japanese Cherry Blossom on the bed next to him, told him that his fiancé had slept next to him. He sighed heavily; wishing he could be there for her through all the sudden changes that were happening. He reached for what looks like a large red envelope on the bed next to his feet. It was opened and Natalie's name was written in bold stylish cursive.

"What's this?" he wondered, opening the envelope, slowly removing what looks like a letter. As he opened up the two paged letter and began to read, he realized that this must have been the reason for her visit to the palace. Shocked by the responsibilities of the letter, he places it back into the envelope and quickly hid it beneath the linen where he'd found it. But then curiosity got the better of him. If he was to marry Natalie, he needed to know what her connections to the Royals were; whether or not they posed a hazard to his future wife. Reaching for the envelope once more, he removed the letter and began reading through it. He read it a second and third time. Hearing footsteps approach, he hid the letter under his pillow and pretended to be asleep.

"Good morning Philip, your breakfast is served," William said. Philip sat up slowly, yawning loudly and rubbing his eyes. William placed the portable tray in front of him.

"Good Morning Will, I have to say that this is your best yet."

"You're most welcome, sir," William said proudly. After breakfast, Philip took his meds and thought about the last paragraph of the letter. It was almost coded and he wondered what it meant.

Chapter 20

Natalie was surprised to see her mother up and about this early at the Manor.

"Mum, you seemed to have disappeared last night," she said staring at her curiously.

Lisa laughed.

"Sweetheart, I thought you might have grown out of being nosy by now. What can I do for you?" She said tucking her hair behind her ears and playfully pinching her nose.

"Mum, cut it out," she laughed trying to get away from her.

"Mum?"

"Sweetheart are you alright?"

She wanted to tell her about the letter and her trip to the Palace Manor but then changed her mind. She knew that this would make things difficult for Philip.

"It's nothing important, I was wondering if you'd like to take a walk with me later over to Tadworth Park. We have lots of catching up to do," she said. Knowing her daughter, she smiled at how little she had changed from childhood. She'd never been able to hide anything from her and Lisa was happy that this hadn't changed. It would also mean that she could be there for her as always.

"Sure sweetheart, is that all?" she asked, staring at her slyly.

"I know that look mum, yes that is all. I'll see you at dinner."

"What about lunch?" her mom calls after her.

"Who eats lunch anymore?" she responded from the end of the hallway. Her mom shook her head and smiled. She wondered what her daughter was up to. Lisa strolled into Maureen's emptied room. She wondered why she was leaving so suddenly. She had met her on her first visit to the Manor and thought she was wonderful. She was always very loyal to Richard and Natalie.

After breakfast, Philip thought about the letter for a long time. He also reflected on all that has happened on this trip. He wondered if it was nature's way of trying to help him with his decision. He also hasn't heard from his uncle and aunt and wondered if they were still on their way to London. He was feeling a lot better and the accident has left him in a conclusive state of mind. There was no doubt that he was overwhelmed and beyond ready to face all fears that would determine whether the beautiful Natalie Baldwin would be his wife.

Prince Ethan had just returned from his visit with the Prime Minister. He thought it was a nice visit and was surprised to find that his wife Rebecca was present. They met at the Prime Minister's home outside the city of London for lunch to discuss the issues that have arisen from plans to convert the ruins of Castlebury into a Public Library, in the city of Birmingham. Their previous meetings were usually argumentative and at first Ethan was reluctant to meet with him. However, he thought that this meeting went well. As he sat enjoying the cup of tea that Jasmine had brought him, he thought of Natalie. He hasn't seen her since that day at the hospital and wondered how her fiancé was progressing. He thought maybe it was time he visited them out of respect. It was almost the eve of the anniversary of his parent's accident and he was overcome with emotion. He got into bed without removing his shoes and thought of his mother, Annie. He remembered the things she had discuss with him, as though she was preparing him in the event that she wasn't around. He had just turned twenty-two and knew that all of England would soon wonder what his plans were for marriage and the throne. He was hardly ready to take on the responsibility and suddenly he wished there were other successors.

As he pondered these things, there was a sharp knock on his door. He wasn't expecting anyone and he wondered who it might be.

"It's Jasmine, your majesty," she called.

"Jasmine? Come on in. I thought you were finished with your duties for today," he said sitting up in bed.

"Yes majesty, this piece of mail arrived this morning and I had forgotten to give it to you. It's from Lady Baldwin and it's marked urgent," she said, handing him a small envelope. He thanked her and when she had left, he tore it open with haste. It was a short note that read...

"Ethan, it is important that we meet tomorrow at noon by Alder's property next to the pond. If you can manage, please come alone." Surprised by the request he wondered what it was about. It's almost impossible to get past his bodyguard and he knew that the only way that this was possible was to invite Lady Baldwin to dinner, here at the Palace Manor. He wasted no time in writing a response to inform her of the new arrangement.

Although Natalie didn't expect a response from Prince Ethan this soon, she was surprised when she checked the evening mail that there was an envelope from him. She tore the letter open and read through it quickly. After reading his response, she thought that maybe she didn't emphasize the importance of their need for privacy. If they were to meet at the Palace Manor, she doubted that they would have any privacy at all. Without hesitation she wrote to him to emphasize the importance that their meeting would need to be as discreet as possible.

When Prince Ethan received a second letter from Lady Baldwin, he began to sense the importance and the need for immediacy regarding Lady Baldwin's pending matter. He wrote to her a second time to inform her that he would see to it that they were alone, and would dismiss his servants for an amount of hours to ensure their privacy. He also ensured her that only those in charge of his safety would be allowed to monitor their visit from a distance. Lastly he informed her that his study where the meeting would be conducted was naturally soundproof and that no one would be able to overhear their conversation. The Prince then enclosed his royal insignia indicating his promise to her and final request to meet at the Palace Manor.

Upon receipt of the Prince's mail, Natalie read through it and responded with her acceptance and confirmation of their visit. She was meeting with him in two days. This gave her sufficient time to properly inform her fiancé. She was hardly prepared to disclose such news to Philip, but she had no other choice. There was no doubt that at some point she would have to make a decision and it terrified her. She wondered if fate had brought her back to England to fulfill her life's purpose, albeit to the one man she swore would be her husband. Would he understand, or would she be forced to choose between her love for one man or country.

Philip was on his mobile when Natalie entered the guest room. He seemed upset and she wondered what was wrong. Seeing that he was occupied, she turns to leave but he called after her and signaled for her to wait. A few moments later he got off the phone and turned to face her. They stared at each other without saying a word and as she was about to speak he brought his index finger to his lips to signal her silence. It's been four weeks since his accident but it felt more like a decade since they had a real conversation. He removed his shirt and Natalie gazed at his handsome features; his blond hair was ruffled and he was beginning to grow a short beard. She's never seen a beard on him and she liked it. Unable to resist him any longer she walked toward him and cupped his face with both hands. Without saying a word to each other, she reached for his lips, kissing him affectionately.

They lay in bed staring at each other. There were tears in his eyes as he whispered.

"I have to go."

She gazes at him, her eyes widened as she searched his face for answers. She thought he needed help getting to the bathroom.

"Oh, okay let me help you," she said, slipping on her robe. Realizing what she'd thought, he chuckled.

"Honey, I meant home, to the States."

Unsure what that meant, she stares at him more seriously.

"You're leaving? What do you mean?" She said becoming more upset with each question.

"My Aunt Becky has suffered a stroke and it has left her unable to speak. I almost lost her. I've also spoken to Eddie, my business partner. He needs me home to sign off on some new contracts for the company." Although she never met Phil's aunt, she knew how much she meant to him. Her heart ached seeing him so distraught.

"Are you planning on going alone?"

He looks at her without responding. He didn't have an answer for her.

"Philip, are you planning on going alone?" She probed, her eyes searching for answers. He wanted to tell her that he'd read the letter that Princess Annie had written to her and believes that she needed some time to think things through, but didn't.

"It'll only be for two weeks, I promise."

"I can't let you go alone, and besides you still need looking after. Dr. Jefferies said that you may at times feel confused for short periods."

He assured her that he will follow up with his Primary Care Physician back home and that he needed to leave after the weekend. After a long conversation, he'd convince her that it was necessary for him to go alone. That was only a few days away and for some reason, the idea of Philip leaving terrified her, but she understood. Everything between them had happened within a very short time and as much as they love each other, she saw this as an opportunity for them to think things through. It was only for two weeks but she knew that she would miss him terribly.

Five days later, Philip boarded British Airways. Her parents were surprised about his sudden travel plans, but understood. She was thankful that her mum had accompanied her to Heathrow to see Philip off. It was difficult seeing him leave and she wondered if it was fate too that was setting the stage to lead her to her destined purpose. Philip disagrees with fate and doesn't see things through her eyes. She had shared some of her fears with him but he only shrugged them off. He believes that everything was based on the decisions we make and nothing more. She had argued with him of the possibility that the decisions we make are predestined and unavoidable. He poked fun at her and accused her of worrying too much and maybe, just maybe he was right. He didn't understand her fears and it took all of her strength to not disclose the details of Princess Annie's letter to him for fear of him not returning to her. As Philip's flight left Heathrow on schedule her mom embraced her tightly. She told her that Philip would be back before she knows it. Unknown to her family, she is the preordained Princess of Edinburgh and her engagement to Philip could decide the fate of England's Monarchy. It's a burden she's carry since reading the letter a few weeks before. The burden to decide on her own was almost unbearable and she felt obligated to share her powerful secret with her mother. As they drove back to the Manor, Lisa glanced over at her daughter often. Her beautiful face was overcome with emotion like when it's about to rain. She wonders what else was troubling her but she didn't pry. As a child Natalie always came to her or phoned her when she was faced with a crossroad. She's now an adult and needs her privacy, even when this means ignoring her daughter's pain, a task almost too difficult to bear.

William stared at the stack of fliers he'd collected of real-estate properties for sale around Thornton Heath still sitting on the table untouched. He wondered if Richard had changed his mind about purchasing a new home. He hadn't mentioned anything since they'd discussed it two weeks ago and he thought that maybe it was just a spur of the moment idea that faded. The eight years that he's been employed at the Manor, he's become much more than Richard's Butler; he was also a close friend and knew when it was time to have another casual discussion with his friend and employer. Lisa entered the kitchen and poured herself some of William's fine English tea. She then sat at the dining table flipping through the pages of the Croydon Guardian. She was surprised to see a short article regarding Richard's Pub on page two of the Guardian. As she read through the article, she was even more surprised to learn of the series of lawsuits that had been filed against the pub, all of which has been thrown out by the Court on grounds of insufficient evidence. She wondered why he hadn't mentioned this to her. William came into the kitchen and was almost startled to see Lisa.

"Good morning Lisa, I didn't know you were here or I would have your breakfast ready."

"Thank you William, but you don't have to worry about me, I'm not Royalty, at least not yet," she joked.

He giggled at her remark.

"Well, remember if you're in my company, you're nothing short of Royalty," he assured. Lisa stood up and bowed at him mockingly and the two engulfed in laughter.

"Well, well, well, Richard said entering the kitchen sharply dressed in a navy blue tux, soft pink shirt and University striped tie.

"Love that tie, Richard. I don't remember purchasing this one."

"It was a gift from Natalie on my thirty-ninth birthday."

"This young lady sure has excellent taste for her father," Lisa said, staring at him seductively.

"I have to agree," William said, pouring Richard a cup of his favorite black tea.

"I'm afraid I'm running late folks; I have a meeting with an interested buyer in less than an hour."

"Buyer, what's for sale?" William asked as both him and Lisa stares at him curiously.

"The Pub, I've finally had it with the public and I put it up for sale," he said sipping on his tea.

"William I knew that you would try talking me out of it. It's the reason I didn't discuss it with anyone."

Before anyone else could say another word, he wrapped a harsh brown in a paper towel. He handed Lisa a pink envelope and hurried out the front door.

"But Richard," William called after him.

"I'll be back in time for lunch," he called and sped out of the driveway.

After Breakfast, Lisa and William chat for a while. He shared with her some of the exciting events that had taken place at the Manor. To Lisa it was like listening to something out of a Novel. She had no idea that Princess Annie had visited the Manor and she wanted to know more about Natalie and Richard's relationship with the Royals. As she listened to William, she realized that she's learned more in a single hour than she could ever be prepared for. Her heart raced as William share with her the details of Natalie and Prince Ethan's tenth birthday, how the kiss they shared sparked rumors throughout the United Kingdom.

"They were born on the same day?"

"You've got to be kidding me?"

"I kid you not," William laughed. Lisa stares at William suspiciously, as he smiles, while engaging her in what some would consider a young woman's fairytale. As she listened, she realized that this was likely the reason her daughter appeared so divided and distraught lately. Learning of Natalie's recent visit to the Palace Manor created new concerns, due to the rumors surrounding the mysterious death of Princess Annie and her husband Prince Philip.

"William, if you don't mind my asking, considering everything, how likely is the chance that my daughter becomes the future Princess?" William refilled Lisa's cup with tea and sat across from her. Natalie was not aware of it but William knew of Princess Annie's Royal Decree-a document she personally wrote, signed and sealed in the presence of Richard and her husband Philip, requesting that Natalie weds her son to make him eligible to be her successor to the throne. Lisa was in utter shock as the Butler discloses highly confidential information to her regarding her daughter's future.

Chapter 21

Natalie awoke to the sound of Cassie barking through the window overlooking her garden.

"Cassie, what is it girl?" She stopped barking for a while then looked over at Natalie. She wagged her tail for a moment and then resumed grumbling and barking. As Natalie climbed out of bed to see what Cassie was fussing about, she felt a mild headache and her eyes were still sore from crying the night before.

"What did you see out their girl?"

Natalie looks out of the window in time to see the blond mane horse having a drink from her garden pond.

"Well, what do we have here? She's been running away from me for years, but one thing's certain, she couldn't stay away from my pond," she said, mesmerized by the beauty of the majestic creature. She's loved this horse at first sight and have hoped that someday she could be hers. Yet, she'd never come this close before and she took it to be a sign. Natalie warned Cassie to be silent. As she opened the garden gate, the horse looked up at her and took a few steps back.

"Hi there, I see that you found me, again," she called. At the sound of her voice, the horse stared at her with her ears pointed up. To Natalie's surprise, she began to slowly approach.

Cassie, still looking out from the window upstairs resumed barking and Natalie motioned for her silence. As the horse approached, she didn't stop until she was only a few inches away from her. As if drawn to her she lowers her head and sniffed Natalie's hair. She could hardly believe it; the horse seems to trust her. She's showed up at a time when Natalie was in great distress and its comforting presence restored her faith. Still in disbelief that this amazing creature was standing in front of her, she reached out her hands and touched her gently. "Who *are you, really*," she whispered. Then someone opened the gate and the creaking sound startled her. The horse ran off but this time she didn't disappear into the wooded area. She just stared at Natalie from a distance.

William approached cautiously.

"Who was that? My goodness I don't remember the last time I'd seen a more beautiful creature."

"Hi Will, it's the horse I always wanted you to catch for me, remember?"

"It can't be, she came so close, at first I thought I was imagining things. I wonder what brought her by," Natalie told William she thought that it was a sign, due to her pending meeting with Prince Ethan. As they were returning from her garden, Lisa was just returning from a shopping errand. She stepped out of the car in style, dressed in a flowing white summer dress and a broad brimmed white hat carrying several bags.

"Mum, you look fantastic; when did you learn to drive?"

"Hi sweetheart, I think you'd better hurry and get dressed. Remember that today we're having that going away party for Maureen. I've seen her and other couples taking photos near Trafalgar Square and I'm sure they'll be here shortly."

"But mum they are not due here till next Thursday." Then she realized that Maureen's party was scheduled on the same day as her meeting with the Prince. Lisa realized that something was wrong.

"What's the matter sweetheart, you look like you've seen a ghost?" Nathaniel York, the Palace chauffeur was coming to take her to the Palace in less than an hour.

"Mum, I have a very important appointment today."

"Certainly darling you'll have to reschedule it. Today is Maureen's party and our guests are due here any minute."

"But I can't, it's with the Prince."

Lisa's eyes widened.

"Lisa, well now you look like you've seen a ghost," William said, observing how lovely she looked in her evening dress. She's without a doubt a beautiful woman and he's enjoyed their chat earlier this morning. Lisa smiled at his remark but as her eyes drifted back to her daughter, her smile faded.

"The Prince, but surely you can't miss Maureen's party."

"Don't worry mother, the meeting is only an hour long, I'll be back in time for the party."

As they stood in the courtyard discussing Natalie's visit to the Palace, William used a remote to let two vehicles into the courtyard.

Five men dressed in chef's outfits came out of their cars carrying large food trays.

"Is this the Baldwin's residence?" One of them asked.

"You must be the party caterer. Yes, you're in the right place," William replied. "Right this way," he said, showing them to the kitchen.

"Thank you gentlemen," Lisa said. As they carried the supplies inside, Lisa notice one of the caterers smile at Natalie and whispered something to the others. She noticed how popular her daughter was becoming and wondered if news of her and Prince Ethan was beginning to get out. Lisa was still in disbelief when the Palace Chauffeur drove off with her daughter. Maureen's friends and relatives were beginning to arrive and Lisa felt alone and awkward as she greeted the guests. Richard arrived a short while later and Lisa felt slightly relieved. She hopes that her daughter returns sooner rather than later, as her outgoing personality would be a big help. As the guests continues to arrive, Richard's mother Annabelle arrived and she greeted the guests warmly; her high-pitched voice echoed throughout the Manor. Lisa was serving champagne when she notices Maureen staring at Annabelle furiously.

"Who invited her?" she said rudely. Thankfully Annabelle didn't hear her. Lisa was surprised by Maureen's reaction and wondered what the history between them was. Lisa also noticed a change in Maureen's attitude; she was much more pleasant when they met several years before.

As Lisa viewed the guestbook, of the sixty invitations sent out, there were more than a hundred guests in attendance and this made her uncomfortable.

"Lisa, there you are," William said, handing her a glass filled with lemonade.

"Are you feeling okay?" he asks.

"I'm perfect, I just didn't expect this many people."

William realizes that Lisa was not accustomed to these types of parties and he showed her to a less crowded area where they could sit for a while. Just then Richard announced that everyone should gather in the courtyard.

"What in the world for?" Annabelle replied and soft laughter followed. They were all familiar with her charming sense of humor.

"Annabelle," Lisa called. Annabelle's eyes widened at the sight of Lisa.

"Lisa, I had no idea that you were in London. My goodness you look lovely."

"I can say the same," Lisa said smiling.

"Where is my granddaughter and her fiancé?" Annabelle asked, looking around the room.

"Philip flew back to the States a few days ago to take care of some business and Natalie is at the Palace Manor. She has an appointment with Prince Ethan," Lisa said in a hushed voice. Annabelle's eyes widened in amazement.

"The Palace, my granddaughter is at the Palace Manor?" Let's have a chat after the party," Lisa replied.

As they strolled into the courtyard where everyone had gathered, Richard stood on the stair of the Manor overlooking the small crowd. He was sharply dressed in a Navy blue tux, and his long-sleeved blue shirt was folded neatly over his wrist. When everyone was gathered, Richard attached a small microphone on the collar of his shirt and tested it with his index finger. When he had everyone's attention, he called Maureen out of the crowd to stand next to him. He smiled at her as she approaches. Lisa notices that there was something comfortable about the way Maureen stood next to Richard.

"Look at her, she's in love with my son. Look at her, behaving as if he's about to propose," Annabelle said in a disapproving tone. Lisa glanced at her watch, it was past two in the evening and she realized that Natalie's been gone for over two hours now and wondered if she'll make the party. Richard made an admirable speech for Maureen, making mention of her loyalty the past seven years. At the end of his speech, Richard presented Maureen with a Chauffeur service achievement; a custom engraved plaque and an envelope she opened before the crowd containing a certificate engraved with a royal seal; the highest recognition that a Chauffeur could receive. The small crowd applauded loudly and others whistled and cheered.

As everyone clears the courtyard and returns to mingling, Lisa saw Richard speaking with an elderly woman and she thought it might be Maureen's mother. She approached them and introduced herself.

"Lisa!" Richard said, "You look lovely. Mrs. Taylor, I would like you to meet Lisa my...

"Lisa, I had no idea. You're as beautiful as I heard. How lovely to finally meet you."

Richard was surprised by Mrs. Taylor's response, and realized that Maureen must have mentioned Lisa to her. As Lisa spoke with Maureen's mom, one of the guests whispered something to Richard and he excused himself. Mrs. Taylor's caretaker had joined the conversation and a short while later Lisa excused herself to take a phone call from her daughter. She was calling to inform her that she wouldn't be back in time for the party. Lisa was a little disappointed but she understood. She knew that her daughter had some major decisions to make and she didn't want her presence in England to conflict with her daughter's life.

It was now six in the evening and some of the guests were beginning to leave. Richard hadn't seen his daughter all evening and searched the crowd to find her. He was certain that she would want to be here for Maureen. Then he spotted Lisa, she was on the balcony speaking with a gentleman he thought he'd recognized from a previous party. She looks happy and he wondered why he suddenly felt a glimmer of jealousy. Lisa noticed Richard staring at her and excused herself from the gentleman.

He smiles as she approaches.

"Hi there, I see that you're enjoying yourself," he said pretentiously.

"That was Ken, he said he's a friend of Maureen's brother-in-law and has been attending your parties for years."

"Hmm, I thought I recognized him," he said sipping on champagne. She looks like a movie star on the red carpet and he wanted to ask her about Natalie, but instead he asked her to dance. She was hardly surprised by the invitation and accepted. Without hesitation she joined Richard on the dance floor.

Maureen's sister watched as Richard waltz Lisa around the ballroom floor. As other couples were beginning to join in, she touched Maureen on the shoulder.

"Look Maureen, this should be your dance. Go ask Lisa if you can cut in," she said boldly.

"It's alright I'm not that great of a dancer anyways," Maureen admitted. After listening to her sister pick on her that she would be single the rest of her life, she was ready to leave, but instead she approached the dancing couple and tapped Richard on the shoulder.

"May I please cut in?" she asked kindly, trying to hide her flushed face.

"Maureen?" Richard said, looking at Lisa then back at Maureen.

"Sure, no problem, he's all yours. I'll go find William," Lisa said. Richard stares after Lisa as he waltzed Maureen across the floor. He wasn't sure how to react to Maureen's sudden interruption and admired how well Lisa handled it. He doesn't mind dancing with Maureen, however, he didn't want everyone else to think that there was something more between them.

"What are you thinking about?" she asked, staring at him seductively.

"I just wanted to thank you for the great party and the wonderful things you said on my behalf."

"Well, they are all true. You've been very loyal to our family and I'll be forever grateful to you. You've also been a wonderful friend to Natalie."

"By the way I haven't seen her all evening. Where is she?"

"Please don't mention this to anyone, but I found out from Lisa that she's at the Palace Manor. She wanted to be here for you but she had an appointment with Prince Ethan." Maureen's eyes widened.

"How's her fiancé handling the news?"

"He left for the States two days ago to handle some professional affairs with his company. I'm surprised Natalie didn't accompany him but they're adults. I'm sure they know what they're doing."

"Certainly," she responded and almost stepped on Richard's feet while glancing at her sister who's been signaling for her to place her hands on Richard's buttocks. She only laughed.

As they danced, a plump blond girl with dimples of about six years old dressed in a beautiful blue evening gown came up to Richard and asked in a loud voice.

"Mr. Baldwin sir, am I next on your dance list?!" Guests laughed at the rude yet adorable remark.

"Absolutely sweetheart, but remember, the next time you need to ask someone to dance, who's already dancing with someone else, the proper approach is, may I please cut in, okay sweetheart?" She smiled proudly at Richard as if he was proposing marriage. Richard kisses Maureen on the cheek and releases her. As he was about to ask the young lady her name, a brunette who appears in her late thirties came hurrying toward Richard and the child.

"Allie Elizabeth Rockefeller Osmond, please come here this instant!" her mother scolded. Allie looks at Richard with tears in her eyes.

"I only wanted to dance with the father of our future Princess," she cried. Richard was surprised at the remark and wondered how she knew that.

"It's alright sweetheart, please go to your mummy," he said, and winks at her. Richard smiled and shook his head as the child left with her mother. He wasn't sure but he thought that he might have heard her name somewhere before.

It was now late evening and almost everyone had already left except Richard's mother; Annabelle, Maureen, Maureen's sister Claire, her husband and another couple. They were all sitting on the balcony conversing with Lisa and William. The others didn't notice when Richard motioned for Lisa to join him. He wanted to see her privately. After excusing herself from the group she went to meet Richard. A gentle wind was blowing and it lifted Lisa's dress slightly above her knees. He led the way into the kitchen and turned off the lights. She had barely entered through the door when took her into his arms and kissed her passionately. This time she didn't resist, she sunk into his arms kissing him madly. A few moments later Maureen came looking for Richard. They were leaving and she wanted to thank him for a lovely evening. She also wanted to give him a letter she had written about their night together. As she was entering the Parlor, Lisa was on her way out to rejoin the others.

"Lisa, have you seen Richard?"

"You'll find him in the Parlor, dear," she replied. After thanking Richard, she handed him the letter. Lisa watched as they embraced each other.

As Maureen and her family were leaving, Natalie was returning from her trip to the Palace. She was relieved to be in time to see Maureen off. Surprised to see the Royal Chauffeur pulled into the courtyard, they all got out of their vehicles and took photographs of Natalie as she stepped out of the Limousine.

"I had no idea," Maureen's sister sneered.

"Well get used to it sweetheart, because you are looking at the future of England," Annabelle boasted.

196

"Maureen, I'm so happy you're still here. I have something for you, please wait, I'll be right back," she called excitedly. After thanking the Royal chauffeur, she ran up the stairs and returned carrying a large picture album.

"These are all the precious moments we've shared and I want you to have it." Then they held each other in a tight embrace, their eyes filled with tears.

"I love you Natalie. You're the closest I've ever come to having a daughter." And as she turned to leave...

"Maureen, you may not be my Chauffeur for now, but please don't be a stranger, I might need you," she admitted. They smiled and blew kisses at each other. After thanking Richard once more, the remaining guests drove out of the courtyard.

"I'm glad you made it sweetheart," Richard said.

"Me too dad," she said smiling. Annabelle cleared her throat as when in the presence of Royalty. They all had one thought in common; how her visit to the palace went?

Chapter 22

Prince Ethan woke early the following morning troubled by the news that Natalie had delivered to him the day before. She had left the letter that his mother had written with him. There was no denying that his mother had written the letter. He's recognized her hand writing the moment that she's removed the letter from the envelope. His mother had set the stage to ensure that he became the next British Monarch. But she's engaged to be married to an American and had told him the night before that she has no intentions of breaking her promise to Philip. He was troubled by her confession. She has never left his thoughts and for many years, he'd hoped that somehow they would cross paths again. As he glances at the letter sitting on the lamp stand, he noticed that it was stamped with the Royal Seal; an indication that the instructions within the letter must be obeyed. Natalie has argued that he doesn't love her and that he was the Prince and could easily find a wife. That may be the case but she's got something wrong; he loves her desperately and he knew that since their tenth birthday, when they shared their first kiss out on the Palace grounds. Then he thought that maybe he should warn her of the potential consequences of rejecting the words of his mother. But then he realizes that this would only push her further away. He knew that he had to see her again and this time he was going to visit her without warning.

As he rushes into the courtyard to find Nathaniel, he almost bumped into his grandmother who was on her way to find him.

"My goodness, aren't we in a hurry."

"Grandmother, I didn't see you."

"I was on my way to see you. I need to speak with you immediately. I've heard from one of the servants that you had a visitor."

"Maybe we can discuss it later, I have some urgent matters to see too," he said and hurries off. The Baroness knew that the Prince was hiding something and it troubles her. Her Grandson is now at the age where the public will begin to question his plans for the throne. She wondered if he remembered that it was custom that if he goes past his twenty-third birthday without marriage, title to the throne would be handed over to the person next in line. Ester opened the door to Ethan's room and noticed the envelope on the nightstand. She removed the letter and read through it thoroughly. Her worst fears were confirmed. Her heart races wild with fear.

"I knew it. I knew she was hiding something from me!" Ester said enraged. As she stormed out of his room, Ethan had remembered the letter and was returning to find it. He grew suspicious when he saw Ester coming out of his room and he wondered if she might have read the letter. He hurried into his quarters and removed the envelope. Suddenly, he realized that if news of this secret letter leaked to the public, it could endanger Lady Baldwin. He had to see her and he must do so quickly. As he entered the courtyard, the Palace Guards saluted him and he signaled for Nathaniel to pull the Limousine into the palace gates. After the Palace chauffeur and the Prince's bodyguard had entered the vehicle, the Royal chauffeur pulled out of the Palace yard onto the highway.

"Where too, your highness?" Ethan didn't respond; he only signaled for him to turn left onto Marden road; then Nathaniel realizes where they were headed.

"But sir, does she know that you're coming?" For a second time, Ethan refused to respond and for the first time since the passing of his parents five years before, he knew that something was deeply troubling the Duke of Edinburgh.

William was surprised to see the Royal chauffeur on the Manor a second time this week and quickly entered the code to let them into the gate. No sooner had they pulled into the driveway, the Prince let himself out and hurried toward the Manor. William stood on the stair and announced to everyone that they had Royal company. Shuffling could be heard throughout the Manor as everyone hurries to catch a glimpse of the Prince. William reached for the door knob with shaky hands to let the Prince in.

"Your Highness, to what do we owe this pleasant surprise," William said gently bowing his head.

"Master William, it's a pleasure to finally meet you, sir. Please tell me, is Lady Baldwin home. I must see her at once, it's rather urgent."

"Certainly sir, you are welcome to have a seat in the Parlor while I find her." The Prince nods as William hurries up the stairs. As he was about to knock on her door, Natalie came out of her bedroom half asleep and in her pajamas.

"What's all the commotion about?" she asked, yawning.

"Natalie, I'm afraid you'll have to hurry, his Majesty is here and wishes to see you. He said that it's urgent."

"He's what... I cannot... I can't... not... not like this..." she said nervously.

"Then I suggest you hurry, it seems urgent. I'll tell him you're on your way," he said hurrying off.

"William dear, I make the rules, remember?" she called in a sweet voice. He laughed then blew a kiss at her and continues down the stairs.

As she was about to return to her bedroom to prepare, she heard footsteps hurrying down the hallway. She peeked in time to see Annabelle disappear down the stairs.

"Oh no, this can't be good," she panicked. Annabelle enters the Parlor and greeted the Prince of Edinburgh, bowing her head gracefully.

"You're Richard's mother, Annabelle, rumor has it that you've recently wedded. May I extend my congratulations to you," he said politely.

"Well thank you, I am beyond honored," she replied. As she sat conversing with the Prince, Natalie entered the room beautifully adorned in a flowing blue, double layered evening gown trimmed in gold. The Prince's focus slowly shifted from Annabelle to Natalie standing in the doorway.

"Lady Baldwin, you look radiant," he said standing.

She blushes at his remark.

"Well thank you, your Highness, it's the best that I can do for now, the fact that you gave me such little time to prepare."

The Prince smiled at her mild rebuke. Just then Richard and Lisa joined them.

"Prince Ethan, what an unexpected surprise," Richard said, shaking the Prince's hand and introducing Lisa.

"I can see where Natalie got her beautiful looks from," he said complementing Lisa.

As the Prince was about to announce the reason for his visit, they were interrupted by the sound of commotion at the front entrance. Richard peeked out of the window in time to see reporters pulling into the gate which was accidentally left open. The Prince's bodyguard and Chauffeur tried to avoid their questions, but they were very determined to gather the reasons for the Prince's sudden visit to the Baldwin's.

"Is the Prince considering Richard's daughter?"

"Is it true she's engaged to an American name Philip?"

"Why did Philip return to the States?"

"Is the Prince here to propose?

"Is it okay if we speak with Natalie?"

Nathaniel and the Prince's bodyguard simply reply with the usual "no comment," as the press continues to probe them for answers. Annabelle loves the attention of the press and didn't waste time as she hurries out front in the hopes of spreading the word of the Prince's interest in her beautiful granddaughter. One reporter notices her approaching and ran ahead to meet her.

As they all became distracted by the press, Prince Ethan took Natalie into another room in the manor and spoke with her privately.

"What are you doing here, your Majesty?"

"Please, it's just Ethan," he said kindly. Then before she said another word, he kisses her affectionately. Then realizing she pulled away from him.

"Ethan, I'm engaged to be married."

"But I love you. We love each other. I've known that for a long time. Don't you remember the promise we made to each other that day in the garden?"

She nods.

"You were meant to be my wife. Every generation of my family for centuries would agree that you were first engaged to me. Even at such a gentle age," he pleaded.

"But why am I just learning of this arrangement," she asked, taking a seat. The Prince sat beside her.

"Almost twelve years ago, when you promised to marry me, I told my mother. I suppose she took us seriously."

"But we were only children, how could they have taken us seriously?"

The Prince smiled at how beautiful she appears, even when questioning life.

"It is customary that, regardless of how old a person is when they make a promise to a member of the Royal family, the promise is written in stone and must be carried out."

Realizing what this meant she sat quietly for a moment fiddling Philip's engagement ring on her finger. Then she looks up at him.

"I wished I'd known; now I'll have to break an American's heart," she said staring at the engagement ring. He almost giggled at the remark but instead he took her hands in his. She knows that the Prince loves her by the way he always looks at her.

"Do you need some time to think about it?" he asked. She nodded yes and he waited in the hallway. A few moments later she came out of the Parlor.

"The truth is that I do love you Ethan and I accept the responsibilities that's been bestowed…"

Before she had finished her statement, the Prince took her in his arms and kissed her savagely.

"Please don't ever scare me like that again, Princess," he teased.

"Do you know what this means?" he asked.

"You are now and have since been the Princess of Edinburgh. You are also now under the protection of England and the Palace Manor is now your home."

Her eyes simultaneously widened with fear and excitement. But he understood the suddenness of the news and he gave her all the time she needed to prepare for her transition.

"A Proper engagement party will be held at the Royal ballroom, at Edinburgh Palace; the home of my future Queen. After my departure, seven Royal guards will be sent to your current residence to ensure your safety, until your transition to Royalty, Majesty," he said smiling proudly. She smiled at his modesty.

"This will take some getting used to," she said, as they headed back to meet the others. The press was still creating a stir and at the sight of Prince Ethan exiting the Baldwin's residence, they tried to approach him, but his bodyguard escorted him safely to his vehicle and they drove away from the Baldwin's residence, uninterrupted.

Natalie's grandmother rushed to her side.

"What was that all about darling?" Annabelle asked impatiently. Without much explaining Natalie took her hands and spoke softly.

"Well, I have good news and some not so great news. Which would you like to hear first?"

"Well, how about the not so great news first, because I'm sure we would all appreciate something lovely to look forward to," Annabelle said.

"Um, how do I say this... as I've just learned, it appears that my engagement to Philip has been voided from the moment it occurred."

"And the great news?" Annabelle asked.

"Apparently, when I was only ten, the Prince and I had made a promise to each other. I presumed that we were only toying around. However, when a promise is made to a member of the Royal family, this promise is legally written in stone. Therefore, from the time I was only ten, I've been legally engaged to be married to the Prince of Edinburg," she said, a smile slowly forming on her face.

"Well, well, well," Annabelle said, embracing her granddaughter. She then took her fantastic discovery to the press. As Annabelle announced the news of her granddaughter's engagement to the Prince... Lisa, who was chatting with one of the reporters, went to find her daughter.

"How marvelous, but what about your engagement to Philip?" Lisa asked.

"I'm sorry mother, I will explain later."

"It's okay sweetheart, this is beyond words," she said, feeling concerned for her only daughter. Puzzled by what all this means, Lisa tries to find Richard and William who seems to have suddenly disappeared. Then she noticed the gate to the back entrance slightly open. As she entered the gate she saw Richard and William having what seemed like a very discreet conversation. The gate creaked behind her and both men glanced at her at the same time.

"Lisa," Richard called.

"Richard, William, what are you up too? Haven't you heard?"

"Heard what?"

"Your daughter is engaged to be married to the Prince of Edinburgh." Both men glanced at each other.

"Wonderful, it's about time. Where is she now," he asked.

"Hiding in her bedroom!" Lisa scolded.

"Richard, please tell me that you didn't know about this all along?" Realizing that he's kept this information from her, she walks away.

"Lisa please, don't say a word to our daughter. I will speak to her at a more opportune time," Richard called.

"Why not?"

"Please, just take my word for it, the information you just learned has placed the throne of England at risk," he warned. She shook her head and went to find Annabelle.

An hour later, when the Press had finally left, the Royal chauffeur pulled into the gate and seven Royal guards entered the courtyard. The Prince had also returned to ensure that the Royal foot guards were properly situated around the manor. Both women watched from the balcony as Richard and the Prince discusses his Fiancé's security protocol. Surprised by the sudden changes taking place around the Manor, Lisa suddenly missed the quietness of her home in Grenada and the golden sunrise and sunsets that graced the sky each day.

"Well, this will take some getting used to," Annabelle beamed. Suddenly our quiet little Manor has become the center of worldwide media coverage."

"I think you're enjoying it Annabelle," Lisa laughed.

"So when are you going to marry my son Lisa? I swear each time he looks at you, the sun stands still," she said observing her lovely attire. Lisa blushed at the remark. Just then Natalie joins them on the Balcony. As she approaches, her mother and grandmother stood with their hands folded behind their backs and bowed gracefully.

"Mother, Grandmother, don't be silly, it's just me and I won't change for anything, not even the Prince," she said, folding her hands. Annabelle laughed at her stubbornness.

"You're your father's daughter," Anabelle said embracing her lovingly.

"Stubborn or not darling you're going to have to get used to it," her mother said proudly.

"Indeed, every young lady in this province would love to be you," Anabelle reminded her.

"William, where are you?" she called hurrying away from the women.

"I wonder what she'll do without William?" her mother chuckled.

Chapter 23

It's been over a week since Philip arrived in the States and couldn't help feeling relieved. He'd taken a direct flight from London Heathrow to Detroit Metro and was spending the week with his aunt and uncle. When he arrived, his Aunt Becky was already released from the hospital a few days before and was resting comfortably. Philip wasted no time in relieving his uncle from the duties of caring for his aunt. As he sat feeding her, her favorite Thai soup, he told her all about Natalie; the woman who captivated his heart, that he almost forgot how to find his way home. She only listened and smiled because she was left unable to speak from the life threatening stroke she'd suffered, two weeks before. She motioned for him to bring her a pen and some paper. She wrote…

"Have you contacted her since you arrived?" He read the note then stood up and walked across the room. Her eyes followed him as he walked in circles.

"I haven't, not yet…." His aunt began writing again and then handed him another note.

"Why in the world not?" he glanced in her direction.

"She's… she's… she doesn't know that I know, but she's supposed to be with someone else mom," he said, feeling upset. The last time he stuttered and called her mom was when he was nineteen and was thinking of joining the Army and needed her approval. She wondered what would make him think that and she wrote him another note.

As she placed the note in his hand, they heard a vehicle pulled into the driveway. It was his cousin Aaron and his wife Aimee.

"It's Aaron and Aimee," Philip said peeking through the window overlooking the driveway. His aunt's eyes lit up at the news. He slipped the note in his pocket and went out front to greet his cousin. They grew up like brothers and were inseparable as kids. It's been almost two years since he'd last seen Aaron and he suddenly wished that Natalie was with him. At the sight of Philip, Aaron embraced him then lifted him up over his shoulders like a sack of potatoes.

"Philip, I can't believe it's you, " he said returning him to his feet.

"Aaron, dude, you look awesome. Last time I saw you, you were quite the chub, what happened?" Aimee laughed at the expression.

"Let's just say, when I met my father-in-law, I knew I had to drop the pounds or have my butt kicked. The dude is like eighty and has a six pack and arms like tree trunks." They all laughed.

"And you must be Aimee, you're beautiful, welcome to the family," Philip said embracing her.

"Thank you," she responded happily.

"Oh by the way, where's dad?"

"He did a last minute errand to the store. I think he's planning a barbecue."

"That's good, he sounds like he's in good spirits," Aimee said. They were about to grab their things from the trunk....

"Don't worry about it folks, I'll get your bags, don't keep mom waiting. It's good to see you Philip; we have some catching up to do."

"You better believe it," he called.

Philip was enjoying the weekend with his family. His Aunt Becky was feeling much better and insisted that she join them in the backyard to watch her husband make barbeque. It was a beautiful evening out and although summer was still four weeks away, it still felt like spring outside. Becky glanced around at her flower pots. Ben's been keeping up with the watering and everything was still in full bloom. She'd been inside for over a week and the warm sun and fresh air breathe life into her. She looked at her family and smiled. They were all home and it was perfect. As they sat enjoying the dessert that Aimee had brought from home, Aaron stared at the television overlooking the entertainment room and his gaze shifted to Philip.

"Hey Phil, why are you on British news?"

"Nice one Aaron," his dad replied.

"No, I'm serious, there's Phil standing next to a very beautiful woman in front of what looks like an English Manor." Philip smiled as they all stared at the television. They had learned of Philip's engagement to the woman who is the promised wife of Prince Ethan, heir of England's throne.

"You were in London? How did you manage to get engage to a Princess?" Aaron joked. They were all looking to him for answers and he was in no mood for Aaron's sarcasm nor was he ready to discuss this with them. He stared at them and without saying a word, he brought a plate of fruit to his aunt and began feeding it to her.

"That sounds exciting Philip, tell us about it!" Aimee beamed.

"Yes Phil, when are you going back for your Princess?"

"Shut up Aaron! You've never taken anyone serious in your whole damn life!" he yelled. Then remembering his aunt's condition, he kissed her on the forehead and apologized.

"Are you alright son?" His uncle asked, looking at him with concern. "We all saw you over the news, are you in some kind of trouble?"

"I'm fine Uncle Ben, I'm not in any trouble. I don't feel that this is the best time to discuss this. I'll tell you about it at a better time. I'm leaving for California in a few days and I'll discuss it before then," he promised.

Two days later Philip boarded his flight to California. He smiled and shook his head as he remembered the funny expressions on his cousin's face as he told them about his amazing experience meeting Natalie. Despite Aaron's constant humor, he had made a good point when he said that he shouldn't give up on Natalie. They all agreed with his decision to remain in California while she decides her future.

It was a six-hour flight from Detroit Metro to California and it was already after midnight when his flight landed at LAX. It was over an hour's drive to Temecula and he had reserve a hotel room at the Hilton for the night. After checking into his room, he ordered dinner and looked at his mobile to see if Natalie had called, but his battery had died. He placed his phone on the charger for a few minutes and when he finally turned it on, there were sixteen missed calls, eleven of which was from Natalie and the rest was from Aaron and his uncle Ben. Fearing that it might have been about his aunt he returns their call immediately. His uncle answered...

"Philip, oh thank goodness, it's your aunt, she's suffered another stroke and they're not sure if she'll make it," he cried.

"No, this can't be," he cried. "I'm on my way, I'll catch another flight and I'll be there by morning."

"No son, don't worry, you must be exhausted, try to get some rest."

"How's she dad?"

"I'm not sure, no word yet, but I'll call you as soon as I do."

"Dad, are you sure?"

"Absolutely, try to get some rest and I'll call you as soon as I can," he said, his voice breaking.

"Okay Dad, I love you."

"I love you too Son." All traces of sleep had left him as he paced restlessly across his hotel suite. As he thought of Natalie, there was a knock on his door. It was room service. After tipping the attendant, he placed his dinner on the small dining table in the corner of the room. It's been a long time since he'd dined alone and it felt strange. He reached for his mobile to phone Natalie but remembered the time difference. A feeling of frustration came over him and he tossed his phone across the bed.

"Oh screw it!" he said, retrieving the phone. He needed to hear her voice and he was going to wake her up. He dialed the number to the manor and Lisa answered

"Hello Baldwin's residence. Philip is that you?"

"Hi Lisa, yes it's Philip, sorry to be phoning so late."

"It's no trouble at all, we're all up anyway. Natalie's grandma is here and she's invited over a few friends. How are you and how's your Aunty? Oh no, I'm so very sorry to hear that. Alright then, nice hearing from you Philip, I'll get Natalie." There was a short silence and a little while later Natalie was on the phone. She sounded wide awake.

"Philip, where have you been?"

"I swore that I'd be waking you up," he laughed.

"Not at all, it's very busy here at the Manor and Grandma is trying to get me drunk, since the engagement was made public," she laughed.

"Really?" he laughed. He didn't realize that she was discussing her engagement to the Prince.

"Sorry to hear but it sounds like you're having fun."

"Philip, I'm sorry but it was the only way to make the time go by quickly."

"No worries, you're forgiven," he joked. After updating her on his aunt's condition, she was heartbroken for him.

"I'm so sorry Philip, please give her my love and take as long as you need." She hesitated to ask... "Would you be able to make it back next week?" There was a short silence before he responded.

"I'm not sure babe." She wanted to explain what had happened in his absence, but it wasn't the time. They spoke for almost an hour before they finally hung up. She'd made him laugh and he was feeling much better.

He already missed her terribly and wondered if he was wrong about remaining in California. He couldn't bring himself to tell her his plans. He knew it was the only way that she would be able to see clearly, to make an informed decision about her future. He was exhausted as he looked at his dinner sitting alone on the table. He'd lost his appetite and moments later he fell asleep.

Philip woke suddenly to a very annoying, buzzing sound. It was only eight thirty in the morning and he wasn't checking out of the Hilton till noon. He realized that he must have set the alarm too early and after resetting the correct time, he went back to bed. A short while later his phone buzzed again. This time it was his uncle Ben and he sounded as though he'd been crying. Then he revealed to Philip that his Aunt had passed away this morning. Not even her previous two infarctions could have prepared him for this moment. She was gone. It was like losing his mother all over again and it hit him as an unexpected storm. After he got off the phone with his uncle, he thought of calling Natalie but he realized that she would want to fly out to be with him and he changed his mind. She had important decisions to make and he didn't want anything to interrupt her. He had to weather his feeling of loss alone for now. Tears ran down his face as he packed his bags for the drive to Temecula. Suddenly he didn't feel like driving himself home and he phoned his business partner Eddie to meet him at the Hilton. He was still exhausted from catching up with the Michigan and London time differences and had called the hotel front desk to arrange for another night.

Philip spent the day indoors thinking about his Aunt who was in every way, his mother. His friends had often mentioned how strongly she resembled his mom. They were born only a year apart and people had often mistaken the sisters for twins. Others would often say that Becky and Uncle Ben are the type of parents that could easily raise an entire village of well-rounded children.

Eddie arrived at the Hilton just before noon. It seemed like a decade since their last meeting and he was relieved to see his Partner. He greeted Philip with a firm handshake and a tap on the shoulder. As they drove home, Eddie filled him in on the company's status and the new contracts that were awaiting his approval and signature. Philip was very pleased by the news. The company had lost several contracts the past year and they had to lay off a few employees. This was definitely going to help turn things around.

"Do you think we'll be able to rehire some of our layoffs?"

"Oh definitely, we should be able to rehire all the layoffs, if they're available and we might have to hire a few more."

"Eddie, that's fantastic news!"

"I'm afraid you're right my friend," Eddie replied.

About an hour later Eddie pulled into Philip's driveway.

"Thanks Eddie."

"As always Mr. Lane, it's a pleasure." Eddie wanted to ask him about Natalie but he wanted to keep things business.

"My condolences to you Phil, I know how much you loved your Aunt."

"Thanks Eddie." As Eddie was about to pull out of the driveway he rolled down his window.

"Philip, if it's okay, I can forward the contracts to your email."

"That's okay Eddie, it's been a while since I've seen the office. I'll come by in the morning."

"Okay boss," Eddie said, trying to cheer him up.

"You know I don't like to be called that," Philip laughed.

He waved as Eddie sped off.

From the moment he entered his home, memories of Natalie flooded his thoughts. He could almost hear echoes of her beautiful laughter filling the hallways, as if the past few months were nothing but a dream. Would she be able to handle the news of his decision? Would she choose him and if not, was he prepared to move on without her? Everything about her was fitting for the role of a leader. She's a fine lady who doesn't need to be endowed in elegant apparel for one to notice her Royal appeal. She's a Princess in every sense of the word and one day soon, a Queen; one that would transform the face of England.

As Philip thought of these things, there was a gentle knock on his front door. He peeked through a window and couldn't see anything but the top of someone's head.

"Who is it?" He asked, sounding annoyed.

"It's me Paul," the person called.

"I don't know anyone by that name."

"We were classmates at University of California Los Angeles," he answered. As Philip swung the door open, he was greeted by a mob of reporters and cameras. A group of reporters scrambled up the stairs asking him multiple questions.

"Is Natalie with you?"

"Is it true you're engaged to the woman promised to be the wife of Prince Ethan; the heir of the British throne?"

"Is she really going to choose to be with you?"

"I didn't know that she had an arrangement with the Royal family, neither did she!" he yelled. He didn't like that they were trying to make him appear foolish as if he didn't have a chance and it angered him.

"I proposed to her first and she said yes, the rest of it is none of your damn business," he yelled and shut the door behind him. He thought he'd left all that attention in London and realized he'd be better off staying indoors until his trip to Michigan in two days. He pulled his luggage into his master suite, flopped on his bed and exhaled loudly. He realized Eddie was right and was about to put in a call to him when his phone rang. The caller ID said it was Eddie. Philip sat up and placed his phone on speaker. When he answered his Partner was laughing hysterically.

"I tried to tell you. They've been showing up at your office every day last week searching for you."

"Who are you talking about?" Philip asked.

"The reporters..." Eddie laughed.

"You know about the reporters; why didn't you warn me."

"C'mon Phil, everyone likes a little attention; I thought you'd enjoy it."

"No Eddie, you like attention, I don't."

"Don't worry, it's good for business. That's free advertising; hopefully we won't have to pay for business advertising for the next few years," he teased. Philip laughed at the idea.

"Eddie, you can forget it. that's not good for business, maybe for you, but not for me. Please forward the contracts to my email. I'll take care of them by tomorrow."

"Will do Boss. Also, our response to the contracts are due next week, so there's no rush."

"Thanks Eddie."

Before getting off the phone, Eddie asked for Philip's permission to make flight arrangements for the employees who offered to attend his Aunt's memorial. Philip's heart was moved by the support of his employees. As he thought of the sudden death of his aunt, he knew his life will forever be changed.

Chapter 24

Since her conversation with Philip the night before, she's hardly slept. After everything they've shared, how was she going to break the news to him that their engagement was over before it even occurred? All of England knew of her engagement to Prince Ethan and she knows that it's only a matter of time before Philip learns. She didn't want him to discover this from the media and there was very little time left which terrified her. As she searched her heart for answers, she remembered her friend, Princess Annie. Most women would consider her extremely fortunate. Yet one thing was certain; all roads led to the throne and her visions, even fate had already decided her future. As she contemplated these life changing thoughts, there was a knock on her door. It was her mother asking her to join her for tea.

"It's rather early mother."

"Early to bed, early to rise, makes one healthy, wealthy, and wise," Lisa responded.

"I don't want any of those except my health," she laughed.

"Well, it's too late my dear, you've always been a modest child and you are worthy," she called, her voice fading as she walked away. A few moments later she joined her mother in the kitchen.

"Where's William?"

"He has some personal business to tend to and has asked Richard for the morning off. He'll be here later today," her mother said, placing a cup of lavender tea on a saucer in front of her.

"Thank you mother, but I miss William," she teased. Her mother smiled and sat next to her.

"I have to admit that it's never been this quiet around here in months," Natalie said. Just then a car drove up to the gate.

"Oops, I think I might have spoken too quickly," she laughed.

"It's probably someone from the press."

"No, it looks like it might be Danica, I wonder what she wants," Natalie said hurrying toward the door. As she opened the door to the main entrance, the guards stood upright to acknowledge her. She then informed them that the visitor was a good friend and they gave the order to open the gate. As Danica approached the entrance of the manor, at the sight of the guards, she appeared uncomfortable. Natalie encouraged her to hurry and she showed her to the kitchen.

"Hi Danica, I want you to meet my mum Lisa."

"Hello, pleasure to meet you. What's happening?" She asked.

"Someone hasn't been watching the news," Lisa laughed.

"You are seated in the presence of Royalty dear. You're looking at England's next Princess," Lisa said, serving her a cup of tea. Danica, who was seated, stood up slowly.

"Wow, you're kidding right?" she said appearing nervous. Realizing that Lisa was serious, Danica glanced repeatedly at the Royal Guards through the window, then she looked at Natalie.

"I believe that I was supposed to show you courtesy majesty?" she said, still unsure.

"Oh please, don't," Natalie assured her.

"When did all this happen?" she asked, appearing slightly relieved. There was something about her tone that Lisa disliked but she overlooked it.

"I know you're probably wondering why I'm here," she smiled looking up from her tea. She reached and removed something from her backpack.

"This here is my mum's final wish. I beg your pardon, but she was Richard's girlfriend who passed away recently. It's kind of a long story but mum had made a final request to Natalie, Richard and myself to spread...her ashes on the edge of the River Thames," she said tearing up.

"I'm terribly sorry for your loss, is there anything I can do?" Lisa asked, handing her a box of napkins. Richard had mentioned your mum to me briefly" Lisa said.

"How very kind of you both, after the way I've behaved toward you, Natalie."

"Don't worry about it, Danni. I'm glad you came back so that we got the chance to reconcile before my transition. Danica, I've never had the chance to ask you your age?" Natalie smiled and her eyes narrowed by how little she knew Danica.

"I just took twenty-two," she said, wiping tears from her eyes.

"You're the same age as my daughter," Lisa smiled. Natalie then explained to Danica that she had to get the Prince's permission to accompany her and Richard to the Thames River. She assured her that if she can't be there, that her mother would be happy to go on her behalf.

"I certainly hope that I can keep my promise to your mum. I only knew her for a short time but I would like to believe that she was a wonderful person."

"Thank you, this means a lot to me, majesty," she replied in a sad yet friendly manner. As they spoke, Richard pulled into the courtyard.

"Alright then, may I please be excused, I need to get on the phone with Ethan," Natalie said standing. Danica smiled.

"I can hardly believe that I'm looking at the future of England," she beamed.

"Does this mean that I'm Royalty too since Richard almost became my stepdad?" Lisa smiled.

Richard overheard her question and responded.

"Absolutely, keep my daughter close and you might very well be. I see you've met Lisa, Natalie's mother. Are we all ready for a splash in the Thames?"

"A splash, Richard, that's not very funny," Lisa said, thinking of Danica.

"This is an emotional time for you both I would think," she scolded him. Danica agreed with Lisa. She'd often wondered if Richard truly loved her mother, but now it was really beginning to show.

"Don't bother, I'll go alone," Danica said, leaving.

"Wait, Danica please I didn't mean it," Richard said following her.

"If you don't mind I'd love to accompany you," he pleaded.

"So would I," Lisa said. She then turned to face them and shook her head in approval.

"Alright then, but I suggest we leave now," she said, sounding a little less upset. Lisa then embraced her. She almost pulled away but unable to resist, she sunk in Lisa's arms and cried. Richard admired how well Lisa responded to Danica. Not only was she beautiful, but caring and his heart ached to be with her.

"I can accompany you Danica," Natalie said happily.

"That's great!" Danica said, smiling again. She was feeling a bit better and was comforted by their unexpected affection.

A short while later Nathaniel, the Royal chauffeur pulled into the courtyard.

"The Royal Chauffeur?!" Danica beamed.

"Well my friend, today you get to enjoy a bit of the Royal treatment," Natalie said motioning for her to enter the Limo. After everyone was seated, Natalie's bodyguard opened the door and helped her into the vehicle. He then shut the door behind her.

"All settled in, Majesty?" asked Nathaniel looking over at his guests.

"He's cute," Danica said. At that, everyone broke into laughter. Nathaniel looked over his shoulder and winked at her.

A half an hour later they arrived at the Thames River. Natalie's bodyguard followed her closely and it made her slightly uncomfortable. She glanced over at him but he didn't make eye contact with her and she realized it was part of his duty. As they walked along the London Bridge overlooking the River Thames, Danica looked around and smiled. She knew that her mother would have truly appreciated the royal company. After reciting the Lord's Prayer, Natalie volunteered to sing the Christian hymn, "Old Rugged Cross." She sang beautifully bringing everyone to tears. Danica then removed the cover from the crystal urn and sprinkled her mother's ashes over the glimmering water. Lisa placed her hand on Danica's shoulder as they walked back to the parked Limo, where the chauffeur awaited. Everyone sat quietly as they drove through London. Natalie broke the silence by inviting Danica to join her and her parents for dinner and she happily accepted.

After Dinner, Richard and Lisa drove Danica back to her flat in Surrey. She'd seen camera men taking photos of them on the bridge earlier and she knew that there would be an article and photographs of her with the Royal family in the paper tomorrow, but she didn't mind. For the first time in forever, she felt a sense of peace. She still couldn't believe that she was treated so well, despite her mother's negative influence on the Baldwin's. As she waved to Richard and Lisa, she felt a sense of closure. Overall, she was thankful for how well she was treated and knew that this was not the end of her relationship with the Baldwin's.

Chapter 25

News of Prince Ethan's engagement to the daughter of England's most beloved Royal Guard spread like wildfire. Visitors and loyal supporters of Princess Annie flooded into England to show their support for the only surviving heir of England's throne. Many had feared and even doubted that the monarchy would continue, due to the Prince's delayed revelation of any romantic interests. Some had even speculated that he might not be interested in continuing tradition. While others thought that he may have feared the responsibilities and fatal sacrifices that monarchs and ancestors before him have endured. News of his engagement debunked all surmisation reawakening the joy that England once felt during the days of their most beloved monarchs. It was only three days until Lady Baldwin's transition to her new life at the Palace and the Prince wanted to be certain that every corner of Edinburgh Palace was ready to be occupied by a long awaited Princess.

Prince Ethan's grandmother, Baroness Ester and her married lover, Prime Minister Godfrey, has been away for over a week. Her plans were to spend some time at her country manor in Wales. However, news of her grandson's engagement to Richard's daughter has forced her to cut her trip short. Isabel and Jasmine, the servants who accompanied Ester to her manor, grew concerned as the Baroness grew more silent each day. They'd seen both her and Prime Minister Godfrey made numerous phone calls. They wondered what it was about. Suddenly, a thought entered Jasmine's mind causing her to shake with fear. She'd seen the Baroness on numerous occasions, entered into the late Princess Annie's room in secret and had tried on some of her royal apparel. Everything, including the death of Prince Ethan's Parents began to race through Jasmine's mind and it almost crippled her with fear. She feared Natalie's life was in grave danger and she had to get word to the Prince immediately.

Every mode of communication to the outside world was in the main room. Since the Baroness was already in bed, she would have to wait till morning to sneak into her quarters to get word to the Prince. She thought of going to the neighbor to use their telephone but she knew that would never work, because every person in these parts are loyal friends of the Baroness. When all lights were out, carrying an old telephone in one hand and a lit candle in the other, Jasmine searched around the dimly lit manor to find a phone outlet. As she tipped toed down the long dark hallway, she felt alone and thought of sharing her fears with Isabel. But Isabel, unlike all the other servants at the Palace, is very devoted to the Baroness. She was alone; the future of England may very well lay in her hands.

As she turned a dark corner, the light of the candle revealed an old outlet slightly covered with cobwebs. Sitting on the dusty floor, Jasmine placed the phone cord into the outlet and was happy to discover a dial tone. She was about to dial the number to the Palace Manor, when someone approached her from behind and covered her mouth. She fought and tried to pry the person's hairy hands away from her mouth, but it was too late. After taping her mouth shut, the stranger bound both her hands behind her back. She was then lifted up and carried a short distance and was placed in a dark room. Seconds later she heard the door being locked, leaving her trapped inside.

As she whirled from her sudden encounter, she wanted to scream but realized it would be no use. As her eyes adjusted to the darkness, she heard someone laugh. She then noticed light coming through a tiny crack in the wall. She peeked through the crack and realized that it was the Baroness's room; she was in bed with Prime Minister Godfrey. She searched around the room in the faint light and spotted a rusty wheelbarrow with a jagged edge. Jasmine rubbed the rope bounding her hands against the sharp edge, freeing her hands. She then squinted her eyes as she removed the tape from her mouth. A few moments later she heard the Baroness speak and she looked again.

"A biracial queen, how absurd, my grandson is out of his mind. How dare he propose marriage to this girl. He's embarrassed the monarchy and the entire history of our beloved country. By the eve of her official engagement to my pathetic grandson, they would both be dead and I shall be queen of England."

Jasmine's fears were confirmed. Lady Baldwin's life is in grave danger and her only hope is locked up in a dungeon, in an old manor in South Wales.

Jasmine searched around the dark room for any sign of escape. As she crawled across the room slightly tapping the floor with her hands, she discovered a hollow area. This might be a way out, she thought. Desperate, she felt around the area and discovered a latch. She lifted it slowly revealing a stair which led to an old storage room on the first floor. Jasmine looked around and found an old door which led to the Manor's vineyards. It was after midnight and pitch black out. Jasmine was finally freed but she had no way of getting out of Wales. Hearing footsteps approaching, she ran through the vineyard and hid herself. Then out of nowhere appeared a blond-maned horse as if beckoning her to climb on. Realizing he was her father's lost horse, on which she'd learn to ride, she ran to her and climbed on.

"Amber, where have you been?" she cried. With little time left, Jasmine nudged the horse and Amber sped off toward the forest. She rode for a long while and suddenly stopped by a pond near a strange manor.

"Amber, where are we?" she asked nervously. The horse responded with a loud neigh.

"Careful Amber, someone might hear us," but it was too late. Jasmine turned around in time to see four guards with the barrel of their guns pointing at her.

"Hands where we can see them ma'am," one guard said.

"Who are you and what do you want?" Slowly lifting her hands…

"I'm Jasmine, servant of Prince Ethan and Baroness Ester. I have some important news to deliver to her Majesty, the Princess." The guards looked at each other.

"But why are you sneaking around here this late at night, couldn't you use a telephone?"

"I'm sorry sir, It's a long story, I'm afraid the Princess's life is in danger."

"Is that so?" asked one guard, hardly believing her story.

After shining their flashlights around in the dark to confirm that Jasmine was alone, one of the guards helped her down from the horse, then they escorted her to the Manor.

The guards escorted Jasmine to a storage house behind the manor. She was warned that any attempt to escape would land her in handcuffs and much steeper penalties. Jasmine pleaded with the men to release her, warning them of the threat against the Princess, but to no avail. They didn't believe a single word she'd said. Jasmine wondered why there were so many guards assigned to this manor. She thought it might be one of the Baroness's other properties but thought that it was strange since she'd never heard of it.

Not realizing that she had arrived at the Baldwin's Manor, Jasmine cried bitterly for hours then finally fell asleep atop an old dusty sofa. The following morning, she was awakened by chains rattling on the old wooden door. She looked up shading her eyes from the sun. Jasmine thought that she was dreaming when she saw Lady Baldwin standing in the doorway and two guards standing beside her.

"Jasmine, is that you, what are you doing here?"

"Lady Baldwin; my lady, is it really you? How did you know?" Jasmine said overjoyed.

"Let's get you out of this dusty storage my friend," she said embracing her.

"This morning I was told that I had a prisoner and was scared to death until I saw your pretty face staring up at me," Natalie said happily.

"I had no idea you live here," Jasmine said relieved. Realizing that Natalie knew Jasmine, the guards apologized to her for the misunderstanding.

"Not at all, you were doing your jobs. I commend you, please keep up the good work. Truly, you would have saved my life if the circumstances were different," she replied.

Jasmine told Natalie that she had urgent news and she invited her inside. She was covered in dust and cobwebs and the Princess invited her to shower before their conversation.

"No majesty, there's no time, we must speak at once," she urged. No sooner they were seated Lisa and Richard joined them at the table. Richard looked at Jasmine in horror.

"Jasmine what happened to you and why are you covered in dirt?" Jasmine's pale cheeks turned bright red.

"Hello, sir, it's good to see you again," she replied.

"Hello Jasmine, I'm Lisa, the Princess's Mother," Lisa said, filling their cups with tea. Jasmine's eyes lit up.

"How wonderful to meet the mother of our future queen," Jasmine beamed. "Mother, Father, Jasmine has urgent news and has been through quite an ordeal to get here to inform us."

"Is that so?" Richard asked, taking a seat. As they sipped on their tea, all eyes were focused on Jasmine. With dirt in her hair, clothing partially torn and her eyes widened with fear, Jasmine revealed her fears to the Baldwin's. As they listened, they thought that Jasmine was mistaken, but as she revealed the details of being bound and locked up in a dungeon in the Baroness's manor, they began to see the truth in her message.

Horrified by Jasmine's report, word was sent to the Palace immediately warning the Prince of the Baroness's plot. Prince Ethan heightened security around the Palace and issued a warrant to have the Baroness and Prime Minister Godfrey arrested. The Prince visited Lady Baldwin's home the same hour to encourage her to make the Royal transition sooner rather than later. Within a few short hours Richard's daughter was transitioned into the unexpected life of a Princess.

The threat against the promised wife of the Prince of Edinburg received international attention. Philip had just returned from laying his aunt to rest and was missing Natalie terribly. He turned on his television and was surprised that almost every channel was reporting the death threat against the new Princess of Edinburgh. Shocked and terrified, he watched the news for several hours to get every bit of information on the woman he thought would be his wife. He was relieved when he heard that she'd moved into the Palace and that every chance was being taken to ensure her security. He would have been due back tomorrow and still felt strange that he'd decided against returning to London. But regardless, he refused to put himself before so many people who relied on her; a woman whose purpose would determine an entire nation's future. To him she was not just someone's wife; she's a Heroine in every sense of the word.

Philip's phone was ringing nonstop. Realizing that the press had figured out his private line, he began to contemplate the television interview he was offered. After all, it was an amazing experience and what they shared was just as important. He owes it to himself to share his experience with the world. He thought that maybe then his phone would stop ringing and the press would finally leave him alone.

Chapter 26

Following her transition to the Palace Manor, the Royal Guards that were stationed at The Baldwin's Manor had returned to regular duty at Edinburgh Palace. Lisa was returning from the mailbox when she noticed a piece of mail from Philip. She realized that he had not returned to England and she wondered how he was handling the news. As she entered the door the phone rang, it was her daughter.

"Hi sweetheart, how are you settling into your new home?"

"Someone's missing mother."

"Who might that be?" Lisa asked assuming it was her.

"William," she replied. I would like for him to join the staff here at the Palace Manor," she said in happy realization.

"I'm sure he'd be delighted because it was only this morning he was wondering if he was out of a job," Lisa laughed. Before she got off the phone, she mentioned the piece of mail that had arrived from Philip and Natalie urged her to forward it to the Palace.

Prince Ethan knocked on Lady Baldwin's door briefly, then entered her room. A long line of traditions has previously been established that potential Monarchs occupy separate rooms until their formal engagement. As he looked around for her, he noticed that she was looking over her bedroom balcony, into a beautiful flower garden watered by an angel fountain. He approached her silently and touched her lower back. Startled, she gasped softly and turned around.

"Prince Ethan, are you always this sneaky?"

"Only around you, my love," he replied. Noticing a glimmer of sadness in her eyes made his heart ache.

"Are you alright?" he asked, placing his hands on her shoulders. It's been two weeks since her move and she was beginning to miss her simple life at the manor. She was also missing Philip but didn't mention it.

"I'm just surprised at the way that everything turned out with Baroness Ester," she said looking away from him.

"We don't have to worry about her anymore. I swear if she wasn't my grandmother, I would have her executed. That poor captain spent more than four years in prison for the death of my parents. I regret that it is only now his words regarding his innocence were heard," he said angrily.

"When I thought that grandmother was truly grieving my parents, I now realize that it was only for her son. She'd meant to kill my mother and spare her son," he said turning away. Seeing his pain, she embraced him from behind. His eyes filled with tears, he turned to face her and kissed her softly.

"When Richard told me that you'd moved away, I had missed you. With each passing day, I was certain that I would never get to remind you about the promise that we had made in the garden. After losing both my parents, I was not myself and I swore that I would never take the throne. I wanted the monarchy to die."

"Why didn't you remind me before?" she asked.

"It's tradition that I wait until your eighteenth birthday, but by then you'd already written your father off and was bound for the Caribbean's." They both laughed at the remark.

"And when I returned, I was engaged to an American."

"Yes indeed, you're quite incredible my lady, but I can't blame him, you're possibly the world's most beautiful woman," he boasted. Natalie blushed. He then took her in his arms a second time and kissed her lovingly... until the morning glories growing in the garden below had closed their pink petals, bidding the night farewell.

Philip's letter arrived the following morning and after reading it thoroughly, five times, she cried. "Though he loves her, he'd released her to fulfill her natural purpose." He didn't fight for her; he simply gave up on their love. They would never race through the streets of London in their Jeep Wrangler, ever again. He was gone. She picked up the phone to place a call to him but she realized that the Prince would learn of it. Tomorrow she would be formally engaged and within two short weeks she would be married and all the world would announce Prince Ethan as the successor of the British Throne. She would no longer have privacy. Her life now belonged to the people of England. She looked at the letter once more. She then warded it up into a ball and tossed it on the floor. She was fed-up with letters. It was the second time in her lifetime that a letter had completely changed her life and she was beginning to get sick of them. As she reached for the phone to place a call to her mother, there was a soft knock on her door.

"One minute please," she called racing to her beauty quarters to apply makeup to hide her reddened face.

"Who is it?" she asked, being careful.

"It's me Jasmine."

"Jasmine, please come in, what can I do for you my friend?" Jasmine smiled and looked up at her. At five feet seven inches tall, Lady Baldwin was almost five inches taller than her favorite Palace help; something that Jasmine always admired about her.

"These over there," Jasmine said pointing to the Palace's mail room. Natalie gasped.

"What's all this?" she said looking at the mailroom almost half filled with bags of mail, flowers and teddy bears.

"These Majesty are fan mail from every corner of England and around the world. They've been opened and were properly inspected by the mail staff before they were presented to you. The people of England adore you and see you as the last bit of hope for the Monarchy. And by the way, there's more and there will be more," Jasmine giggled.

Shocked, Natalie slowly lifted her hands to her mouth.

"And to believe I was just beginning to get sick of letters." Natalie and Jasmine engulf in laughter.

"Almost forgot, here's a list of twenty beautiful young ladies along with their photographs. Among these, you will choose twelve to be your handmaids," Jasmine said.

"Handmaids? You and Master William are quite enough help."

"Trust me, your Majesty, you'll need all the help that you can get; including someone to begin reading these letters to you so that you can begin replying to them. Unless you want to read them all by yourself," she teased.

"Reply to them?" But Jasmine had already disappeared down the hallway.

The thought of her impending status exhausted her. As she glanced at the clock on the wall, she realized that her parents were late arriving. Prince Ethan had ordered the head servant to employ fifteen more servants and now Lady Baldwin feels like she's completely surrounded by strangers. Her parents would help her to feel more at home and she could hardly wait till they arrived. Overwhelmed, she flopped down on her very large comfortable bed and began looking through the list of young ladies, vying to be her handmaid. Within a few short minutes, she'd selected eleven of the twenty young women who stood out being both humble and genuine. Jasmine was surprised by how quickly she'd made her selection and as she looked through the list.

"You've only selected eleven. But you need one more," she insisted.

"Yes and I'm looking right at her."

"Whom, me, you wish me to be your handmaid?"

"I couldn't imagine a more trustworthy friend. After all, it is only true that you've saved my life." Stunned by the invitation Jasmine embraced Lady Baldwin so tightly that she could hardly breathe.

"Jasmine, can I have my hands back now?" Jasmine looked up at her.

"Yes you may, Majesty," the two laughed heartily.

"Does this mean I can immediately quit my current duties?" Lady Baldwin stared at her squarely and she knew what that meant.

"Oh," she said and hurried off with the list to contact the ladies among whom has been selected to be handmaids to Lady Baldwin. Natalie giggled, "She's quite the character isn't she?"

Cassie barked in agreement.

Jasmine peeked through the kitchen window and spotted the gardener and Prince Ethan's horse trainer conversing which gave her a brilliant idea. She placed her current duties on hold and hurried to the Palace yard.

"Sir, sir Henry, can I have a minute of your time please?"

"Certainly, what can I do for the lady who saved the future of our beloved country?"

"Well, thank you sir, but I only did what anyone would," she replied.

"Not anyone my dear, one day soon you'll be properly recognized for what you've done," he said proudly. Jasmine smiled.

"Is that you Jasmine?" called the gardener joining in the conversation.

"Sure is. I need both your help with a very important project," she said.

"Anything for the noblest woman in our land," the horse trainer replied.

"Although the Prince had already chosen a horse for our lady, I believe that there's another horse that has won her heart and would make a much finer choice than that of Gregory the Clydesdale." After discussing the whereabouts of Amber; the blond mane horse with Henry and George, they agreed to find Amber and bring her to the Palace to be the official property of Lady Baldwin.

Over the course of a matter of days, the Palace Manor became the busiest place on earth as new faces arrived and arrangements were made to prepare the home of the future King and Queen of their land. Jasmine pounded on Lady Baldwin's door for the fiftieth time that day. This time she didn't answer and Jasmine entered without permission.

"It's about time you'd figured it out," Natalie teased.

"What is it now Jasmine? Is it time to get dressed, time for tea, time for dinner or is it time for a boring walk around the Palace yards?"

"No my lady, it's time to meet the new faces of Edinburgh Palace."

"Now it's my turn to say oh oh!"

"I promise you'd get used to it my lady. Shall I assist you in getting dressed?"

"Does anyone realize that I've been dumped by my American fiancé?"

"Yes Majesty but now you shall be Queen, a more desirable, much needed calling. One of which you are more worthy than any other."

"You're a friend like no other Jasmine. I will forever be grateful to you. Not only am I ready to meet the staff, I am now prepared to embrace my true calling; my destined purpose." A wave of wholeness swept through her as Jasmine assisted Lady Baldwin in preparation for her first meeting with the new Palace staff.

Endowed in royal apparel, led by a confident Jasmine, Lady Baldwin was introduced to the new members of her home. Among the staff, standing single file in a separate line are the lovely young women whom she'd chosen to be her handmaids. As she approached them, each member introduced themselves by stating their names and their position in the Palace individually. Unknown to them,

Prince Ethan observed the proceeding from the balcony above, paying close attention to any, even the slightest negative reaction from any member of the staff. He looked pleasingly at his future wife as she strolled gracefully, greeting each member with the gratitude of a saint. After the introduction, each staff member excused themselves and resumed training for their respected position.

"My lady, you did wonderfully," Jasmine beamed.

"Yes indeed, and they all appear to love you," Prince Ethan said proudly, entering the room. Jasmine bowed gracefully at the presence of his Majesty. She bowed gracefully once more and exited the room. Lady Baldwin narrowed her eyes and smiled at Ethan.

"You look magnificent," he said, taking her hands and waltzing her across the floor.

"You are terribly late," she joked.

"Yes, I've been visiting with your parents. I have to say, I've never seen Richard more in love. And he's managed to keep it hidden for all these years." Natalie listened as he continued. I swore that he was a permanent bachelor, but not after what I've seen when your mum entered the room. Richard's face lit up like a Christmas tree."

"Are you poking fun at my parents?" she asked, playfully stepping on his toes as they danced.

"They're a lovely couple. I must say, Prince or not, I'm sure that your mum would be looking at me very closely," he teased, kissing her face all over.

The following morning, Jasmine and the handmaidens hurried back and forth to prepare Lady Baldwin for the day ahead. It was the day of her formal engagement to the Prince. The first moment of Royalty, one that England had long awaited. Her Parents arrived a day later than expected and she was slightly relieved to be surrounded by familiar faces. Her mother insisted on helping with her daughter's preparation but instead, the Palace staff kept her entertained and stuffed her silly with the finest meals and more tea than any one person could possibly refuse. Finally spoiled and overly indulged, Lisa fell asleep in the entertainment room and was gently escorted to her bedroom which was prepared by Kate, her new assistant.

For the first time in months, the sun shone beautifully, warming the cool weather, casting its golden reflection across the Palace yards. The Royal guards each carrying a golden trumpet had taken their place forming two lines at the main Palace stairwell which led to the Royal balcony, overlooking the large courtyard. Thousands of guests by invitation, from every part of the United Kingdom crowded the palace gates to witness the beginning of one of the most important moments in the history of England.

"Where's Lisa?" Richard asked, searching anxiously.

"I beg your pardon sir but she's resting in the west wing," Kate replied. Richard thanked her and hurried off. When he found Lisa she was fast asleep and he didn't want to wake her. Just then he heard his daughter approaching. She was almost unrecognizable in a flowing purple gown enshrined in gold and diamond trimmings. She was searching for her mother. At the sound of her daughter's voice, Lisa stirred tiredly and sat up.

"There you are. Why aren't you both in the courtyard taking your places?"

"We're about to sweetheart," Richard replied, embracing her.

"Don't worry, we'll be there. Shouldn't you be with the ladies…?" No sooner he'd completed his statement, four handmaids entered the room and called for Lady Baldwin urging her to come quickly.

"Please Kate, give mum a hand, I'll see you both in the courtyard," she called hurrying off. Less than a minute later Kate, Lisa's handmaid, had her dressed and her and Richard took their places next to the Prince on the Royal Balcony.

At the sight of the twelve handmaidens leading Lady Baldwin down the main stairwell, the Royal guards sounded their trumpets. All eyes were now focused on Richard's daughter as she graced the stairwell, unrecognizable as the sun shone on her, causing her diamond studded gown to immerse in a glowing reflection all around her. She appears as an angelic vision bringing tears of joy to her mother's eyes. She knew that from the day she was born that her daughter was destined for a great purpose. As the sound of the trumpets subsided, Richard, speaking in place of Prince Ethan's father presented the couple to the crowd. As it is custom, Jasmine, the head handmaid, presented Richard with a small pillow on which laid a magnificent engagement ring. The crowd watched silently as

Jasmine handed Lisa a ribbon filled pillow on which sat a glistening engagement crown. At the sound of a single guard sounding the trumpet, before an anxious crowd, Prince Ethan knelt before Lady Baldwin and for the second time in history, he asked for her hand in marriage. Assured by her visions, Princess Anne's letter and the words of her mother...

"You are destined for greatness." She said...

"Yes your Majesty, I shall be greatly honored to be your wife." At that moment, Richard handed Prince Ethan the engagement ring and he placed it on his Princess's finger. Her mother then lifted her hands gracefully and placed the First Crown of Royalty on her daughter's head as an indication of her agreement to marry the Prince. At the sight of their new Princess wearing her crown, the Royal guards sounded their trumpets once more and the crowd went wild with excitement. With the Princess of Edinburg by his side, the Guards led a Royal Procession through the streets of London where they waved to the citizens of England. After their public appearance, the successors of the British Throne were led through the Palace courtyard, into the main ballroom where they danced gracefully before their guests. As other guests began to join them on the ballroom floor, Prince Ethan whispered...

"Let's get out of here," and she agreed. As they shoved through the crowd...

"There's my beautiful granddaughter," Annabelle said, embracing her tightly.

"Annabelle, I see that we meet again," said Ethan, slightly annoyed to be interrupted. As Annabelle introduced Natalie to her friends, she heard a familiar voice. It was Brent. Her cousin Katie was standing next to him as he spoke with Richard. Brent didn't notice her but she realized that he was asking about her and she wanted to get away, but it was too late. Her cousin Katie noticed her and came hurrying toward them. Prince Ethan whispered in her ear...

"Mingle, I'll return shortly." He then approached Lisa, took her by the hands and escorted her to the ballroom floor.

"Forgive me, my lady I almost forgot my manners," he said smiling as he waltzed Lisa across the floor, catching everyone's attention. Richard looked on enviously, then lifted his glass to Lisa and Prince.

"Cousin Natalie, I can hardly believe my eyes," Katie said. As she was about to greet her cousin, William approached and bowed before her.

"William, where have you been all evening?"

"Looking at you my lady; I couldn't be more proud."

She blushed at his sterling bona fide expression.

"William, if anyone asks why I've chosen England, please tell them that I did it all for you." He smiled and kissed her hands affectionately.

"Katie, do you remember William?"

"How can I forget the man I almost married when I was only five?" Katie replied.

"Five? How is it I never knew that you almost stole my girl Will," said Brent joining the conversation.

"Well, it would have been well deserved," Natalie replied. Realizing what she meant, everyone laughed.

"Can I borrow you for a minute?" asked Kate. As Natalie was about to respond, one of her private guards entered the room.

"Your Highness, you must come quickly," he said urgently, taking her by the hand and leading her through the crowd.

"Is something wrong?" she asked. But he didn't respond and continued to lead her through the halls. Then he stopped and pointed to the Prince's chambers.

"My Lady, your Prince awaits," he said smiling for the first time since they met.

"I could slap him, I thought something was wrong," she said relieved.

"Slap him, that sounds mighty fetish," the guard said winking at her.

"Did you just wink at me, sir?"

"You'll get used to it, Majesty."

"I'll tell you what, you'd learn proper manners for your superiors," she teased.

"Soon enough," he smiled and hurried off. She shook her head and entered the Prince's chamber where a handsome Prince awaited.

"How dare you?" she scolded, pretending to be annoyed.

"I love you even more when you're annoyed," he replied, removing her crown and tilting her head back gently.

"We are not yet married," she reminded him.

"Then I shall be all the more grateful when we do," he replied. As he removed her diamond studded dress and carried her to his bed, she felt like the weight of a thousand pounds had dropped to her feet. As he kisses her, her dreams begin to unfold and she feels like a Dove that has been freed to save a Nation.

Chapter 27

It's been almost three weeks since her formal engagement. The Princess has embraced her new life and with each passing day, she is slowly being reborn into a world that was once foreign to her. With no one to reflect the roles of leadership, she feared the unknown. Reflecting on her visions of Prince Ethan's mother, her parent's words and the hopeful expression on the faces of the people during her first public appearance as their Princess, instilled within her a passion to bring about much needed change.

The Princess awoke to a very familiar sound. Cassie barked and tried looking out the window but they were too high for her and she whined irritably trying endlessly to see outdoors. One of the handmaidens heard Cassie's whimpering and entered the Princess Chambers to see what was wrong.

"Hi there, what's the matter girl? " asked Camille, gently patting her head.

"I think she might have heard one of the horses," the Princess replied, tossing about restlessly.

"I beg your pardon Majesty, I didn't mean to wake you," she said apologetically.

"Not at all, I was already awake," she said sitting up in bed.

"I think I'm going to go for a horseback ride this morning. After all, I still haven't visited the trails. I heard they are marvelous," she said, removing her sleep mask.

"Shall I find the maidens to help assist you, my lady," she asked.

"Thank you Camille, but it's alright, I'll manage," she assured her.

"I would be delighted to help pick out your clothing to be sure that you're properly attired," Camille said smiling.

"That would be alright I suppose, since I'd received less than a standing ovation when I walked through the Palace in my bikini yesterday."

"That's exactly what I was implying your highness," she replied, holding back laughter.

"Well, you tell them that it won't be the last time, so they'd better get used to it," the Princess replied.

"Duly noted majesty, and besides I thought it was an excellent bikini. Did you purchase this one from California?" she teased. Besides Jasmine, Camille was quickly becoming one of her favorites. She adores her free spirit and supportive sense of humor.

As she was about to escort Gregory from the horse's stable, she heard a familiar sound. The Princess looked in the stall next to Gregory's and couldn't believe her eyes.

"It can't be, how in the world did you get here?" she asked, patting the face of the blond mane horse. Recognizing the Princess, the horse neighed playfully. After replacing Gregory back into the stall, she led the blond mane horse into the yard and climbed onto her.

"Her name is Amber," Jasmine called.

"How do you know?"

"She's a runaway that used to belong to my father."

"No way, you've got to be kidding me. Are you saying that I'm stealing your horse?" She said, placing both her hands on her hips. Jasmine giggled...

"I wouldn't think so Majesty, she hates me anyway. William told me how you two met, a very charming story, she's all yours now." Jasmine watched as Abbie sped off disappearing down trail with the Princess barely hanging on. But Just as she was about to panic, she heard Amber returning and this time the Princess was sitting as a professional jockey with her hips slightly elevated, holding tightly onto the reins as the horse sped through the open trails. A few moments later, Jasmine watches as the Prince leads his horse Victor onto the trails, following closely after his future queen as they race through the narrow trail.

"Richard, do you think they can manage, they're the youngest couple in history to have taken the throne," Lisa said preparing for her date with Richard.

"I'm certain of one thing. Our daughter was ready from the time she was five. I'll never forget how she ran her poor nannies ragged, with her authoritative attitude," he punned.

"Did it occur to us that when our daughter made that forbidden call to you here in merry Ole London, that she was setting the stage for the future of England," Lisa said, taking his hand.

"Well darling, little did we all know that this call was the writing of History, as we raise a Monarchy greater than the world has ever seen," Richard said kissing the woman he loves.

About the Author

Natlie Bartholomew Pitt has seen some of the world's most beautiful horizons. From dawn till dusk, the view from her windows have always been the soft yellow ray of the sun as it casts its golden reflection on the bay at sunrise. Then just as faithfully at dusk, displays its multicolored memory of the day's joy-cascading remembrance on the twilight sky at sundown. Natlie is an American socialite, romance novelist, children's book author, comedy writer and educator. Natlie found her writing cues and momentum in the midst of life's most daunting episode...while assisting her artist husband as her twins climb over her back and play with her hair. During unplanned downtimes, readers can find Natlie on Twitter via @NatliePitt, entertaining her Twitter audience with beautiful inspiring words and her untimely humor. Natlie lives in Southern California where she is surrounded by exquisite beauty that instills a fire in her heart to release her most imaginative work.